bile A

2

2

D1476393

FEVER PITCH

KENZIE GILMORE CRIME THRILLER
BOOK 6

BIBA PEARCE

2000693389

NEATH PORT TALBOT LIBRARIES

Copyright © 2023 by Biba Pearce. All rights reserved. No part of this publication may be copied, reproduced in any format, by any means, electronic or otherwise, without prior consent from the copyright owner and publisher of this book.

Liquid Mind Publishing
This is a work of fiction. All characters, names, places and events are the product of the author's imagination or used fictitiously.

KENZIE GILMORE CRIME THRILLER SERIES

<u>The Kenzie Gilmore Crime Thriller Series</u>

Afterburn

Dead Heat

Heatwave

Burnout

Deep Heat

Fever Pitch

Storm Surge (Coming Soon)

Do you like Audiobooks? Find the Kenzie Gilmore Crime Thriller series on Audible here:

Neath Port Talbot Libraries

CL AFiC

Date 11 23 PR

CC Mob

Health Post Failed Deliveries

1

Saturday never happened.

Kenzie wanted it to. Desperately. She'd been looking forward to their date, but Keith, her editor at the *Miami Herald*, had other ideas. Reid, and their tentative reconciliation, would have to wait.

"I need you up there before the weekend," the hard-nosed newspaperman had told her. "There's a massive buzz about this wedding. Most of Washington's political elite will be there, as well as President Sullivan himself. If you can get a comment..."

He didn't need to elaborate. She knew her job. It might seem like the celebrity wedding of the year—a beautiful French supermodel marrying the President's youngest son—but there were undercurrents of suspicion, malice and distrust. Warner Sullivan and his father were estranged, and it was no secret the family didn't look kindly on the marriage. Emmanuelle Lenoir was the illegitimate daughter of the late cartel boss, Maria Lopez, something Maria had been at pains to hide. Like most big secrets, it couldn't stay hidden forever.

Kenzie had broken the story. Indirectly. Her researcher, Raoul, had told their editor. She didn't blame him. He'd been new and eager to please, and Keith could be very intimidating if you got him on a bad day. Or even on a good day, for that matter.

A pang of guilt sliced through her as she stepped off the airplane and took her first gulp of New York air. It was not something she felt good about, breaking a trust. Even if it was that of the infamous cartel boss. Kenzie had given her word, and that meant something.

Still, in this industry, if you didn't splash it over the front page, somebody else would, and MARIA LOPEZ'S SECRET LOVE TRYST had been a scoop she couldn't afford to lose. A scoop her editor would not allow her to lose.

The hard, white sun blazed down on the runway, shimmering like a mirage. Heels, boots, suitcases, voices. Rolling, clacking, talking all at once. She longed for the calm of her hotel room.

It had been an early start, the sun not yet up in Miami when she'd boarded the plane. Breakfast served at 30,000 feet in plastic containers, acrid coffee, synthetic milk. Normally, she didn't mind flying. It was a means to an end. New places, new faces, new stories. Plots to unearth and truths to find. But this flight lacked the familiar buzz of excitement. It might be because every mile was taking her further and further away from where she wanted to be. From *whom* she wanted to be with.

She'd heard the disappointment in Reid's voice when she'd told him.

"Sure, if you have to go."

"It's only for a week. We can get together when I get back."

"Okay."

"It's a celebrity wedding. Ridiculous, really. The entertainment reporter should go, not me."

A silence.

"Reid, I'm sorry about this."

"It's okay. Catch you when you get back."

And that was it. He'd sounded tired, like he was done waiting, done hoping.

That's all they seemed to do. Wait. And hope.

Kenzie walked into the arrivals terminal and turned toward the baggage claim. She had to grab her suitcase. A celebrity wedding called for a designer wardrobe, so she'd packed her few items of clothing reserved for such occasions. An off-the-shoulder Oscar de la Renta cocktail dress. A Carolina Herrera poppy-print gown. Glittering shoes and leather purses. If she were to rub shoulders with fashionistas and charm the President and his entourage, she had to look the part.

Kenzie Gilmore, award-winning investigative reporter. That's who she was this week. Everything else, including her love life, could wait. Would have to wait.

She collected her suitcase from the conveyor belt, squeezing in beside frazzled parents with one eye on their luggage, the other on their tired, irritable children; businessmen and women with bony elbows and caffeine-withdrawal scowls; and the occasional over-excited tourist.

New York.

The terminal was heaving. Summer was in full swing. Kenzie walked diagonally across the concourse to the nearest exit. A line of taxis catered to an even longer line of travelers. Reluctantly, she joined it.

"Never changes," the man in front of her grumbled. "I've wasted hours of my life in this line."

Had she? How many wasted hours had been spent at airports around the world? Mexico City. Rio de Janeiro. London. Rome. Paris. And further flung places on the globe. Manilla. Bangladesh. Johannesburg.

No, not wasted. Empty. Empty hours.

A means to an end.

The line was moving steadily, but she still had some time to go. Taking out her phone, she called Liesl. Liesl Bernstein was a reporter for the *New York Times,* originally from Florida. They'd studied journalism together after Kenzie's accident had seen her dreams of becoming a police detective crash down around her.

Liesl had pulled her out of that slump, infused her with a passion for the truth. For reporting the truth. For putting her thirst for justice into an article. Into a feature with award-winning potential.

Liesl was the real deal. One of those naturally curious people. Always questioning. Always observing. Nothing escaped her razor-sharp intuition. Like Keith, she was a born newsperson. She could sniff out a story from a hundred miles—and often did. She could write, too. Liesl had a way with words. Kenzie had learned the skill, but Liesl had been a natural.

The call rang out to Liesl's voicemail.

Hello, you've reached Liesl Bernstein from the New York Times. Leave a message and I'll get back to you.

Liesl couldn't even record a voice message without adding the *New York Times*. It was who she was. Not a friend, a sister, a wife. Only ever a reporter. Kenzie, a fellow student, now a peer, a respected colleague, was probably the closest thing she had to a friend.

It sounded familiar.

Finally, she was at the end of the line. "The Sheraton Hotel. Times Square," she told the driver, who took off even before she'd closed the door.

New York. Always in a rush.

The last time they'd spoken, Liesl had told her she'd tracked down the man who'd drugged, then brutally raped ballet student Gail Winslow back in 1998. Jeff Dooley, his name was. Except Jeff Dooley had turned out to be a married man from Queens. A leather worker who'd died from asbestos poisoning several years ago.

That's as far as they'd gotten. Kenzie planned to look into it in her free time while she was here. Gail deserved justice. Her rapist deserved to be punished for what he'd done to her and probably to a number of other young women. Men who roofied girls and then took them to two-bit motels to rape them didn't stop at one. They didn't suddenly get an attack of conscience and repent.

Kenzie was confident there'd be other women out there with stories like Gail's. Lives that had been shattered because they'd accepted a drink from a handsome stranger. The star quarterback, that's what Gail had said he'd looked like. Blonde, tall, good looking. A flirtatious smile, twinkling eyes. *Can I buy you a drink?*

The Sheraton in Times Square wasn't much to look at from the outside, but inside, it was an oasis of calm. Contemporary and elegant, and above all, convenient. Right in the center of New York, it made getting around easy, and Kenzie didn't want the hassle of trying to negotiate traffic if she could help it.

"Any messages?" she asked the stylishly dressed woman behind the check-in desk. Kenzie had left a voicemail for her friend yesterday with her arrival details. Liesl hadn't picked up then either, but that wasn't unusual. Her friend always got back to her, though, which she hadn't done this time.

"Um, let me check." The woman clicked a mouse under the counter. Gone were the days of messages in pigeon-holes. It was all electronic now. Notes stored on a hotel database, readable by anyone who had access. More secure, or maybe less secure. "Yes, there is a message."

"Oh, great." She smiled. Of course Liesl hadn't forgotten. They'd arranged to have lunch, after all.

"It's a reservation. 1:45pm. Connolly's on West 45th Street."

"Thank you." Kenzie hadn't heard of it, but Liesl would have chosen somewhere they could hear each other talk. At least it was only a few blocks away, easily within walking distance.

Kenzie dropped off her suitcase and laptop bag in her hotel room, ran a brush through her travel-weary hair, applied a smattering of make-up, then set off. It was warm, pleasantly so. Not the moist, all-encompassing heat of Miami, but a dry heat that made her think of alfresco dining and outdoor bars. She wondered what kind of place Connolly's was.

To her surprise, it was a traditional Irish pub. It looked nice, but more suited to a cozy winter meal than a light lunch. Not Liesl's style at all.

Strange.

Kenzie went inside and looked around but couldn't see her friend.

"I have a reservation," she told the host who came to meet her. A long, polished bar ran down one side of the pub, a dining section on the other. It was stuffy inside, despite the front door being open. A television screen above the bar showed a soccer match that—judging by the rainy weather—looked like it could be happening across the pond in Ireland.

"This way." He headed off to a dark corner of the restaurant. Then Kenzie got it. This wasn't a catch up so much as a clandestine meeting about Jeff Dooley. It must be. Why else would her friend have reserved a table in such an establishment, and way out of sight of the doors and windows?

She felt a surge of excitement. Had Liesl found something else? Did she know who Jeff Dooley really was? Could she point Kenzie in the direction of Gail's rapist?

Kenzie checked her watch. 1:55pm. Liesl was ten minutes late. Understandable in New York traffic. She ordered a drink and browsed the *Herald's* latest news on her phone.

Congressman Leonard was up to his old tricks. A new initiative. Modernization of the tram system. An upgrade that would benefit thousands of commuters. There was even a comment by the mayor. She gave a snort. Funded no doubt with dirty money from Leonard's longtime supporter, Del Gatto.

Now Liesl was twenty minutes late. Kenzie frowned and took out her phone. She sent a text, but it didn't go through. Calling made no difference. Liesl's phone was off. Sighing, she leaned back and continued reading. She'd give it till half past, then go back to the hotel. Liesl knew where to find her.

Kenzie had just moved on to the next article when a loud screech followed by an ear-splitting crash had her jumping out of her seat.

"What the—?"

She ran to the door, followed closely by the host and the bartender, who'd turned away from the game. Two cars had collided not fifty yards from the restaurant.

"I hope nobody's hurt." Kenzie darted out onto the sidewalk for a better look. A crowd had gathered around the two cars. There was a scream, and a woman cried, "Oh, my God. Somebody call an ambulance!"

A horrible feeling crept over Kenzie, who broke into a run. A crowd had formed, blocking her view. "Excuse me." She elbowed her way through.

God, no. Please, no.

Liesl lay in the road, her body bent and crumpled like a crash test dummy.

"Liesl!"

Kenzie dropped to her knees beside her friend and took her hand. Her brain was telling her what her heart refused to believe. The unnatural angle of Liesl's head, the way her neck was twisted to the side. Eyes closed, chest still. A tiny trickle of blood leaked from the corner of her mouth.

Kenzie pushed her fingers into Liesl's neck. *Please, find a pulse. A tiny one. Anything.*

But there was none.

Her friend was dead.

2

Kenzie felt the pavement press into her knees. The crowd swirled around her as if in a dream. Muted voices. Car horns. Sirens.

"Out of the way, miss."

She scrambled back and watched in horror as two medics tried to resuscitate Liesl, but she was non-responsive. Eventually, the one glanced at the other and shook his head.

Tears welled, and she swiped angrily at her eyes. What had just happened? *How* had this happened? She wobbled to her feet, looking around as if for the first time. The two cars meshed together, their fenders a twisted mess of metal. One vehicle was empty, the other had a woman inside, sobbing. A beat patrol officer who'd stopped to help was speaking to her. Kenzie slid closer so she could hear what was being said.

"Can you exit the vehicle, ma'am?"

The crying woman gingerly got out of her car. There was a gash on her forehead, and she clutched her left shoulder. The airbag had deployed, probably saving her life.

"I didn't see him," she sobbed. "The car came out of nowhere and crashed into me."

Him?

Kenzie looked around. Where was the driver of the second car?

Wrenching her brain out of its shocked stupor, she fished out her phone and took some photographs of the crash. The two vehicles. License plates. The sobbing woman. And of course, Liesl, who was now being lifted into a body bag. The sound of the zipper brought on a flood of nausea. Kenzie doubled over, retching, but nothing came out.

Oh, God. Liesl. How? Why? She couldn't process what had happened.

Sirens pierced her stupor. The NYPD had arrived.

Kenzie stood where she was and watched them swarm onto the scene. Brusque voices ordered everyone back, and a cordon went up. An officer began waving traffic on, guiding impatient motorists around the wrecked cars. The smell of exhaust fumes made her feel even more nauseous.

New York. Always in a rush.

She watched as an officer picked up Liesl's purse, which had fallen beside the body. No evidence bag. They weren't treating this as suspicious. Just a grim nod as he handed it to a female colleague. An unfortunate accident. A pedestrian caught in the wreckage.

Was that all it was?

Kenzie turned back to the second car, the one that had hit Liesl. Still empty. The driver was nowhere in sight. Had he been frightened and made a run for it? Had he been drinking? Was that why he'd disappeared? Or had it been deliberate?

She shook her head, trying not to overreact. Not everything was a conspiracy. Sometimes, things were as simple as they looked.

Kenzie took a few steps back. That's when she saw the phone. It lay in the gutter, several yards from Liesl in the body bag. Outside the police cordon.

Kenzie hesitated. It could be Liesl's. If she'd been holding it in her hand when she was hit, it could have skidded across the road in that direction. No one had noticed it yet.

Slowly, deliberately, she moved towards it. Bending, she sank down to pick it up. She'd just slipped it into her pocket when a cop came up to her. "Excuse me? I believe you were one of the first on the scene?"

She straightened up. "Er, yes. I was waiting to meet her in the pub. The victim is... was a friend of mine."

"You know this woman?"

A nod. "Her name is Liesl Bernstein."

He wrote it down. "And your name?"

She hesitated. "Kenzie Gilmore."

He glanced up. "Address?"

"I'm staying at the Sheraton."

His eyes narrowed. "You not from New York?"

"No. Miami."

"Then the victim—?"

"Oh, she's from New York. She worked for the *New York Times*." It defined her.

"A reporter?"

"Yeah." Kenzie bit her lip. A damn good one, too.

"Do you have a minute to give a statement?"

"I didn't see anything," she said. "I heard the crash, ran out of the pub, and saw a crowd of people. When I pushed through, I saw my friend lying on the ground. I could tell she was..." A lump formed in her throat. "I could tell she was dead the moment I saw her." A wave of sadness mixed with anger and bitterness swept over her. Why did this have to happen? Why Liesl?

"You didn't see the crash?" He sounded disappointed.

"No."

"Okay. I'm sorry for your loss." An automatic response, like he'd said it so many times it had lost all meaning.

"Thank you."

The cop moved away, on to the next bystander.

Kenzie watched as Liesl's body was lifted into an ambulance. The purse was handed to the medic. The doors shut. Her friend was gone.

Kenzie walked back to the hotel in a stupor. Pedestrians jostled her, but she hardly noticed. Her mind swirled with unanswered questions.

Why had Liesl's phone been dead for days? It was totally unlike the *New York Times* reporter to have her mobile device switched off. Rule number one: be contactable. What if a source called? What if something happened? A terror attack, a shooting, some other disaster. Their bread and butter.

She sighed. What a way to make a living.

How many times had she put her life at risk over the last few years? Too many to count. Luckily, she'd had someone looking out for her.

Reid.

A pang hit her in the chest, and she caught her breath. What was he doing now? Did he hate her for disappearing yet again? Had she ruined any chance she may have had with the gruff Miami detective? She quashed an overwhelming urge to talk to him, to tell him what had happened. She was overwrought, that's all. Emotional. He'd be at work now. Too busy to talk. She'd try him later. Maybe.

Liesl had no one. At least nobody Kenzie knew about.

She fingered the phone in her pocket. Cold. Silent. Useless.

Or maybe not.

As soon as she got back to the hotel, Kenzie took out the device. She pressed the power button, but nothing happened. It was dead. Broken? Or just out of battery?

She feared the worst. Why would Liesl have it in her hand?

Still, she plugged it into her charger and set it on the bed stand. A light flickered. She exhaled. Good. It wasn't damaged.

No. Not good. Liesl was dead. Kenzie stared at the phone for a full minute, her eyes burning. Then the tears came.

Liesl lived on the Upper West Side in a fancy apartment block with a concierge, underground parking, and an elevator with a one-hundred-and-eighty-degree view of the city. Kenzie stood outside, looking up. The only problem was she didn't know the apartment number—which was why she'd brought the gift. She was hoping the concierge might help her.

Kenzie entered the marbled lobby, the wrapped present under her arm. She'd just gone through the revolving doors when a dark-haired man careened into her.

"Oh, I'm sorry." She gasped as his elbow poked her in the ribs.

He hurried on, not bothering to look up.

How rude.

Rubbing her side, she took a moment to compose herself. Recessed lighting gave the lobby a sophisticated air, as did the wide, marble-topped reception desk, the fancy flatscreen computer, and the burly concierge-slash-security guard standing behind it.

He looked up. "Can I help you?"

A smile. A batter of eyelids. "I hope so. I've got a birthday present for Liesl Bernstein."

He didn't smile back. "You can leave it here."

"I'd really like to give it to her." She tossed her blonde hair over her shoulder. "She's a friend."

The guard's gaze dropped to her chest. "Your name?"

"Kenzie Gilmore." There was no point in lying.

"I haven't seen you before."

"I live in Miami. I'm here for the week and thought I'd surprise her."

He took in her tanned arms, her strategically chosen T-shirt with *South Beach Miami* emblazoned on the front, then gave a nod. "Apartment 114, eleventh floor."

"Thank you."

Her smile vanished as she took the elevator to the eleventh floor. Liesl's phone had been locked, so she hadn't managed to get much off it. Only a missed call that had flashed up on the locked screen. Kenzie had jotted down the number but hadn't called it yet. The elevator pinged, and the doors sighed open.

She got out and looked up and down the plush corridor. The carpet under her feet made no noise as she hurried to Apartment 114. She wasn't even sure what she was doing here. Guilt, maybe?

It had been her idea to meet. It had been she who'd asked Liesl to look into the rapist. Was it her fault her friend was dead?

Gulping back the bitter taste in her mouth, she reached the door to Liesl's apartment. To her surprise, it was slightly ajar.

Her heart skipped a beat. Had Liesl left in such a hurry she'd forgotten to lock it? Gingerly, Kenzie pushed open the door and gasped. The apartment was a mess. Overturned chairs, cushions scattered on the floor, a deep slash in the base of the couch. Cabinet doors open and a vase lying on its side on the table, water dripping onto the carpet.

The place had been ransacked.

3

Kenzie knew she shouldn't, but she did anyway. She went inside. If the police scolded her, she'd just have to plead ignorance.

The door was open. I didn't know she wasn't there.

Kenzie glanced around at the mess. Someone had given the place a good going over. What were they looking for? And why? Kenzie rubbed her forehead. None of this made sense.

Five minutes, and then she ought to sound the alarm. Any longer, and it would be obvious she'd had a look around. Hell, she might even be blamed for it.

Careful not to touch anything, Kenzie took a quick look around her friend's apartment. The living room had been gutted. Every cabinet and drawer was open, the contents spewed across the floor.

She stepped over the mess and poked her head into the kitchen. Refrigerator door ajar. Cabinets open. Tubs of flour and other foodstuffs upturned on the floor. She didn't go in, just surveyed the mess from the door. Her footprints would show up in the flour covering the floor. Already, there were scuff marks where the perp had stood. Hopefully, the police could get something off of those.

Next, she went into Liesl's study, a smaller second bedroom. A glass and steel desk glinted in front of the window, the ergonomic chair on its side. Kenzie blinked. She could almost see her friend sitting there working on her laptop, phone glued to her ear.

I read your piece on Maria Lopez. Brilliant stuff, darling. Let's get together soon and catch up. When are you in New York?

Liesl's laptop. Where was it?

Kenzie scanned the room. Liesl hadn't had it with her when she'd died, or they'd have found it. It wasn't in the living room or her study.

Finally, the master bedroom. Bed disheveled, bedding on the floor, mattress askew. Like the living room, the closet was open and Liesl's clothes were scattered over the floor. Same with the chest of drawers. Whoever had searched the place had done a thorough job of it.

No laptop, though. Could the burglar have taken it?

Carefully, Kenzie backtracked out of the apartment. She left the front door as she'd found it, slightly ajar, and ran back to the elevator. As soon as it got to the ground floor, Kenzie burst out and ran across the lobby.

"Excuse me," she panted, clutching the desk. "My friend's apartment has been burglarized!"

The guard shot out of his seat. "What?"

"The front door was open, and the place has been ransacked."

"Miss Bernstein?"

"She's not there." Kenzie squeezed her eyes shut. Nor would she be coming back. "I think you'd better call the police."

"Wait here. I'll take a look."

"I'll call them!" she called, as he took off for the elevator. What she really wanted to do was get out of there, but there was CCTV in the lobby and leaving would only make her look suspicious. It would be better if she hung around and waited for the cops to show up.

Taking out her phone, she dialed 911.

"Could you repeat it one more time?" the fresh-faced officer who was the first to respond asked, his forehead crinkled in concentration.

Oh boy.

Kenzie took a deep breath. "I came to visit my friend and when I got up to her apartment, I found the door ajar. I went inside to see if she was okay, but she wasn't there. The apartment was a mess, so I ran back downstairs and told the security guard. Then I called 911."

"You didn't go into the apartment?"

"Only to check if my friend was there."

He stuck his tongue out as he made a note.

"Would you like my contact information?" she prompted. Ideally, she'd like to leave before the real cavalry arrived. This would be the second crime scene she'd been at today.

"Um, yeah."

She gave her name and contact details, then left. More police officers, probably detectives, were arriving as she exited the building. The rookie cop had let their only witness go, but once the rest of the department caught up with what had happened here, and connected the burglary to Liesl's death, they'd call her. They'd have to. She was the only lead they had.

Kenzie caught a cab back to the hotel. She used the time to place a call to her researcher, Raoul, back in Miami. Right now, she needed his help.

Raoul picked up on the first ring. She could hear him typing on his keyboard, and knew he was balancing the phone between his shoulder and ear. "Kenzie, how's New York?"

"Raoul, I need a favor," she began.

He sniggered. "I'm good, thanks for asking."

"Sorry," she said. "Raoul, something's happened, and I need your help."

His tone changed. "The wedding?"

"No, not that. Um... a friend has... been killed." Just saying the words made her cringe. Out loud, they seemed more real. More definite.

Still, she didn't think she was jumping to conclusions. Killed was a strong word, and the accident alone might not have persuaded her, but the burglary along with it... That was too much of a coincidence. Like Reid, she didn't believe in them.

"Oh, shoot. I'm sorry, Kenzie. I didn't know."

"That's okay. She was a reporter for the *New York Times*. Liesl Bernstein."

"What do you need me to do?"

"She was killed in a road accident today." A lump formed in her throat. "Hit by a car. I'd like you to run the plates if you can?"

"Give them to me."

Kenzie read out both numbers. "One of the drivers is missing, fled the scene. The other, a woman, was questioned. It's the missing one I'm most interested in."

"Got it."

"I'll also send through some photographs that I took at the crime scene."

"Crime scene? Are you saying your friend was murdered?"

Raoul was quick.

"Kenzie?"

She sighed. "I'm not ruling it out. Someone broke into her apartment. I've just been there."

"What's going on?" he asked.

"I don't know. Something, though."

"Does this have anything to do with the wedding?"

"No, completely separate. Liesl was working on something else for me. A historic rape case."

"Gail Peters?"

"That's the one, although she was Gail Winslow at the time."

"You think your friend discovered something? Something that got her killed?" He voiced what she'd been thinking.

"I don't know, Raoul. Gail was assaulted twenty-four years ago. It seems a long time for her rapist to still be around, but—" She petered off.

Raoul did the calculation. "If he was in his twenties then, he'd be in his fifties now. It's possible he's still out there."

"I guess so." She frowned. "Anyway, how would he know Liesl was looking into him?"

"Maybe she was asking around and he got wind of it? You never know."

"True." She thought for a moment. Had the fake Jeff Dooley somehow found out that Liesl was on to him? Was that what her friend wanted to talk to her about? Was that what got her killed?

She took a deep breath. "See what you can find on those license plates. I'll do some digging on my side. I think her laptop was stolen from her apartment, but I've got her cellphone."

"Be careful, Kenzie." She heard the concern in his voice.

"I will. Talk to you soon." They hung up.

The taxi dropped her outside her hotel. Times Square. A buzzing hub of activity in the city that never slept. The intersection between Broadway and 7th Avenue.

It was hotter than before. She glanced up at the skyscrapers stabbing at the cobalt sky, then blinked, her eyes watering. The subdued lighting in the hotel foyer was a welcome relief.

Kenzie sat in the hotel lounge, sipping a cold drink and composing herself. Her phone rang. She glanced at the number. It was private. That only meant one thing. The police.

Ignoring it, she kept sipping her drink. They'd want her to go down to the station and give a statement. Standard procedure. Except that was the last thing she felt like doing. Going in voluntarily was a trick the police used to get suspects and persons of interest in the interrogation room. She wasn't falling for that one. If they wanted to speak to her, they could come here, to the Sheraton.

The call diverted to voicemail. She thought about her previous conversation with Liesl, running it through her head.

"I looked into your witness. He was there. The motel kept computerized records. I got a name for you."

"Yeah?"

"Jeff Dooley. That's not his real name. Jeff Dooley was a leather worker in Queens."

"Was?"

"Yeah, Jeff died five years ago from asbestos poisoning. He never worked in sales, and he was sick for a long time."

"You don't think it could have been him?"

"This guy was five foot four and prematurely balding. Didn't you say your witness said he was six foot and blonde?"

"Yeah." A high school quarterback was how Gail had described him.

"Not your man."

That was the last time she'd spoken to Liesl. After that, her friend had gone offline. Until her death outside the pub.

Kenzie finished her drink and stood up. She could wait for the cops to show up or go to Queens and talk to Jeff Dooley's wife. Sitting still wasn't an option. Too much time to think, to dwell, and she didn't want to do that.

Making her decision, Kenzie picked up her purse, paid her bar tab, and headed for the door. It was time to retrace Liesl's steps and find out what she'd discovered.

4

QUEENS, located across the East River from Manhattan, was a commuter area for young professionals and families wanting to get away from the constant bustle of the city. It took forty minutes for Kenzie to get there in a cab.

Jeff Dooley's wife lived in a well-maintained, red brick apartment block near the subway. Kenzie dismissed the cab driver—she'd take the train back—and crossed the road. The building towered above her, blocking out the sun, the sky an unrelenting blue behind it. Pressing the buzzer to flat 9, she silently thanked Liesl for texting her the address all those weeks ago.

A woman's voice. "Hello?"

"Hi, my name is Kenzie. I believe you spoke with a friend of mine a few weeks ago about your husband. Could I ask you a couple of follow-up questions?"

She heard shuffling, and then the woman said, "I remember. Come in." The door clicked open, and Kenzie stepped inside. The hallway was narrow with an elevator on one side and a flight of steps directly in front. She took the stairs. Apartment 9 wouldn't be more than one or two flights up. Two, as it turned out.

Mrs. Dooley, slim, slightly bent, and in her sixties, was waiting on the landing when she reached the top. "What did you say your name was again?"

"Kenzie." She held out a hand.

The woman shook it, her grip weak. "What you wanna know about my husband for?"

"I'm trying to trace a man who knew him," she said. Mrs. Dooley teetered against the doorframe, and Kenzie got a whiff of booze.

"What man?"

"Shall we go inside?" Kenzie suggested.

"Yeah, alright." The woman turned and walked back into the flat. It was surprisingly neat, with clean, but well-used furniture; a sturdy, worn dining room table; and some old landscape prints hanging on the walls. Nothing fancy.

"Have you lived here long?" Kenzie tried to make conversation.

"Since I was married, so yeah, a long time. Both my kids have left home. It's just me, now." She gazed over Kenzie's shoulder into the past.

Kenzie perched on the edge of a crumpled, leather armchair. "Mrs. Dooley, I'm trying to find a man who knew your husband, Jeff. I'm afraid I don't know his name. All I've got is a description." It was tenuous, at best.

"Oh, yeah? What did he look like?"

"Tall, blonde, well-built—or he would have been at the time. Did your husband know anyone who fits that description? Someone he worked with, maybe? This man would have looked like a high school quarterback."

Mrs. Dooley frowned. "It's been over five years since my Jeffie passed, but I don't remember anyone like that."

Kenzie grimaced. Granted, it was a long shot, but you never knew what random things people remembered. She recalled several occasions where witnesses had mentioned irrelevant details that later turned out to be vital in cracking the case.

"I can take a look through my photo albums," Mrs. Dooley said wistfully. Kenzie got the impression she was glad for the excuse.

"That would be very helpful." Kenzie wasn't in a rush. When the woman didn't move, she prompted, "Should I wait?"

"Dearie, some things have to be done in private."

Kenzie nodded. Memories were sacred. Private. The woman didn't want a stranger pouring over them, diluting her emotions. Kenzie pulled out her business card and wrote her cell number on the back. "You can reach me here. I'm staying at the Sheraton Hotel."

The woman glanced at the card. "You a reporter?"

"Yes, but this is a personal matter." She wasn't working for the *Herald* now. Liesl's death wasn't just another news story. "Please call me if you find anything."

"Tall and blonde, you say?" The woman raised an eyebrow.

"Yes and built like a quarterback."

A naughty grin, a hint of the woman she used to be. "I think I'd remember someone like that."

Kenzie smiled, even though she didn't hold out much hope. "Thank you, Mrs. Dooley. Don't get up. I'll show myself out."

On the way back to Manhattan, Kenzie received a text message from Raoul. According to police reports, the vehicle belonging to the missing driver had been reported stolen two days ago. The owners lived on Long Island, and the vehicle had disappeared from outside their house during the night.

She waved a sweaty strand out of her face. Annoying that they couldn't trace the driver, but it did prove one thing, this was no accident. Whoever stole that car had done so with the sole purpose of running Liesl down.

The NYPD would know about the stolen car. Along with the burglary, they'd upgrade Liesl's death to 'suspicious.' Somehow, she doubted the detective in charge would be as open to working with her as Reid was.

She messaged Raoul back.

Can you look into Jeff Dooley? Known associates. Friends. Employers. Rapist assumed his name.

She got a thumbs up in reply.

The subway took her right back to Times Square. As she emerged from the muted, underground world, she was once again hit by the frenetic activity on the surface. For the second time that day, she was grateful for the calm oasis of the hotel.

Kenzie hadn't walked more than a few steps across the lobby when two men approached her.

"Miss Gilmore?" the taller one asked.

"Yes."

"I'm Sergeant Randal. This is Detective Adams. We'd like to ask you a few questions."

5

KENZIE LED the two police detectives into the plush hotel lounge. They looked out of place amongst the chandeliers, poseur tables, and laughing guests. The tall one, Randal, had a serious, earnest face with worry lines engraved into his forehead, and a slightly frazzled appearance. His partner, a foot shorter and at least ten years older, looked pissed off with life in general.

"Shall we?" She gestured to a table by the window.

The tall one grunted, and they sat down.

"Miss Gilmore," Randal began. "I believe you were at Liesl Bernstein's apartment earlier today."

"Yes, I was."

"Could you describe your relationship with Miss Bernstein?"

"I'm—I was her friend. We were at college together in Miami."

"Is that where you're from? Miami?" He knew very well it was. Even if her T-shirt didn't scream it, he'd have done a background check on her back at the station.

"It is."

"And what are you doing in New York?"

"I'm working. I'm a reporter for the Miami Herald, and I'm covering the wedding."

He scowled. "What wedding?"

She arched an eyebrow. "Warner Sullivan's wedding. This Saturday."

"Oh, yeah." She could tell he didn't give a rat's ass about the President's son's upcoming nuptials and liked him all the more for it.

"What were you doing at Miss Bernstein's apartment?"

"Visiting her. Like I told you, she's a friend."

"Except you were also at the scene of the car accident earlier that day in which your friend sadly died." The earnest eyes plowed into hers. Sergeant Randal was a lot smarter than he looked.

"Yes, I was." She cleared her throat. It was time to come clean. "I'm afraid I thought her death was suspicious, so I went to her apartment to see if I could find anything that would give me an idea as to who would want to harm her, but when I got there, I discovered it had already been searched."

The detective studied her intently, his gaze locked on her face. She shifted uncomfortably. The silence dragged on. She knew what he was doing. Years working with Reid had taught her that if you let the silence lengthen, someone would step in and fill it, hopefully divulging more information than they intended.

Eventually, he gave up waiting. "What made you think her death was suspicious?"

Kenzie glanced at his partner, silently judging her. "The missing driver. At first, I thought maybe he'd been drinking or something, which was why he fled the scene, but when I saw her apartment..." She faded out.

"You think the two incidents are related?"

It was her turn to fix her gaze on him. "Don't you?"

There was a brief pause.

"When last did you speak with Miss Bernstein?" Randal was changing the subject.

"About two weeks ago. I called to tell her I'd be in New York this week and that we should meet up."

"Do you know the date of that call?"

"I can check for you." He nodded, so she took out her phone, scrolled through the call register until she found it. "Here." She showed him her screen. He leaned over and took a look.

"And that's the last contact you had with her?"

"It is. I tried calling her when I arrived, but her phone was off. I left messages, but she didn't get back to me."

"What was she doing on West 45th street?"

"We were meeting for lunch."

"So you did have contact with her?"

He was trying to catch her out, but it wouldn't work. You couldn't outmaneuver the truth. "No, she left a message for me here at my hotel. The receptionist gave it to me when I checked in."

Randal nodded to his partner who got up and left the lounge, no doubt to follow up on her statement.

"We didn't find a phone on Miss Bernstein's body." His gaze returned to her face. "You wouldn't know where it is, would you?"

Kenzie swallowed. "No, sorry. I didn't find anything in her apartment either."

"You went in?"

"Briefly. The door was open."

"Touch anything?"

"Only the door handle."

He tilted his head to one side. "And did you find anything that made you think her death was suspicious?" He didn't trust her. Not one bit.

"I noticed her laptop was missing. Maybe whoever broke in took it."

"Why would they do that, do you think?"

"I don't know. It could be something she was working on." The thought had occurred to her when she'd seen the mess in the apartment. It was possible this had nothing to do with the rape of Gail

Peters, and everything to do with a story Liesl was investigating. "You might want to talk to her editor at the *Times*."

He pursed his lips. "Miss Gilmore, excuse me for saying this, but you seem to have a knack for involving yourself in police business. I spoke with a detective in Miami, a Lieutenant Garrett, who vouched for you, but just so you're aware, we don't appreciate that kind of thing here in New York."

"What kind of thing?" she asked politely.

"Taking matters into your own hands. Investigating. Vigilantism. Whatever you want to call it. I know you're a big shot reporter, but this has nothing to do with you."

Now, there they differed. "Liesl was my friend."

"I know, and I'm sorry for your loss, but leave the police work to us. We know what we're doing." While Randal seemed capable, he didn't have all the facts. There was no way the detective could know about the mysterious stranger known as Jeff Dooley, or the Formosa Hotel where he'd raped a young Gail Peters. She wasn't about to tell him, either. Twenty-four years after the crime, he'd laugh in her face.

She gave a curt nod. "Fine by me, detective. I'm here to work, anyway."

His eyes narrowed. "Good."

Adams returned, and Kenzie saw him nod at his partner. The receptionist had confirmed her story. Randal got to his feet. "Thank you for talking to us, Miss Gilmore. You stay out of trouble now. I don't want to see your name on any more police reports."

That suited her. "Understood."

After a parting nod, the two men marched out of the hotel.

Kenzie had barely gotten back to her hotel suite when her phone rang.

Reid.

She already knew what he was going to say. "Hello?"

"Kenzie? What the hell is going on up there? Are you in some kind of trouble?"

"It's nice to hear from you too," she said.

He wasn't listening. "I got a call from a NYPD detective by the name of Randal. Something to do with you being at a crime scene today?"

The weight of the day pressed down on her, and she sighed. "My friend Liesl, the one who works for the *New York Times*, died earlier this afternoon. She was on her way to meet me when a car ran a red light and barreled into her." She stifled a sob. "There was nothing I could do."

A silence.

"I'm sorry, Kenz." His voice softened. "Are you alright?"

"Yes, I think so. Reid, I think it was something she was looking into that got her killed." She hesitated. "Something *I* asked her to look into."

"You? What's this got to do with you? I thought you were covering a wedding."

"I am."

He hesitated. "I'm confused. What's this case you asked her to look into?" She heard voices in the background. He must still be at the station.

"It was Gail Peter's rapist."

"Gail Peters? Jacob Peter's wife?" Jacob was the victim in a homicide investigation Reid had looked into last month. It was how Kenzie had met Gail and found out about the sexual assault.

"Yes," she whispered. "I thought while I was up here, I'd look into it."

"Wasn't that decades ago?"

"Yes, but a man like that—"

"Kenzie." He cut her off. She could hear the exasperation in his voice. "Does Gail know you're looking into this?"

"No."

"Don't you think you should ask her? She might not want to dredge up the past."

He had a point. Still... "A man like that doesn't stop at one, Reid. I bet you he's raped several women over the years."

"Do you know that for a fact?"

"No, I haven't had time to look into it. I was meeting Liesl when... when she was killed. Her apartment was searched, her laptop stolen. The police have been here, and I—"

He groaned.

"What?"

"You're doing it again."

"Doing what?"

"Involving yourself in something you shouldn't."

"How do you know I shouldn't? Maybe this man is still out there. Maybe it's time someone brought him to justice."

"It's been over twenty years."

"Twenty-four."

He sighed. "He may be dead for all we know."

"If that's the case, he can't hurt anyone else. But until we know that for a fact, I won't give up. Besides, if this is connected to Liesl's death, he's still very much alive."

"What's his name?" Reid asked, reluctantly.

"Jeff Dooley. At least, that's the name he booked the room under at the Formosa Hotel. Where he raped Gail back in '89."

"Not his real name?"

"No, the real Jeff Dooley is dead. Five years ago. Asbestos poisoning. I've just spoken to his widow."

"Okay." He sounded tired. "I'll look at the police records and see what I can dig up."

She smiled her first real smile that day. "Thank you, Reid. I mean it."

"Take care, Kenzie. Look after yourself."

"I will."

That was one promise she intended to keep.

6

The glass and cast-iron luxury condo in Greenwich Village sparkled like a jewel in the midmorning sun. It was easily the most impressive building on the street. Kenzie's interview with Emmanuelle was at ten o'clock. She was right on time.

Owing to her previous relationship with the supermodel, and the fact she'd warned Emmanuelle and Warner about the scandal about to engulf them last year, the couple had allowed her to be part of a handful of reporters invited to cover the wedding. Keith had been beside himself when he'd heard. Kenzie had never seen him so excited over a celebrity wedding.

"This is beneath us," she'd grumbled.

"It sells newspapers. People don't want to read about murder and mayhem all the time."

"I've just come off a case. I need a break."

"So, go to New York. Do some shopping. It'll be good for you." She'd thought of Reid and how she'd have to let him down. Again. "You're one of my best, Kenzie. I need you on this. Besides, you've got a history with the bride. Don't let me down now."

She'd sighed. "I won't."

Unlike the first time Kenzie had met Emmanuelle here, she was allowed up to the suite. The gruff doorman, who Kenzie didn't recognize from before, pressed the elevator button and waited until the doors opened and she'd gotten inside before he backed away.

When the elevator came to a halt, she understood why. The doors opened inside the couple's apartment. Theirs must be the only suite on this floor.

Emmanuelle floated toward her on a cloud of lavender essential oil. She wore a fluffy white robe and the barest smattering of make-up, yet she looked stunning. Her coral-tipped hand waved a greeting. "Hello, Kenzie."

"Emmanuelle."

They walked into the sitting room, and the bride-to-be sunk into the chair opposite Kenzie. "Gregor, get me an espresso." She turned to Kenzie. "Would you like anything? Gregor makes an excellent coffee." She batted her eyelids at the burly bodyguard, her full lips playing with a smile. It was very French. He nodded and turned to do her bidding. Kenzie wondered if anyone ever refused her anything.

"I'm good, thanks." She took out her notebook. One of the conditions of the interview was no phones, no recording devices, no photographs. They'd buy those from the professional photographers hired to cover the event.

"How are you feeling?" Kenzie smiled, hoping Emmanuelle wouldn't see how forced it was. Today she was in reporter mode. The events of the day before had been pushed firmly from her mind. Compartmentalized, for now. She'd continue grieving for her friend later, but right now, it was all about the woman sitting in front of her.

"Go for the human-interest angle," Keith had said. The blushing bride-to-be, living in the shadow of her cartel mother's legacy, about to be married to the son of the most powerful man in the world. It was newspaper gold.

A nonchalant shrug. "I'm okay. It feels like I'm preparing for a fashion show. You know, the hair and make-up, the dress, the walk down the aisle."

Kenzie supposed a wedding did resemble a fashion show. Paris Fashion Week, maybe. A saunter down the runway, but unlike the designer shows, the whole world would be watching. America's equivalent to a Royal Wedding.

"Are you excited?"

"Of course." Emmanuelle was hard to read. Like a book with the pages stuck together. You didn't want to pry them open for fear of tearing them. Kenzie would never say it, but Emmanuelle was very much like her mother. Maria had taken a while to warm up, but then they'd come to an understanding. They'd pushed each other's boundaries and settled somewhere in the middle. That area where neither was wholly comfortable, but not vastly uncomfortable either. It had worked. Kenzie strove to find that middle ground with her daughter too.

"Who are you wearing?" Kenzie asked, because everyone would want to know.

"Monique Lhuillier. Have you heard of her?"

Kenzie knew a thing or two about designers. "She's from L.A., isn't she?"

"Oui. She's one of my favorite designers. Sophisticated, yet playful, you know? Like me." A coquettish smile.

Kenzie wasn't sure she could picture the pouty Emmanuelle being playful but nodded dutifully. Gregor put two espressos down on the coffee table.

"Gregor is from Ukraine," Emmanuelle said. "He's upset by what is happening in his country right now."

"I'm sorry." Kenzie glanced up at him. The bodyguard gave a curt nod, then stepped back to retake his position by the door. Not the Secret Service, then? A private security company.

"I thought the Secret Service was supposed to provide security for the President's family," Kenzie said.

"Warner doesn't like it. He says it feels like his father's watching him." She sighed. "But we'll have to for the wedding. President Sullivan's insisting on it."

"Where is Warner?" Kenzie turned the conversation to her fiancé.

A wave of the hand. "I don't know. We're not seeing each other this week. It's bad luck."

"I thought that was the night before the wedding."

"I have friends coming later. We have some festivities planned. Warner has his own itinerary."

For a woman about to be married, she was incredibly controlled. But then, she was no stranger to the limelight. Used to being on camera. Used to being a star.

"Are you looking forward to being a married woman?"

A hint of a smile. "Of course."

"Will you keep modeling, or will being a politician's wife take up most of your time?"

The oval eyes hardened, as Kenzie had known they would. "I have my own career. Warner knows that."

"I'm glad to hear it. Is it true that Warner wants to follow in his father's footsteps?"

"I don't know. You'll have to ask him."

Kenzie pursed her lips. Emmanuelle was hard work. "I'm asking you what you think?"

"He hasn't said anything to me about it. At the moment, he is focusing on his business interests."

"In the Far East?" She'd read that Warner was making waves in China, causing some consternation because he was on the board of a large Chinese bank, a clear conflict of interest with his father's policies regarding the country. But then, it was public knowledge that Warner did not get along with his father. The youngest son was something of a black sheep, carving his own way.

"Amongst other places."

Emmanuelle, Kenzie decided, would make an excellent politician's wife. She had a fantastic poker face, and she'd gotten better at it in the last year. When they'd first talked about her birth mother, a woman she hadn't known existed until recently, she'd put up a good front, but Kenzie had been able to see behind the eyes. The flicker of uncertainty, the anxious hand gestures, the furtive glances toward her boyfriend. Now all her tells had disappeared. As she lounged against the leather-backed chair in her bathrobe, she was the picture of serenity.

"Let's talk about Fashion Week."

Emmanuelle perked up. Fashion Week was in September and would be Emmanuelle's first modeling appearance after coming back from her honeymoon. The couple was keeping the destination a secret, which Kenzie respected, but the fashion world would be curious to see what effect marriage had on the supermodel.

She let Emmanuelle ramble on about the designers, the couture, and the latest season's trends, interjecting now and then to ask a question to which she didn't really want to know the answer. Eventually, she brought the conversation back to the wedding.

"Will you keep your name?"

"Professionally, yes, although otherwise no. I'll be Mrs. Warner Sullivan." A flutter of eyelashes, a secret smile. Perhaps she was excited to be married, Kenzie thought. She was just very good at hiding her emotions.

"What about your adopted parents? Are they going to be there?"

"Of course. They are my family. I have no other." Now that was a statement worth printing.

"Are they here, in New York?"

"They arrive tomorrow."

Kenzie smiled. "Did you choose the wedding venue?"

The couple was tying the knot at The Plaza. The popular celebrity wedding venue was on 5th Avenue, not far away.

"We chose it together. I would rather have gotten married in the French town where I grew up, but we didn't think it was fair to the guests." Personally, Kenzie thought that sounded like a much nicer idea.

"I'm sure it'll be the event of the season."

"For what Warner is paying, I hope so." She chuckled, a rich throaty sound. Then she glanced at Kenzie. "You will be there?"

"I wouldn't miss it for the world." Was that a flash of vulnerability in the otherwise carefree facade?

"Good. The media isn't always on my side. It'll be good to have someone in my corner."

Kenzie was touched. Even though Emmanuelle acted tough, there was a softness about her once the layers were peeled back. She'd seen it in the first interview, and she saw it now.

"I'll be there," she repeated. "It's all going to be fine."

7

KENZIE STOOD outside the Formosa Hotel and stared up at the run-down, narrow brick building. Squeezed in between two other buildings, it looked like it was holding its breath. This was where Gail Peters had been raped all those years ago. According to Gail, she'd waited until her assailant was in the shower and then climbed out of a window.

Kenzie squinted up at the fire escape. She must have used that to get down.

The buzzer gave a hoarse cough, and a few seconds later, the peeling door clicked open. A musty smell greeted Kenzie as she walked inside. There were no windows, just a dark hallway with a tiny office on one side, set back into the wall. A lamp struggled away in the corner.

A rotund woman with frizzy red hair squinted through the Perspex. "Can I help you?"

"Hello, are you the manager of this establishment?"

"No sweetie. I'm just the help. His lordship doesn't work mornings."

"Right. And his lordship's name would be?"

"Malcolm Lord." Her eyes glittered at the play on words. "Who wants to know?"

"Oh, my name's Bianca Glover. I'm a blogger for *The Beat*, an online publication. I'm writing a piece on historic hotels near the East River." The secret to lying was to keep it as close to the truth as possible. Bianca was a new pseudonym, but a good one. She might use it again.

"Oh, yeah?" The woman looked her up and down.

"I'd like to ask Mr. Lord some questions, but I can come back this afternoon. He'll be in then?"

"Should be, yeah."

Kenzie thanked her and left. Even though she hadn't been inside for long, it felt good to be back in the fresh air. Something about the place was stifling. Kenzie shrugged it off. It was probably psychosomatic, since she knew what had happened there.

It was another beautiful day in the city, the sky a cloudless, cobalt blue above the skyscrapers. Kenzie decided to take a walk and explore the area. She meandered through Little Italy, browsing the various stores, restaurants and cafes. She breathed in garlic and rich tomato sauce, and her stomach rumbled. Drawn by some colorful red tablecloths, she stopped for lunch at a sidewalk cafe. A signboard read, *The Best Spaghetti Outside of Italy*.

"I'll have a glass of your house white, along with a bowl of the spaghetti bolognaise," she told the waiter, who'd appeared almost immediately. He nodded his approval, then hurried back inside. She was in New York, one of the most vibrant cities in the world. She may as well make the most of it.

While waiting for her food to arrive, Kenzie's thoughts turned back to Liesl. The crash... her friend's body in the road... the missing driver... the burgled apartment. She shook her head. It seemed so surreal, like a dream. No. A nightmare. One she wouldn't wake up from. Liesl was dead and wouldn't be coming back.

Think. Kenzie ran a hand through her hair. Liesl's apartment had been searched not an hour after her death. There must be a connection there. She just had to find it.

"What did you find out, Liesl?" she muttered, pulling out her friend's cellphone. After staring at it for a long moment, she placed it on the table. Last night, when she'd gotten back to the hotel, she'd called the number on the screen. It had diverted to an automated voicemail account. No name. No clue as to whom the number belonged. A burner, most likely. No way of knowing. Not unless someone answered.

What about the purse? Liesl's purse had gone with her to the morgue. When would they do the autopsy? Had her family been notified? Did Liesl even have a family? She'd never mentioned any parents or siblings.

Kenzie exhaled, trying to dispel some of the tension that had gripped her since her friend's death. She'd never get a hold of that purse. Sergeant Randal wouldn't let her near it. It was unlikely Liesl had brought anything with her to lunch, anyway. The New York Times reporter was too careful for that. Purses could be snatched. Any valuable information would be on her phone or laptop, behind a digital lock and key.

A couple strolled past, hand in hand. Kenzie thought about Emmanuelle and Warner, soon to be Mr. and Mrs. Sullivan. Warner, the youngest son of the President, determined to forge his own path. Emmanuelle, the beautiful French girl, outwardly tough but with a vein of fragility running through her stony exterior.

Would Emmanuelle rise above her mother's infamous legacy and create the life she wanted, or would she forever be known as the illegitimate love child of the most notorious cartel boss since El Chapo?

That remained to be seen. Kenzie bet Emmanuelle was willing to try, and she admired her for that. Overcoming adversity wasn't easy, particularly with the press ready to pounce on every wrong move. The irony wasn't lost on her. Kenzie was partly responsible for that.

It'll be good to have someone in my corner.

Kenzie hoped she could be that someone. A friendly face in the crowd. Not judging, just reporting. The food came, and she dug in. The signboard was correct. It was excellent. All the walking had worked up an appetite.

She was just finishing up when Raoul called. Wiping her mouth on a napkin, she answered her phone.

"Kenzie, I've been looking into Jeff Dooley."

"Yeah?" She took out her notepad and pen. "What did you find?"

"He wasn't a very interesting guy."

No surprises there.

"He worked for a leather manufacturer on the East River for most of his adult life, until the asbestos got him."

"Company?"

"Vitale Leatherworks. They still exist. I have the address if you want it."

"Shoot." She typed the address into her phone. "That's near to where I am now. Maybe I'll pay them a visit."

"He sued them after what happened," Raoul said. "There was a court case, but he lost. Neither he nor his wife received any compensation from Leonardo Vitale or the company."

"I see. When was this?"

"Shortly before he died."

"Okay, thanks."

"I couldn't find out much about his friends or known associates, however, he did belong to a bowling team. They did quite well in the club league for a while. Team Ten they were called. The last mention of them was four years ago."

"Send me the address," she said. "It might be worth checking out." Someone there may have used his name as an alias when they went on the prowl.

"I'll text it to you," Raoul said. "Kenzie, be careful. If this person did kill your friend, he's dangerous."

"I know. Don't worry, I will be."

8

VITALE LEATHERWORKS WAS LOCATED on the border of Little Italy and Chinatown in a warehouse building near the East River. At one point, the whole district had been industrial, but recent rejuvenation had made it trendier, and the warehouses were now interspersed with boutique stores and sidewalk cafes.

Kenzie knocked on the office door and waited. She could hear noises from inside. The hum of machinery, the splutter of a printer. Footsteps on an uncarpeted floor. The door opened and a young man in his early twenties appeared. "Can I help you?"

"Oh, er... hi." She was thrown by his age. Tall, broad-shouldered, with dusky blonde hair, he stood awkwardly, watching her. "My name's Kenzie. I'm looking for Leonardo Vitale."

"Dad is on the factory floor," he said. "I can call him if you want."

"Thank you, that would be great."

"Wait here." The young man turned and walked through an adjoining door into the factory. Kenzie took the opportunity to look around. A more experienced manager wouldn't have left a stranger alone in the office, but she wasn't complaining.

A large steel table and two chairs stood underneath the window, covered in paperwork. A box of empty binders told her the kid was doing the filing for his father. Perhaps he was being trained to take over the family business. She leafed through some of the documents. Invoices, orders, bank statements. Nothing out of the ordinary.

On the walls, above the filing cabinets were some old photographs. A glimpse into the past. This was obviously an established family business. Some of the pictures were in black and white and, judging by the style of the people in them, Kenzie guessed they'd been taken in the late fifties or early sixties.

She heard footsteps and backed away from the desk. The connecting door opened and a middle-aged man strode in. He was an older, wiry version of his son. Also tall, but with less hair. "Sorry to keep you waiting." He flashed a smile, eyes crinkling at the sides. "Tony told me there was someone waiting to see me. What can I do for you, Miss—?"

"Winslow. Kenzie Winslow." She smiled and shook his hand, watching him for a reaction. There was none. The son hadn't returned. Perhaps he'd taken his father's place on the factory floor. "I'm sorry to interrupt."

"No problem. As you can see, we're very informal. Do you want to sit down?" He gestured to one of the vacant seats.

"Thank you." Stepping gingerly over the box of binders, she sat down. "I won't take up much of your time. I flew in this morning from L.A." She paused to let that sink in. "I came to ask you about an ex-employee, Jeff Dooley. I believe he worked for you right up until his death five years ago."

There was a pause.

"You a lawyer?"

"No, sir. I'm trying to find out more about him. I—I believe he may have been my father." It was a cover story she'd come up with on the way over here. It did mean she was compromising Jeff Dooley's reputation, but at the same time, pretending to be Gail's illegitimate daughter would allow her to ask questions without appearing suspicious. And if, by some chance, Leonardo Vitale was the man who'd used Jeff's name

at the hotel, it might shock him into a reaction. That is, if he remembered Gail.

The look of surprise on his face told her she'd shocked him. Was it
because he recognized the name or because the nerdy Jeff Dooley
wasn't the type to have fathered an illegitimate child?

"What did you say your name was?"

"Kenzie Winslow." She gave an embarrassed cough. "I know this
sounds crazy, but my mother's told me so little about him. They weren't
married, you see."

A sympathetic nod.

"It's not a big deal these days, but back then..." She shrugged. "Anyway, she's passed now, so I thought I'd try to find out a little more about
my biological father."

Was that a look of relief on his face?

Vitale cleared his throat. "Jeff worked here for nearly twenty years.
He was one of my best employees. In fact, I regarded him as a friend.
We were all very upset when he got ill."

They seemed unlikely friends, considering how different they
were.

She gave a sad smile. "Thank you. That means a lot." She hesitated.
"Asbestos poisoning, wasn't it?"

His face slumped. "Yeah, it was never clear how he got it, although
we do have asbestos ceilings here in the building. The rest of the work-
force was unaffected, so it couldn't be proved the factory had made him
sick."

She shrugged, not wanting to dwell on that for too long. "I guess
some people are more susceptible than others."

He gave a stiff nod. "We've since had the ceiling replaced."

"Good to know." She smiled, making sure he noticed her dimples.
"Mr. Vitale, this is going to sound strange, but did you know Jeff Dooley
was having an affair?"

He shook his head. "I didn't. No offense, but he didn't seem the
type. I met his wife several times over the years, at work functions and
so on, and they seemed happily married."

"That's okay. It would have been very early on, about twenty-four years ago." She gave a self-conscious grin. "Probably just a one-night stand. My mother didn't tell me how they'd met. I turned twenty-three this March." Okay, that was a stretch, but she'd been told she looked young for her age.

He thought for a moment, and she wondered if he was doing the math. "I'm sorry, no. It could have been before he started working here."

"Could be." She bit her lip. "Oh, well. Thanks for talking to me, Mr. Vitale. I appreciate it."

"You're welcome. Sorry I couldn't be of more help."

She got to her feet, her gaze roaming over the photographs on the walls. "You've been around a long time."

"Yes." He stuck out his chest. "This is a family-run business, Miss Winslow. It was started by my grandfather back in '53. He was an Italian immigrant."

She gave an interested nod. "Is that him?" She pointed to one of the more faded photographs of a man in overalls standing proudly beside a shiny new sign that read Vitale Leatherworks.

"Yeah, that's him. He was originally from a small town in Puglia." That would explain the lighter coloring. She knew several Southern Italians who sported blonde hair.

Her eyes widened. "Would my father—Sorry, I mean Jeff Dooley—be in any of these pictures?"

"Why, I think he might be." He walked over to the back wall and scrutinized a group photograph. "Here he is. Back row, second from the right."

Kenzie smiled and joined him in front of the picture. Then she frowned. "That's Jeff Dooley?"

"Yes, that's him."

"Oh." She rubbed her forehead.

"Is something wrong?" he asked.

"No, I mean, yes. He's not at all like my mother described."

"Oh? What did your mother say he was like?"

"She said he was tall and handsome with blonde hair. She said he looked like a high school quarterback."

Maybe it was the fluorescent lighting in the office, but she was sure Mr. Vitale paled. "That doesn't sound like Jeff," He massaged his chin where gray-blonde stubble was beginning to appear. "Jeff was short with dark hair."

"That is so strange." She shook her head.

Mr. Vitale made a sympathetic sound at the back of his throat. "Maybe your mother was romanticizing him, you know, for your benefit."

"I guess..." She turned away from the wall.

"I'm sorry," he said again.

"That's okay. I appreciate you talking to me." She flashed him a somber smile and headed for the door. As she left, she spotted a picture hanging beside the light switch. It had been behind her, so she hadn't noticed it before. In it, Leonardo Vitale stood with his arms around another young man, huge grins on their faces. They were dressed in full football gear, shoulder pads, the works, and held up a big silver cup between them.

9

"Raoul, I need you to look into Leonardo Vitale." Kenzie lay back against the pillows in her hotel room, phone to her ear.

"He's Jeff Dooley's boss, isn't he?"

"He was, yes. He fits the profile. Tall, blonde, good looking. Or rather, he would have been twenty-four years ago. And he played for his college football team. I saw a photograph on his wall."

"Seriously?"

"Yeah, although he didn't react when I mentioned Gail's name."

"You told him about Gail?"

"I said I was her daughter. Kenzie Winslow. That was Gail's maiden name."

He exhaled noisily. "You took a risk, Kenzie. What if it was him? Now he knows you're onto him."

"He doesn't know who I am. Kenzie Winslow won't get him far. He thinks I'm a twenty-three-year-old from L.A."

"Still, considering what happened to your friend..." He didn't need to continue. She got the message.

"I'll be careful, okay?" She thought of the congenial factory owner.

"I have to say, though, that despite fitting the description, Vitale didn't seem the predatory type."

"You never know with people," Raoul cautioned. "Gail would have been taken in too."

Again, he had a good point. Perhaps Leonardo was just an excellent actor. Still, she usually had a sixth sense about these things, and even though her brain was telling her he warranted further scrutiny, her gut wasn't convinced.

"See what you can dig up."

"Will do. How's the wedding?"

"Preparations are in full swing," she replied. "I've got an interview with the celebrity wedding planner tomorrow."

"Good luck."

"Thanks. I'll be in touch."

She was just dozing off when her phone rang. It was Reid. Groggily, she answered.

"Did I wake you?" His voice was gravelly, like he'd been shouting a lot. He was probably still at his desk, typing up reports.

"No," she lied. "Did you find anything?"

"Kenzie, I looked into sexual assaults in New York going back twenty-five years and there are too many to count."

Her heart sank. "That's depressing."

"Yeah, so I refined my search to those that occurred around the same time as Gail's, in the same neighborhood."

Hearing something in his voice, she sat up. "Yes?"

"I found three other women who reported being sexually assaulted in the same year as Gail."

She caught her breath.

"Two of those said their assailant used a date rape drug."

"That could be him," she whispered.

"Uh-huh. That's what I thought. So I extended my search to the following year and found another one. The victim reported being picked up in a bar and drugged before being taken to a hotel and sexually assaulted."

"Same guy?"

"Could be."

Kenzie sucked in a breath. "Did any of the victims get a rape kit done?"

"Unfortunately not."

"Damn." No DNA.

"Obviously, I couldn't look at every report in the last twenty-four years," Reid said. "So, I skipped to the NYPD's current unsolved rape cases."

"Yes?"

"There was a similar attack three years ago. The victim reported being drugged and taken to a nearby hotel where she was raped."

"Three years ago?" She shook her head even though he wasn't there to see it. "It's not likely to be the same assailant though, is it? Twenty years is a long time."

He hesitated. "Normally I'd agree with you, but the victim said her assailant's name was Jeff."

Kenzie felt a surge of adrenaline.

It was him.

She knew it. Felt it with every fiber of her being. She thought of Leonardo Vitale. Tall, strong, crinkling brown eyes. Could he be the serial rapist?

"Can you give me the victims' names?"

"I can, but are you sure you want to go there? This guy could be dangerous."

"Now you sound like Raoul."

"Kenzie, I know you. Please, be careful. It's not worth getting killed over."

"I'm not going to get killed. Nobody knows I'm here." Okay, that wasn't strictly true. The police knew, but she'd used an alias for her other inquiries. "This man needs to be stopped. If he's still doing it, if he's still raping women, someone's got to bring him down."

"You're not a cop, Kenzie."

She grimaced. Why did he have to remind her of that? "I know."

"What are you going to do when you find him?" She liked that he said *when*, not *if*. He knew her too well. She wouldn't give up, not now that she had a lead, like a bloodhound with a scent.

"Go to the police, of course. What else would I do?"

There was a brief pause.

"Take care, Kenz. I mean it."

"I will. I'll keep you posted. Thanks, Reid. I appreciate this."

After they hung up, Reid sent the names through. Four women.

1989
   Silvia Ferri
   Milena Kownacki
   1990
   Freya Andersen
   2018
   Monica Stoller

She stared at the names for a long time. The first three women would be Gail's age or older. Mid-forties, with husbands, families. They'd have moved on with their lives. Would they want to dredge up the past just for the sake of catching a man who'd assaulted them in their twenties?

It was worth a try. Take Gail, for example. Her life had been destroyed because of what had happened. Unable to achieve intimacy, she was childless, and her marriage had broken down. Her husband had had affairs, seeking the affection she couldn't provide. Now in therapy, twenty-four years later, she was finally beginning to deal with what that man had done to her.

Were the others like that too? Nursing wounds they could not heal.

Monica Stoller, the most recent victim. Her attack had only been three years ago. Still fresh in her mind. She would remember the man who'd bought her a drink.

Buzzing, Kenzie forwarded the names to Raoul and asked if he could locate their addresses for her. Reid wouldn't give her that information, but he'd know she'd locate the women herself. Raoul would still be awake. Her research assistant was a night owl, never far from his computer.

She got a thumbs up in reply. Finally, they were getting somewhere.

Reaching over, she switched off the light, but it was a long time before she fell asleep.

10

Romantic. Timeless. Sophisticated. That's how she'd heard The Plaza described, and it was accurate. The iconic luxury hotel overlooking Central Park was breathtakingly stylish, and Kenzie admired the French Renaissance château-style building as she walked up the carpeted steps to the front entrance.

The lobby was vast and elegant. Guests swirled around pulling Louis Vuitton luggage, their Manolos clacking on the shiny marble tiles. There was a twinkle as a poodle in a diamond collar sauntered past, as dazzling as its owner. Kenzie breathed it all in.

Turning around, she spotted several suited musclemen hovering by the door. Bouncers. Hired security guards to protect the glamorous clientele. One had his eye on her. She was lurking. Looking around, she was relieved to see the wedding coordinator gliding toward her.

"Kenzie?" the woman asked politely, a practiced smile on her Estée Lauder face. She wore a red skirt suit, a Hermès scarf, and black pumps with four-inch stiletto heels that shone brighter than the polished marble. Kenzie immediately felt dowdy in her charcoal-gray pants suit and flats.

"Yes. Hanna?"

A self-assured nod. "It's good to meet you. Please, come this way."

The guard turned away as she followed Hanna into the glittering depths of the hotel. "Let's start in The Grand Ballroom as that's where we're holding the reception."

Kenzie gazed in awe as she was led from The Grand Ballroom to The Terrace Room and The Oak Room. A team of event planning specialists were already setting up the reception area for the upcoming nuptials. Kenzie wondered how much Warner Sullivan had spent on the occasion. Or was the President picking up the tab?

Emmanuelle had money, but her parents were modest French villagers. They wouldn't be able to afford The Plaza. Kenzie doubted even the supermodel's salary extended this far.

"What is your security like for the event?" Kenzie asked.

"The couple has hired their own security," Hanna told her. "We will obviously accommodate them. I believe the Secret Service is also involved."

That figured. The President didn't do anything without his personal security present.

"We only allow invited guests into the wedding area," she continued, "and they show ID when they arrive." Kenzie nodded. It sounded reasonable.

"Do the bride and groom have the penthouse suite?" she asked.

"I can't divulge where they'll be staying, but they've spared no expense." She smiled.

That would be a yes, then.

They talked briefly about the catering, the cake, the bridal bouquet, and of course, the arrangements for the big day. When her phone rang, Kenzie answered it, grateful for the distraction.

"Hi, Raoul?" She held up a finger to the wedding coordinator. *One minute.*

"I've got those addresses for you."

"Great, will you send them through to my phone?"

"Already have." It vibrated in her hand.

"Thank you."

She turned back to Hanna. "I'm so sorry. I have to go."

"But we haven't seen the spa and wellness center yet." The disappointment in her voice was real.

"Oh, that's such a shame. I'll have to come back some other time." She made her excuses, accepted Hanna's business card, and left. Flashing a parting smile at the guard who'd been watching her when she'd walked in, she darted through the revolving doors and out into the sunshine.

Monica Stoller lived in New Canaan, an affluent suburb roughly an hour's train ride from New York City. The double-story property was situated on a wide avenue adjacent to a leafy park. Children's voices drifted over on the evening breeze. From what she could find online, Monica was a junior associate at a New York law firm. Kenzie checked her watch. It was nearly seven o'clock. With a bit of luck, Monica would be home.

She pressed the buzzer and waited, listening for footsteps from inside. There were none. Perhaps the lawyer was working late or had gone out for drinks after work.

The door swung open, startling her. Looking down, Kenzie saw the occupant was barefoot. "Oh, hello. Are you Monica Stoller?"

The petite woman, dressed in workout clothes, gave a half-nod. "Who are you?"

"My name's Kenzie Gilmore." She hesitated. This was always the tough part. "I was hoping to talk to you about what happened three years ago at the Formosa Hotel." She waited, expecting the woman to close the door in her face.

Instead, Monica frowned. "Why?"

"The same thing happened to a friend of mine. I want to find out who this man is and stop him."

There was a pause. Monica's small but intense blue eyes studied her. "You think I might know who he is?"

Kenzie caught her breath. "Do you?"

"No."

She exhaled, disappointed. "Would you mind talking to me about it? I know it's not the easiest topic, but it would really help me to find out what you remember."

Monica's chin jutted out. "I've put it behind me."

"I know, and I'm sorry to ask you to dredge it up again. I wouldn't be here unless it was important."

She sighed. "How did you find me?"

"Police records."

Monica frowned. "Are you a cop?"

"No, I'm actually a reporter, but this isn't work related. As I said, it's personal."

The narrowed eyes told Kenzie the lawyer wasn't convinced. "How do I know my story isn't going to end up as a tabloid headline?"

"Because I work for the *Miami Herald*, not a New York publication, and my friend was raped twenty-four years ago, by the same man who raped you. He's been doing this a long time, Monica, and I thought someone should put a stop to it." She looked directly at the lawyer. "Will you help me?"

Monica gnawed on her lower lip. Kenzie was about to give up, when the woman gave a stiff nod. "You'd better come in."

"Who is it, babe?" called a female voice from inside the house.

"It's work," Monica called back, flashing Kenzie a warning look. "Why don't you come into my study, it's more private there? Oh, and would you mind removing your shoes? We have a no footwear policy in the house."

"Okay." Kenzie smiled at the taller woman who'd appeared. She was striking, with short, cropped hair and high cheekbones. She wore an apron that said 'Baking Queen' on it and was holding a spatula.

"This is my partner, Ingrid," Monica said.

"Pleased to meet you." Kenzie took off her shoes and placed them in the rack by the front door. "I apologize for the interruption."

Ingrid gave her a curious glance, then turned to Monica. "Supper will be ready in twenty minutes." Monica nodded, and Ingrid went back to the kitchen.

"I won't take up much of your time." Kenzie followed her down the hallway to the study.

Monica closed the door and gestured for her to sit down. Kenzie eased herself into a leather chair. "Now, what do you want to know?" Monica perched on the edge of the desk.

"Why did you drop the charges?" The police report specified that Monica had initially called the police, but then decided not to pursue it.

She waved a hand in the air. "Because of my work. I had just graduated from law school when it happened, and it was my first year on the job. I didn't want a rape case hanging over my head, particularly since I specialize in representing women in corporate harassment cases. It... well, it wouldn't have looked good."

Kenzie understood Monica's reasoning, except it meant the perpetrator went unpunished. Free to assault other women.

"Did you get a rape kit done?"

Monica hesitated. "Yeah, but I didn't use it."

Kenzie breathed in. "There's no mention of it on the police database."

"I got it done at a private clinic. I have the results right here." She nodded to a wooden filing cabinet.

Kenzie followed her gaze. "You do?"

"I got an FBI friend to run it through CODIS, but they didn't find anything."

Kenzie stared at her. "So you *did* try to find him?"

"I was angry, and I knew if I didn't do the rape kit, the evidence would be lost. Ms. Gilmore, I'm a lawyer, I know the value of evidence."

"Of course. It's just... I'm relieved, that's all. Because when we catch him, we'll be able to compare his DNA to your sample."

"When?" Monica gave a soft snort. "You think you can find this man?"

"I do." She was good at finding people. She'd done it before. Missing individuals, victims, perpetrators. The hunt. That's what she excelled at.

"Okay." Monica leaned back and studied her. "I'll tell you everything I know, because I agree with you. This man should be behind bars, but I want it in writing that you're not going to publish one word of what I tell you."

"In writing?"

"Yes, I'll draw up a contract right here, right now, and you'll sign it. Otherwise I'm not saying another word."

"Okay," Kenzie readily agreed. If that's what it took to find this guy. She wasn't doing this for the paper.

"Alright then." Monica moved around to her desk chair, opened her laptop, and quickly typed up a basic contract. Five minutes later, the printer spat out a page. Kenzie signed on the dotted line. "There."

Monica sat down again. "I'll make this quick. I was out with some friends after work. I'd just started this job, so we were celebrating. I'd had a few drinks when this man approached me at the bar. He was good looking, charming, well-dressed." She scoffed. "Back then my sexual orientation was less clear. Anyway, he hit on me. It was pretty blatant, so I turned him down."

She paused, her gaze locking on a landscape picture hanging on the wall next to the desk. A trickling stream, people lazing on the bank, blue skies. It was a tranquil scene. Maybe she was drawing from it. "When that didn't work, he apologized. Asked if he could try again. This time with a better opening statement."

Kenzie arched an eyebrow. "He knew you were a lawyer?"

Monica shrugged. "He must have overheard us talking."

"What happened next?"

"We started up a conversation. I have to admit, I found him interesting. A stockbroker; worked in the city. He was writing a novel, played part-time in a band. Probably all bullshit."

Kenzie was inclined to agree. Some men knew exactly what to say to get a girl interested. Didn't she play the same game when scouting for information for an article? Get them to trust you, to open up. Tell them what they want to hear. "What then?"

"He bought me a drink." She swallowed, the memory still raw. "It gets a little hazy after that."

"I'm sorry. Just tell me what you remember."

"He must have spiked my drink because it went straight to my head. I felt woozy, confused. I remember him leading me out of the bar and into a taxi."

"He put you into a cab?"

"Yeah, but he got in too. I remember him telling the driver I'd had too much to drink. It was weird, like I was fully conscious, but my body wasn't responding. We went to this fleabag hotel. It wasn't far, only a few blocks away."

"Name?"

"Winston Heights Hotel." She shivered. "I'll never forget it."

Kenzie gave a sympathetic nod. That must have been terrifying. To know what was going on but unable to do anything about it.

Monica's eyes fled back to the painting. "I must have passed out because the next thing I remember is waking up in the hotel room, naked."

Kenzie cringed inwardly.

"He was lying next to me. When he felt me stir, he smiled and asked if I wanted to do it again." Monica's voice was brittle, like it might break.

Kenzie shook her head. The audacity of the man. "What did you do?"

"It took me a few seconds to put it all together. The drink, the hotel, what he meant." She shuddered. "I lashed out."

"You hit him?" Kenzie's eyes widened.

"Yeah, I fucking went for him." Her face hardened. "I used to take self-defense classes, so I knew a few moves. He tried to pin me down, but I kneed him in the nuts. He yelled and released his grip. That's when I grabbed my clothes and fled."

"You didn't ask the receptionist for help?"

"What receptionist? All I saw was a sweaty man with food stains on his vest. I ran out of the hotel and never went back."

Kenzie couldn't imagine how that felt. "I'm so sorry you had to endure that. Is that when you went to the police?"

"I went home first. I cried for ages, then pulled myself together. I figured if he'd raped me, then I wanted proof. At first, I thought he might have been kidding." Her voice dropped. "He wasn't."

Kenzie watched her, admiring the way she kept her emotions in check.

"I did the rape kit privately because I didn't want anyone to know. The nurse advised me to speak to the police. I did but regretted it instantly."

"Why is that?"

"Their attitude." She took a deep breath. "They were totally indifferent. There were so many more serious crimes that I was an afterthought, an inconvenience. I got some harassed female officer straight out of the academy, who barely knew what she was doing, which is when I left. It was the right decision."

Kenzie sighed. "I understand. At least you have his DNA."

"Yeah, and I'll be hanging onto that until you have something to compare it to."

Kenzie gave an approving nod.

"Remember our agreement. Even if you find this man—when you find him—my name is not to be mentioned."

Kenzie leaned forward. "You have my word."

11

THE WINSTON HEIGHTS Hotel was nowhere near as glamorous as its name suggested. In fact, it was little more than a dingy motel, tucked away in a noisy alley of Manhattan, next to a Chinese takeout joint. The type of establishment that rented rooms by the hour.

The sweaty man in the stained vest hadn't changed either. He looked up as Kenzie entered, put down the food wrapper he was holding, and wiped his mouth on the back of his hand. She couldn't work out what he was eating, but decided she didn't want to know. A red glow from the takeout sign next door pulsed through the filthy window, illuminating half of the man's face, giving him an almost otherworldly, demonic appearance. "Can I help you?"

"I hope so. I'm looking for information on a guest who stayed here three years ago." She pushed a small piece of paper with the date toward him and watched his face twist in recognition.

"What you wanna know about that for? You a cop?"

"No. A reporter."

"Can't help you, lady. I don't want my hotel to be in any newspaper."

"Looks like you could use a little publicity." She looked around.

The hallway was musty, the glass above the reception desk was so smudged you could hardly see through it, and there were unidentifiable stains on the threadbare carpet.

He pondered this for a moment. "What you wanna know?"

"Can I see your surveillance footage of that night? The night when the girl was assaulted."

"I don't have any. That's what I told the cops."

"The police asked for it?"

"Yeah, some woman cop. Young thing, nice ass."

Kenzie grimaced. "Why didn't you have any?"

He shifted in his seat. "The camera was broken at the time." That was a lie if she'd ever heard one. Unlike Monica, this man was no good at hiding anything. His eyes kept drifting to the left, where a camera was mounted on the wall facing the desk.

"What is your name?" Kenzie asked.

"Bob Smulder."

"Bob, I know that camera was working that night, and I'm willing to pay you to show me the footage."

He wavered. "How much?"

She hid a smile. "A hundred bucks." Catching Gail and Monica's rapist on camera was worth a hell of a lot more, but she didn't tell Bob that.

He licked his lips. "Okay, but don't tell the cops. I don't want them coming back here."

"I won't."

She watched as he got up and disappeared into a back office. It didn't take long. Kenzie bet he knew exactly where the footage was hidden. Somewhere no police officer would find it. Less than a minute later he was back with a disc. "Here you go."

The only problem was she didn't have a CD player on which to view it. "Um, would you mind if I viewed it here? That way you can hang on to it."

A hundred bucks and he got to keep the tape. He gave a nod and opened the case, taking out the disc. Slotting it into the side of his computer, he beckoned for her to come around.

Kenzie opened the wooden door leading behind the reception desk and wrinkled her nose at the smell of stale food.

"What name did he check in with?" she asked, even though she knew.

He didn't have to think about it. "Jeff Dooley."

"You remember him?"

"Yeah. He seemed like a decent guy. Sporty, you know?"

The star quarterback.

"Were you here the night he brought back the woman?"

"Nah. If it's late, I leave 'em to it."

Kenzie squinted through the dirty glass at the front door. "How do they get in if you're not here?"

"They have a key." He shrugged. "I'm only upstairs. They can call if there's a problem."

She nodded. The video footage came up on the computer screen. It had a sinister reddish tinge, thanks to the takeout sign. The door opened... a figure entered the hallway. It was a man, and he was alone. Kenzie studied him. Broad shoulders, sports jacket, cap pulled low.

Damn. She couldn't see his face.

Turn around.

The guy paid cash, took the keys, and headed toward the stairs where he disappeared from view. Kenzie ground her teeth in frustration. "What about later? Do you get him leaving the building or coming back with the girl?"

"You still don't see his face," Bob supplied. Obviously, he'd watched the footage too. Back then. After it happened.

"Can I see it?"

"Sure." He wound the disc on until later that night. Same dingy hallway. Same reddish glow. The tall man came into view. Head down, face turned away from the camera.

"He knew," Kenzie whispered. "He knew it was there."

"Anyone with eyes in their head could see there's a camera there," Bob snorted.

Still, this guy knew without looking up. Not once had he lifted his head toward the surveillance camera. "Has this guy ever stayed here before?"

"Not that I remember."

"Could you check for me?"

"Lady, I already gave all my records to the cops. If he'd stayed here before, they would have found it."

Not if he'd used a different name.

She stared at the screen. He'd lost the jacket and was wearing a black T-shirt and jeans. "What about later on? When he brings her back."

Bob forwarded the footage again. It was only a few seconds on the disc, but several hours in real time. Hours during which Monica was being chatted up, drugged and brought back in the cab. The front door opened. In walked the man, his arm around a petite, bushy-haired woman.

Monica.

She was leaning against him, her head on his shoulder. It looked like she was drunk. He supported her, kicking the door closed with his foot, his arm never leaving her waist.

Kenzie watched as he led her toward the stairs. There was no sound, only the visual. She imagined Monica groaning, the sound of her feet scuffling as she stumbled over the threadbare carpet, her rapist's soothing tones.

Kenzie glanced at the timestamp at the bottom of the screen.

Eleven forty-three.

"Hang on. Can you wind it back?" Something had caught her eye.

"Sure."

He did so. Kenzie stared at the jerky movements as they moved backwards toward the door. "Okay, run it from there."

He let it run. Kenzie watched carefully. "There!"

Bob paused the video. "What?"

She stared at the screen. "Is that a tattoo?"

He leaned forward. "I don't see anything."

"In the glass. Look at the reflection." It was on his left arm, and as he walked past the reception desk, the reflection picked up an inked design on his bicep.

Bob whistled softly. "You've got good eyes."

"It is, isn't it?"

"Sure looks like it."

She squinted, trying to see what it was, but couldn't make it out. The reflection distorted the image. A black smudge on his skin. She took out her phone. "I'm going to take a photo, okay?"

He sat back as she took a few shots. "What you gonna do with it?"

"I'm going to use it to find this man."

He frowned. "But you can't see Jack-sh—"

"I can see enough," she interrupted. "Thanks for your time, Bob. Here's the hundred dollars." She put the money down on the desk.

Eyes gleaming, he pocketed it. "You won't tell the cops, will you? I don't want them coming back here, asking all kinds of questions."

"I said I wouldn't."

He didn't respond, no doubt thinking about what he was going to do with his hundred bucks. Kenzie left the smelly office and saw herself out.

Gail Peters, née Winslow, answered the telephone with a breathless, "Hello?" It was late evening, but Kenzie wanted to speak with her tonight.

"Gail, it's Kenzie Gilmore. How are you?"

"Oh. Hello, Kenzie. I'm good, thank you." Kenzie heard curiosity in Gail's tone. She was wondering why, weeks after Kenzie had helped solve the mystery of her missing husband, she was now calling again. "Is something wrong?"

"Nothing's wrong," Kenzie hastened to inform her. "I just have a question to ask you. I hope it's not going to upset you."

Gail hesitated. "Is it about Jacob?"

"No, it's about the man who sexually assaulted you back in '89."

Silence.

It dragged out. Agonizingly. Broken by a male voice in the background asking who was on the phone. Kenzie recognized it as belonging to Detective Monroe, a veteran officer at Sweetwater Police Department in Miami where Reid worked. She was glad they'd got together. Gail needed someone stable in her life, someone she could rely on.

"It's Kenzie Gilmore," Gail responded with a wobble.

"Kenzie? What does she want?"

"Gail, I'm in New York." Kenzie steered the conversation back to the reason for her call. "I've since discovered that Jeff Dooley, the man who assaulted you, has done the same thing to three other women that we know about." And probably dozens they didn't. "The last being three years ago."

A shocked gasp. "That can't be him."

"I think it is."

"But... it was so long ago."

"I know. He used the same alias."

Another silence. Longer than the first.

"Gail," Kenzie sliced through it. "Do you remember your attacker having a tattoo on his left arm?"

Gail gasped. "Oh, God."

"Is that a yes?"

"Yes, it *is* him." She spoke in a hoarse whisper.

Kenzie fizzed with adrenaline. "Do you recall what it was?"

Gail thought for a moment. "A skull and a gun. No, not a gun. A knife. Two knives. Like crossbones." Her words fell over themselves as the memory came flooding back. "Horrible thing. I remember because I asked him about it at the bar before... you know."

"I know." Kenzie's heart pounded. "What did he say?"

Gail hesitated. "I'm afraid I can't remember. I'm sorry. Is it important? It's important, isn't it?"

"Well, I've got an image of a man on a surveillance tape who I think might be him. His face is hidden, but there is a tattoo." She hesitated, then asked, "Would you mind if I sent it to you?"

A shuddering breath. "Why are you doing this, Kenzie? Why are you looking for him?"

"Because he can't be allowed to get away with what he's been doing for the last twenty-odd years. I'm going to find out who he is so he can be punished."

Gail's voice grew warm. "I knew my story had affected you. I felt it when I told you. But are you sure this is wise? What if he's dangerous?"

"Who's dangerous?" Monroe's voice in the background.

"I'll be careful," Kenzie promised. "Can I send you the photograph?"

"I don't know if I'll be able to identify him after all this time. I've spent most of my life trying to block him out."

"I understand if you don't want to." Kenzie held her breath, willing Gail to be strong.

"No, it's alright. I want to help. Send it to me."

Kenzie exhaled. "You're sure?"

She heard Gail suck in air. "Send it, Kenzie."

"Okay. Thank you, Gail."

"Don't thank me just yet."

Kenzie hung up and sent through the photograph she'd taken from the surveillance footage at the hotel. It wasn't the best photo with the bad lighting, the poor quality of the camera, and the face that remained hidden. Kenzie was hoping Gail's memory would be good enough to recognize his build, his stance, or the tattoo. Anything that would confirm it was the same guy.

Her phone beeped. Wow. That was fast. She glanced down and her heart skipped a beat.

It's him.

12

Ensconced in her hotel room, Kenzie went online and browsed tattoos. There were many variations of the skull and crossbones. Skull and rifles. Skull and swords. Skull and knives, as Gail had said. Most were military. Had the rapist served in the armed forces?

Kenzie thought about this for a while. It could explain why he'd evaded capture for so long. Weren't soldiers trained to do that? It might also explain the build. Tall, strong, broad. A man who knew how to handle himself.

On the other hand, lots of people got military-style tattoos these days. The whole military angle might be throwing her off-track. Still, it was worth bearing in mind. Kenzie thought back to Leonardo Vitale's office, but she couldn't recall anything military. No photographs with fellow squad members. No awards. No military memorabilia.

Only the gleaming, silver cup. College football.

Did he have a tattoo? He'd been wearing a long-sleeved shirt when she'd last seen him. Maybe she'd pay him another visit tomorrow to try to catch him off-guard. It was with that thought in her head that she fell asleep.

. . .

Kenzie snorted in disgust when she drew back the blinds the following morning. The sky was covered by a thick silver-gray blanket of clouds. *That* did not fit into her plans. If Leonardo hadn't been wearing a T-shirt yesterday in eighty-degree sunshine, he certainly wouldn't be today.

Still, with no other leads, she ate breakfast at the hotel, then walked the short distance to the Leatherworks factory in Little Italy. Not wanting to rush into anything, she hovered outside for a while. Watching.

Leonardo arrived on foot, shortly after nine o'clock, wearing a shirt and trousers. Same as the other day. There was no skin on display. From her hiding place behind a delivery van, she stared hard at his left arm, but couldn't see anything through the pale blue material.

She wondered where he lived. Originally, Leonardo's grandparents would have had accommodation adjoining the factory, but with the gentrification of the area, it was more likely they'd moved further afield. More space, lower prices.

Kenzie was about to go inside, when she saw his son arrive. The lanky teenager sauntered over to a coffee cart by the East River. He seemed to be in no rush to get to work. Changing her mind, Kenzie approached him.

"Hi again." She smiled disarmingly.

He turned, startled. "Oh, hello."

"How's the coffee here?" she asked.

"It's good." He blinked several times. "Are you here to see my dad?"

"My hotel's nearby," she explained. "I was just taking a walk."

He gave an uncertain nod.

"How do you like working for the family business?" she asked, keeping him talking.

"It's okay. Dad's training me to take over one day."

"Impressive."

He shrugged.

"Don't you want to?"

"Oh, yeah. I do. I mean it's the family business, right?"

"But you wanted to do something else?" He seemed reluctant.

"I wanted to play pro football." His face twisted into a grimace. "Then, I hurt my knee."

"I'm sorry."

"Yeah, it's a bummer. Now I'm stuck working here."

She felt genuinely sorry for him. Kenzie knew what it was like to have your dreams crushed by something outside of your control. It sucked.

"Did your dad play?" she asked. Seeing his surprise, she elaborated. "I saw a photograph of him holding a trophy in his office."

"He played at college," the kid said. "Like me."

"Was that before he went to the military?" It was a shot in the dark. She was just throwing it out there.

The kid frowned. "Dad wasn't in the military."

"Oh, right. Sorry. My mistake. I thought I saw a photograph of him with a tattoo on his shoulder."

"Nah, couldn't be Pops. He doesn't have any tattoos."

"I was obviously looking at the wrong man." She laughed, seemingly self-consciously. "Anyway, I'll let you go." She threw him a parting smile and headed off toward Chinatown.

So much for that. Kenzie traipsed back to the hotel, suddenly weary. She hadn't slept well last night, the possibilities swirling around in her head. She'd had bad dreams too, of dim hallways, grubby men in wifebeater vests, and in the background, a girl screaming.

This case was getting to her.

Not wanting to be alone in her hotel room, she sat in the hotel lounge and ordered a coffee. It was lunchtime, but she had no appetite. Tourists came and went. Laughing. Chatting. Flushed with excitement. She found the activity reassuring. It helped dispel the creepiness that had settled over her the night before.

Opening her laptop, she wrote up some notes on the wedding. Keith had already published two of her articles since she'd been here, so she checked the online version of the newspaper to see if they were there.

Inevitably, Liesl crept into her mind. How far had the New York Times reporter got with the inquiry? Last time they'd spoken, Kenzie had thought she'd come to a dead end. The Formosa ... Jeff Dooley ... his widow in Queens ... Had Liesl also gone to see Leonardo Vitale? The leather worker hadn't mentioned it, neither had his son.

Kenzie ran an agitated hand through her hair. What about the burgled apartment? Had the police made any headway? There was no point in calling Detective Randal or his sidekick Adams, they wouldn't tell her anything. What she needed was a source. Someone who worked for the police department, who she could talk to about the investigation. Liesl would have had a contact. Reporters always did. Kenzie tapped her finger on the keyboard. If only she had a name.

There was one person who might be able to help her.

Taking out her phone, she dialed Reid's number. He'd be at the station. Maybe he could find out what was going on. To be honest, she just wanted to hear his voice. To her surprise, the call diverted to his personal cellphone. He picked up just as she was about to end the call.

"Kenzie?"

"Hi." She hated that her voice was suddenly breathless.

"Where are you?"

"I'm at the hotel. Why?"

"In your room?"

Now he was acting weirdly. "No, I'm in the lounge, working. Why?"

"Oh, right." The line went dead.

Confused, she stared at her phone. Then, a gruff voice behind her said, "There you are!"

"Reid?" She sprung up. God, it was good to see him. Resisting the urge to throw her arms around his neck, she asked, "What are you doing here?"

"I came to see you."

"But—?" She shook her head at a loss for words. He wore jeans and a sweatshirt, his hair messy from the flight, but he looked great. "Why?"

"I had vacation days. It was about time I took a break."

She gazed happily at him. He didn't seem to notice her reaction. "Kenzie, I spoke with Monroe, then I did some more digging. This could be bigger than you think."

"What do you mean?" She gestured for him to sit down, still dazed he was actually here. In New York. To see her.

He remained standing. "I looked into homicides in the New York area, in particular where the victim had been raped, and a date rape drug had been found in the autopsy."

"Yes?" Kenzie held her breath.

"There were two. Both victims were found in dingy hotels. One being the Formosa."

13

"Someone died at the Formosa?" Kenzie stared at him, shocked by the news.

"They found her body in a room," Reid said. "She'd been strangled."

"As well as sexually assaulted?"

"Yeah. The medical examiner found Rohypnol in her system, just like what happened to Gail."

"And Monica Stoller," Kenzie murmured.

Reid nodded. "Have you checked out any of the other victims on that list I sent you?"

"Not yet." She told him about the visit with Monica. "She has his DNA, Reid. When we catch this bastard, we can run it against him."

"That is helpful," he agreed. "But we have to find him first."

"I've got a shot of him on camera." She picked up her phone.

His eyebrows shot up. "You do?"

"It's not great quality, but this was taken the night he raped Monica." Kenzie showed him the screen.

"Where'd you get this?" Reid took it from her and scrutinized the grainy picture.

"From the owner of the Winston Heights Hotel. Monica told me that's where it happened."

"Can't tell much by the photo, other than he's keeping his head down. He knows the camera's there."

Kenzie nodded in agreement. "I watched the whole recording. He doesn't look up once."

"Do the police have this?" Reid handed the phone back.

"No, the owner told them the camera was broken."

He frowned. "Why?"

"He didn't want them sniffing around. It's the kind of place that accepts cash payments, and I doubt they all get declared on his tax return."

Reid gave a knowing nod. "Lucky for us he still had it."

"It doesn't help much but look—" She pointed to the reflection in the glass. "That's a tattoo." Reid leaned in. "I called Gail. Her rapist had a military tattoo on his left arm. A skull and two crossed knives. See, you can almost see the design if you look closely. It's the same guy."

"Good work," said Reid, impressed.

She smiled ruefully. "The only problem is my one and only suspect doesn't have any tattoos."

"Suspect? You mean you've got someone in mind?"

"I did, but not anymore." She shook her head at the phone. "It can't be him."

"Who did you think it was?"

"The real Jeff Dooley's boss, Leonardo Vitale. He runs the family business in Little Italy, and for a while, I thought it might be him. He fits the description, but he doesn't have a tattoo."

"He could have had it removed," Reid suggested.

"Maybe, although his son confirmed he didn't have one, and the kid must be in his early twenties."

"So, you've ruled him out?"

"Yeah, I guess so. I'm all out of leads." She threw her hands in the air and sank back down onto her chair. Reid eased his tall frame into the armchair next to her and stretched his legs out in front of him. "What now?"

She looked across at him. "I'd love to know what the police have."

"You've spoken to the cops?"

"Briefly." She told him about Liesl's apartment and the missing laptop.

"You think it's related?"

"Reid, the place was ransacked. It wasn't your run-of-the-mill burglary. These guys were looking for something."

"Her laptop?"

"I'm guessing so.

"Makes sense." He raked a hand through his hair, smoothing down the wayward strands. "What was she working on? Do you know?"

"No, I haven't had a chance to contact the paper yet. I doubt they'd tell me, anyway. I work for the *Herald*." She gave a wry grin. "Rival newspapers aren't open to sharing information."

He frowned. "How are we going to find out?"

Kenzie hesitated. "I do have her phone."

"What?" He fixed his steely gaze on her. "How'd you get that?"

"At the scene of the accident. It was lying outside the police cordon. Liesl must have dropped it when she was hit." Kenzie didn't want to think about that. "I picked it up. I was going to hand it over, but—"

"You thought you'd see what was on it first?" Reid finished for her.

Flushing, she gave a nod. "The cops don't know about Gail's sexual assault, okay? It happened twenty-four years ago. If I'd said anything, they'd have laughed at me."

Reid scowled at her. "So you took evidence from a crime scene and kept it."

"It wasn't a crime scene at that point," she pointed out, lifting her chin a notch. "The cops were treating it as an accident."

"Semantics. You should have—"

She held up her hands in a gesture of surrender. "I know, okay? I'm sorry."

"No, you're not."

She sighed. "It's too late now. The phone is compromised. Besides, I can't get into it. It's locked, and I don't know her passcode."

Reid massaged his forehead.

"But I did take down the last missed call. It was on the screen."

He glanced up, arching his eyebrows. "You call it?"

She gave a contrite nod. "I got an automated voicemail. I don't know who it belongs to."

"The police would have been able to find out."

"I know,." She tilted her head. "Can you find out?"

There was a long pause.

"I could, but we're going to play this straight. We're going to pay the lead detective a visit. What was his name?"

"Sergeant Randal." Kenzie sighed, but she knew he was right. She didn't have the resources to track down the owner, and Reid was out of his jurisdiction. "What if it's a burner?"

"Then they won't be able to find out who the number belongs to, but you can bet they've traced Liesl's last movements. That's what I'd do. If you have the phone, they'll work it out and you'll get into even more trouble."

Damn, he was right. In the shock of her friend's death, she hadn't thought of that. "They're not going to be happy with me."

"No, but then we know something they don't."

"About the rapist?"

"Exactly."

"You're going to tell them what Liesl was looking into?"

"Yeah."

"But..."

"If we ever find this guy, we're going to need their help." She recognized the no-nonsense tone in his voice. He wouldn't be dissuaded. "The scumbag has killed two women, Kenzie. It's not limited to rape anymore. He's a dangerous predator."

She couldn't fault his logic. "Okay, if you must."

"And... I might be able to find out what they've got on the burglary."

She relented. "That would be useful. When do you want to do this?"

"How about now?"

The NYPD Midtown South Precinct was an unforgiving brown concrete and brown-brick building situated on West 35th Street. Sergeant Randal headed up the Detective Squad, responsible for homicides in the local neighborhood, which included a large part of midtown Manhattan.

Kenzie and Reid walked across the busy street and up the three steps to the front entrance. A young officer at a security desk greeted them. "We'd like to speak to Sergeant Randal," Kenzie informed him.

He glanced at her, and then his gaze shifted to Reid, who held up his ID. "Lieutenant Garrett, Sweetwater PD in Miami." The man scrambled to his feet. "Yes, sir. If you just wait here, I'll call Sergeant Randal."

Kenzie raised an eyebrow. Reid grinned. "Works every time."

Not five minutes later, Sergeant Randal strode into the lobby. His suit was crumpled, his thinning hair wispy, and judging by the dark circles beneath his eyes, he hadn't slept a wink. Still, he had a look of intense curiosity on his face. "Lieutenant Garrett, I'm Sergeant Randal." They shook hands. Then his gaze fell on Kenzie. "Miss Gilmore?" The curiosity changed to confusion as he glanced between the two. "You're here together?"

"Yes." Kenzie shot him a triumphant smile.

He frowned. "How can I help you?"

"Actually, it's us who can help you," Reid replied, turning the discussion around.

"Oh?"

"We have some information you should be aware of."

"I see." He fixed them with a hard look. "Won't you come through to my office?"

They followed him through the body scanner, across the lobby, and up a flight of stairs. "We're on the second floor," he said. "But the elevator takes forever."

A few moments later, they were ensconced in his overly warm office, while he took a seat behind a scratched wooden desk. The window was open a few inches, but still didn't let in enough air. He saw them glance at it.

"Doesn't open any wider than that," he supplied, with a shrug. "Maybe they think we'll throw ourselves out of it." With his deadpan expression, Kenzie wasn't sure whether he was joking.

Reid snorted.

They sat down. "Now, what's the information you have?"

Reid cleared his throat. "I believe you spoke with Kenzie before in connection with Liesl Bernstein's death."

A nod. "We questioned her."

Reid looked pointedly at her. "She has something she'd like to add. Go ahead, Kenzie."

Kenzie narrowly avoided rolling her eyes at him. Time to come clean. "I have Liesl Bernstein's cellphone."

At his exasperated look, she continued, "I'm sorry that I didn't give it to you before. It was wrong of me to keep it."

Randal frowned so hard crevices appeared on his forehead. "How did you get it? Did you take it from her apartment? Do you have her laptop too?"

"No! And no." She shook her head. "I found her phone on the street where she had the accident. She must have dropped it when she was hit."

"It wasn't on," Randal said. "We pinged it."

"I switched it on," she said. "After I charged it up."

"We didn't pick that up."

"Only briefly. It's locked."

He shook his head. "Can I see it?"

Kenzie dug in her purse and pulled out the device, setting it on top of the pile of folders in front of him.

Opening his drawer, Randal pulled on a pair of forensic gloves. Kenzie heard Reid grunt approvingly beside her.

Randal picked up the phone. With a gloved finger, he switched it on. The missed call flashed on the screen. "Know who this number belongs to?"

She shook her head. "When I called it, nobody picked up."

Randal studied Kenzie. "You realize I could book you for withholding evidence."

Reid cut in. "You don't know that it is evidence yet," he said matter-of-factly. "Besides, it was outside of the police cordon. If Miss Gilmore here hadn't found it, your men would have missed it entirely. You could say she's assisting you with the investigation."

Randal pursed his lips, his dark eyes darting from Kenzie to Reid and back again. "I don't know what arrangement you two have going on down in Miami," he said. "But here in New York, we don't collaborate with members of the public."

"Can I have it back, then?" Kenzie asked.

His grip tightened around it. "No, ma'am. You may not."

"We also know what Miss Bernstein was working on at the time of her death," Reid said, turning the conversation back to the victim.

"But if you don't want to collaborate, we'll just leave," Kenzie added, earning herself a scowl from Reid.

Randal's gaze narrowed. "If you have information pertinent to this investigation, you should share it."

"We're not sure it has anything to do with her murder," Reid said. "But we thought—"

"Murder?" Randal interjected. "How do you know she was murdered?"

"Let's see." Kenzie scratched her chin. "She was mowed down in the street, the driver fled the scene, the car involved was stolen, her apartment was searched, and her laptop stolen. How's that for starters?"

Randal glared at her, unamused. "Okay, fine. We are treating her death as suspicious. What information do you have?"

Reid nodded for her to continue. Kenzie took a deep breath. "I asked her to look into a sexual assault that happened twenty-four years ago."

"Twenty-four years?" He scratched his head, clearly unsure where this was going.

"Yeah."

"Just wanted to make sure I heard you right. Go on."

"It happened in a hotel called the Formosa, downtown. The victim was picked up in a bar, her drink spiked, and taken back to a dingy hotel room where the rapist forced himself on her. In the morning, she climbed out of the window and fled."

Randal shook his head. "I'm sorry, but what has this to do with Miss Bernstein's death?"

"Liesl was looking into it for me," Kenzie said. "She went to the Formosa, spoke with the manager, and got the name of the rapist."

The New York detective stared at her. "And you think he's responsible for her death?"

"I don't know," Kenzie shrugged, glancing at Reid for help. "All I'm saying is that since then, we've discovered several other women who have been raped in the same way."

Randal pursed his lips. "This is New York. Unfortunately, what you're describing happens a lot."

"The man's name was Jeff Dooley," Reid supplied. "Look it up. It's on the police database." He lowered his voice. "In addition to the rapes, two women were murdered. The last victim was discovered by the maid at the Formosa Hotel. Also on the system."

Randal sucked in a breath. "Same hotel?"

"Yes. The rapist is a murderer."

Randal closed his eyes, briefly, as if wishing them away. Unfortunately, they were still there when he opened them again. "You think this man, this rapist and murderer, is responsible for Miss Bernstein's death?"

"He's killed before," Reid said with a shrug.

"She was looking into it," Kenzie reminded him. "Maybe she found out who he was, and he killed her to silence her."

There was a long pause as Randal digested this. "Do you have any proof? Anything that shows Miss Bernstein was investigating this guy?"

Kenzie fidgeted in her chair. "Only what she told me on the phone."

"Which was?"

"That she traced Jeff Dooley to an address in Queens. His wife told her Jeff died five years ago from asbestos poisoning."

Randal exhaled. "So, it wasn't him?"

"Exactly. The real rapist was using his name. That's as far as she got."

Randal stretched his neck. Kenzie could tell he was tiring of their story. Basically, they had nothing other than the cellphone. Except that wasn't strictly true. "I've got a photograph of him." She reached for her phone.

Randal's head snapped up. "Of the rapist?"

She nodded. "I took it from the surveillance footage at another hotel where a woman was sexually assaulted three years ago."

He shot her a skeptical look. "How do you know it's the same guy?"

"The reservation was under Jeff Dooley."

The detective's eyes widened, and he stretched out a hand for the phone. Kenzie passed it to him. Studying the photograph, he said, "Can any of the victims confirm it's him?"

"One already did," Kenzie replied. "I haven't spoken to the others yet." She didn't mention Monica by name, as she'd made it quite clear she didn't want to be involved. "The tattoo is a skull and crossed knives, by the way. The first victim remembers it well."

Randal grunted. Kenzie interpreted that as a good sign. It was probably the closest thing she was going to get to a thank you. Eventually, he put the phone on the desk and leaned back in his chair. "Okay, we'll look into it."

"You'll look into this rapist?"

"Yeah. I'll put one of my men on it."

Kenzie glanced at Reid. One of his men? With no background information, no prior knowledge of the case? Her heart sank.

Reid got to his feet. "Would you mind if I looked into it?"

Not to be outdone, Randal stood up. Reid was taller. "Well, that's not really how..."

"How you do things in New York? I know. Call it a professional courtesy. The first victim resides in Miami, so you could officially second me to the case. Call it inter-agency cooperation."

"Let me think about it," Randal said, after a pause. "I'll have to clear it with my boss."

"Okay, here's my card." Reid placed it on the folders, right in front of the New York detective. "I'm in town for a couple of days, and I'm offering to help you out. I know you've got your hands full here."

Randal gave a stiff nod. "I'll let you know."

"Do you think he will?" Kenzie asked as they left the building.

"Yeah," Reid said with a wry grin. "It's a cold case, and he doesn't have the manpower. If we can close this case for him, we'll be doing him a favor. He's got nothing to lose."

"I hope so." Kenzie bit her lip. "Otherwise we're just going to have to solve it without him."

14

"You wanna grab some lunch?" Reid asked on the way back to the hotel. He hadn't eaten since he'd left Miami that morning and his stomach was rumbling.

"Sure. I know this great Italian spot."

"Sounds good."

She led him through the vibrant streets of Little Italy to the restaurant she'd dined at before. Remembering her, the waiter beamed. "So good, you had to come back, eh?"

Kenzie grinned. "You got me."

Reid raised an eyebrow. "Making friends already?"

"It is seriously good food."

They ordered the house special and some soft drinks, and Reid leaned back, taking in the surroundings. "The last time I was in New York was over fifteen years ago."

"For work?"

"No, I came on a wild weekend with some colleagues. Didn't see much of the city."

Laughing, she asked, "Where are you staying?"

"Your hotel."

"The Sheraton?" She seemed surprised.

"Yeah, thought it would be easiest. Is it a problem?" He tried to read her expression, but couldn't.

"No, it's just the newspaper's putting me up. It's not cheap."

"I can afford it." He glanced up at the dissipating clouds. The sun forced its way through.

Kenzie took off her cardigan. It was an aquamarine that brought out the blue in her eyes. As usual, she was dressed casually, in jeans and a T-shirt. Her hair hung loosely around her face, something she was doing more often these days. She always used to wear it up in a no-nonsense ponytail. He wondered what had brought about the change. The fresh air, or maybe it was the warmth, brought a pretty flush to her cheeks. Not that he noticed.

"How's your cabin coming along?"

"It's getting there. I think I was being more of a hindrance than a help," Scoffing, he said, "The site supervisor hinted I should leave them alone to finish the project." A construction crew was rebuilding his cabin after it burned to the ground in a wildfire last year. He'd been helping them rebuild, which he enjoyed. The manual labor took his mind off work—and Kenzie—but he could understand the foreman not wanting him there micromanaging every little detail.

Kenzie chuckled. "When will you be able to move in?"

"Not soon enough." He was sick of staying at the Gator Inn, a flea-bag motel in the Glades, not far from his cabin.

"And the department is okay without you?"

"Yeah, I've left Vargas and Diaz in charge." They were both very competent detectives. Besides, they weren't investigating anything big, only a couple of burglaries that had hit the neighborhood.

"How is Willie doing? Has he gotten over Shannon?"

Willie Vargas had recently split from his ex-fiancée, who had seduced him with the sole purpose of using his access to hack into the police database. He'd fallen for her hook, line and sinker. He'd even asked her to marry him. Understandably, her betrayal had come as a shock. Not just to Vargas, but to all of them. It would take Vargas some time to recover.

"He's okay," Reid frowned. "As well as can be expected under the circumstances."

Kenzie gave a sympathetic nod. "Poor guy."

The food came and Reid dug in. "Damn, this is good."

"Told you so."

"You're not hungry?" She was barely eating.

"Not really. Besides, I've got to fit into a cocktail dress tonight. I've been invited to a pre-wedding soiree at The Plaza. Emmanuelle asked me to be there."

"You two becoming friends?" Reid raised an eyebrow.

Kenzie shrugged. "Of sorts. I think she looks upon me as a friendly face."

"Because you forewarned her about the scandal involving her mother?" If he remembered correctly, Kenzie had flown to New York to warn Emmanuelle that the story about her biological mother, the infamous cartel boss, Maria Lopez, was going to break, allowing her some time to prepare for the media onslaught.

Kenzie gave a nod. "She trusts me."

"Can she?" Reid cocked his head.

"Of course."

"And if Keith asks you to publish something detrimental?"

Kenzie shrugged. "Emmanuelle knows I'm writing about the wedding. But if there's ever something she doesn't want printed, we'll cross that bridge when we come to it. I'm open to negotiation."

"Keith's not." Her editor was not known to make allowances for sensitive dispositions. A story was a story. His job wasn't to worry about the consequences of what he published. Only the content.

"No, he's not," she admitted with a sigh. "Besides, President Sullivan is going to be there tonight." She shot him a cheeky grin. "I want to get a selfie."

Reid laughed. It felt good. As he sat here with the sun on his face, good food in his belly, and Kenzie opposite him, he felt happier than he'd been in a long time. Even with the pall of the rapist looming over them.

"I wanted to talk to you about your friend, Liesl," he said, after he'd finished eating.

"Oh, yeah? What about her?" Kenzie had abandoned her lunch and ordered a cappuccino. He ordered an espresso.

"If she was killed by this guy, the fake Jeff Dooley. How'd he know she was onto him?"

"I've been thinking about that too," Kenzie said. "I retraced her steps from the motel to Dooley's wife in Queens, and then to a leather-worker not far from here. The suspect I told you about. He employed Dooley for years."

"Okay, let's go through it step by step." Reid stretched his legs out under the table. He wanted to understand everything she'd done so far. Two heads were better than one.

"I never actually met the guy at the Formosa," Kenzie said. "But I spoke with the receptionist who told me his name was Malcolm Lord. He'd only had the hotel for ten years, though, and Gail was raped twenty-four years ago."

Reid nodded. "What about Dooley's wife?"

"She was going to look through some photographs for me," Kenzie recalled. "To see if any of her husband's friends or colleagues fit the rapist's description."

"You think they must have known him?"

"You'd have to, to impersonate someone, right?"

He nodded. It made sense.

"Anyway, Dooley's employer, Leonardo Vitale, is tall, fair haired and well-built for his age."

Reid arched an eyebrow. "He fits the profile."

"I did think it might be him at first, but like I said, he doesn't have a tattoo." She sighed in frustration. "And yet, someone ran her down in the street and searched her apartment."

"Hmm..." He scratched his chin. The stubble was already starting to grow on account of not being able to shave that morning. The flight was too early. "I might pay our friendly neighborhood detective another visit in the morning," Reid said. "I want to take a look at his files on the burglary."

Kenzie's eyes gleamed. "That would be very helpful."

"In the meantime, let's talk to the owner of the Formosa. I want to take a look at where it all started."

"I'd love to come with you, but I've got to get ready for tonight. I've got a hair appointment at the hotel salon in an hour."

He couldn't resist a grin. This was the other side to Kenzie, the reporter side. He admired her ability to morph into someone else in order to get a story. Tonight, she'd be a glamorous socialite, no doubt in a designer gown, looking like a million bucks. He felt quite envious that he wasn't going to be there to see it. "That's okay."

"It's not much to look at," Kenzie warned him. "Neither is the other hotel, the Windsor Heights. They're both dives."

He knew the type. "Places where suspicious activity won't be so easily noticed. Bringing a drunk woman back is not going to raise many eyebrows."

Kenzie gritted her teeth. "Exactly." He sensed her anger. Unfortunately, it didn't sound like they had much to go on. Still, he'd solved cases with less, and he was going to do his utmost to find this rapist-slash-killer and get him off the streets. "If you're back before I leave, you can update me then."

"Sure." It seemed he'd get to see her in all her finery, after all.

15

REID PUSHED OPEN the peeling door to the Formosa Hotel and entered the dimly lit hallway. The first thing he noticed was there were no guest rooms downstairs. Reid remembered Kenzie telling him that twenty-four years ago, a young Gail Winslow had climbed out of the window in order to escape. To do that, she must have used the fire escape. There were no windows down here, just a flickering light in the ceiling above him, and a muted lamp behind the reception desk.

It smelled musty, like sweat and mold. A man in a New York Knicks sweatshirt sat behind a desk in a tiny office, separated from the hallway by a protective screen. Somewhere in the background a television played. It sounded like a sports game, judging by the cheering.

"You Malcolm Lord?"

Narrowed eyes. "Who wants to know?"

"Lieutenant Reid Garrett." He held his ID card up against the screen.

"Miami? You're out of your jurisdiction, aren't you?"

"I'm working with the NYPD," he replied gruffly. "I'm looking into the murder of a woman whose body was found on these premises five years ago. Her name was Rebecca Wilson."

"Not that again." Lord shook his head.

"Can you tell me what happened?"

An annoyed grunt. "Some dude strangled her in the room. I found her body out back near the dumpsters. That's all there is to tell."

That was never all there was to tell. Reid took a step closer to the screen. "Talk me through it."

"Why? I've already been through this with the cops." He shot Reid a beleaguered look. "Talk to them."

"I have," Reid retorted. "I'd like to hear your version of events."

An exasperated sigh.

The hotel proprietor pushed himself off his chair. It was then Reid noticed the crutches against the wall. Malcolm Lord was handicapped. Reaching for them, he opened the connecting door.

"You'd better come in."

Reid walked into the cramped office. It was barely bigger than his hotel bathroom and twice as cluttered. The desk had an ancient computer on it, along with food wrappers, newspapers, a book of sudoku puzzles, and two sets of glasses.

"Take a seat."

There was a bar stool positioned against the wall, so Reid perched on that. Malcolm Lord toppled backwards into his chair again, emitting a loud grunt.

"What happened?" Reid nodded to his foot. Even with shoes on, he could see that the ankle was twisted inwards. It looked painful to walk on.

"Motorcycle accident." He scowled. "Damn stupid too. Came off at close to eighty miles an hour. Nearly lost my whole darn leg." He shook his head, regret written all over his face.

"Bad luck," Reid murmured.

"Yeah, they said I'd never walk again." He smirked. "They were right. That's when I bought this place. Had to make a living somehow."

"When was that?" Reid asked.

"Nearly eleven years ago now." He sighed. "Feels longer than that."

The light in the hallway flickered as if to remind him of this. "Damn electrics," he muttered. "Whole building needs rewiring."

The place was in a terrible state. Reid couldn't understand why people would pay good money to stay here. He supposed it was cheap and central, and you could rent a room for a couple of hours. There was a market for everything.

"Tell me about this girl," he prompted, not wanting to stay too long.

"She wasn't staying here," Lord said. "One of the guests brought her back. I didn't hear them come in. A couple of years before that happened, I had the place fitted out with keycards. Made my life a whole lot easier. Now I leave 'em to it and go to bed."

"Mm-hmm." Reid scratched his head. "Who was the guest?" Even though he knew. It was on the police report.

"Name was Jeff Dooley," the proprietor said. "I remember because I had to say it over and over again to those cops. I told them, I didn't see him come in with her."

"But you must have checked him in earlier that day?"

"Well, yeah."

"What did he look like?"

"He was a good-looking dude. Tall, well-built, like he worked out, you know?"

"Hair color?"

"Fair. Lighter than yours."

Reid nodded. "What else can you tell me? Did he have any defining marks or scars? What about a tattoo?"

"Not that I could see. It's dark in here and I only saw him for a few minutes. He paid cash."

Of course.

"Gave his name as Dooley. That's all I can remember."

It was exactly what was in the police report. "What about the morning you found the girl? Can you tell me about that?"

"It was around seven a.m. I went out back for a smoke and found her lying there on the concrete next to the dumpster. At first, I couldn't believe what I was seeing. She was so still, like a doll. Then I called 911."

"Did you touch the body?"

"No, man. I watch TV. I know better than to do that."

Reid nodded. "What was she wearing?"

He frowned. "I think it was a dress. Yeah, a short dress and no shoes. That's it. Her shoes were missing."

Reid frowned. "Both of them?"

"Yeah, because the CSI guys found them under the bed in Jeff Dooley's room. That's how they knew it was him."

Reid didn't remember reading anything about shoes in the police report, but then he'd just skimmed it. He'd been so shocked by what he'd read, he'd printed out the reports, gone home and packed, and jumped on a plane that same day. Those reports were now sitting in his hotel room.

"One other thing," Reid said, before he got up. "Twenty-four years ago, a woman was sexually assaulted here. The man who raped her also gave his name as Jeff Dooley."

Lord hung his head. "Yeah, I know. A reporter chick came around a couple of weeks ago asking about that. I didn't own the place back when it happened, but the records were on the system, so I just kept them."

Thank God he'd had the foresight to do that. "Do you remember this reporter's name?"

"Er... Lisa, Linda, something like that."

"Liesl?"

"That was it, yeah."

That was proof Liesl had indeed been to the Formosa. "You showed them to her?"

"She wanted to know who stayed here on one particular night, I can't remember the date. I wrote down a bunch of names, and he was one of them."

Reid frowned. "You didn't tell her about the murder?"

"She didn't ask."

Reid shook his head. If he had, Liesl might have contacted Kenzie sooner. Or reported it to the police. She might still be alive.

"What?" Lord shrugged. "I'm not going to willingly divulge that kind of information, am I? I don't want no reporter sniffing around. It's bad enough the cops are still bothering me." He scowled at Reid, who raised his hands.

"Okay, okay. Calm down. We're done here. Thanks for your cooperation."

Lord gave a sulky nod, and shifted, reaching for his crutches.

"Don't get up," Reid said. "I can see myself out."

"Her shoes were missing?" Kenzie stared at the police reports spread out over the bed. The shoes had been mentioned, but he'd glossed over the detail in his hurry to get to New York.

"Yeah, when the killer dumped her body, he left them in the hotel room. The CSI team found them under the bed."

"Sloppy. Is that how they linked him to the killing?"

Kenzie stood in the center of his hotel room in a scarlet off-the-shoulder dress with a slit up the side that showed a testosterone-inducing amount of thigh. The delicate silk hugged her figure to the extent that he could see every curve in her body. Reid found he was struggling to stay focused on the conversation. "Uh-huh. Yeah."

She frowned. "I'm surprised he overlooked that detail."

Reid was too, to be honest. It was a rookie mistake. Not the actions of an experienced perpetrator. "If he'd disposed of the shoes, they wouldn't have known he was involved."

"Until they searched the rooms. Checked them for DNA."

"Hotels are notoriously bad for DNA." He glanced away as she smoothed down the dress. "Evidence is nearly always contaminated."

"If it's the same guy, he's normally more careful." Kenzie's thought process mirrored his own. "He's been active for twenty-something years. You don't get away with that without being careful. In all that time, we've found only two women who've died. So why did he kill them? Did they struggle? Did they threaten to go to the cops? Did they know him?"

Reid tilted his head thoughtfully. "There could be more victims we haven't connected to him."

"There could be, but there are far more women he raped and didn't kill. I don't think this guy is a killer. Not really. I think he only kills if he has to."

"What's this got to do with the shoes?"

"The night he killed Becca Wilson... maybe he was in a hurry? He dumped her body behind the hotel, no attempt to hide it. He left the shoes in the room. It's sloppy."

"You have a point." He thought about what she'd said. "I'll look into the other victim. The conditions of her death might be able to shed some light."

"Good idea. I wish I could do it with you." Then she sighed and did a small pirouette. "How do I look?"

"You look—" He hesitated. "Beautiful."

"Thank you." She met his gaze, then quickly glanced away. "Let's hope the President thinks so."

Reid raised an eyebrow. "You're going to interview him?"

"No, but I would like to get his thoughts on the wedding. Plus, it's the first time he and his estranged son will have been seen together in public in a long time. Everyone's dying to know if they've buried the hatchet."

"I didn't know they'd fallen out."

She rolled her eyes. "Don't you read the newspaper?"

"I'm not interested in politics."

"Well, let me enlighten you. Warner Sullivan is on the board of a major Chinese bank, which could have repercussions for the White House. The President can't be seen to be a hypocrite, not after he's just banned the export of high-performance chips to China." Reid felt his concentration begin to wane and fought to stay focused. "Why is he going then?"

Kenzie tilted her head. "To support his son. That's the official line, anyway."

"And unofficially?"

"Unofficially, I think he's going to talk to Warner about his relationship with the Chinese. He'll try to persuade him to resign his board position. Warner will refuse because he hates being told what to do, especially by his father."

Reid just shook his head. "What time will you be back?"

"Late. Although, it depends."

"On what happens?"

Kenzie gave a small grin. "Exactly."

Reid hesitated. He wanted to ask if she'd stop by later, when she got back. But she'd be tired, eager for bed. The tangle of words died in his throat. "Have fun, and I'll see you in the morning."

16

KENZIE WALKED through the double doors into a dazzling wonderland. The soiree was held in The Edwardian Room at The Plaza and was a precursor to the wedding. The guest list included politicians, dignitaries, minor royals and celebrities, and anyone else who deserved a nod but wasn't invited to the wedding.

Kenzie didn't know anybody, but that had never stopped her before. As a reporter, she was used to arriving uninvited and introducing herself to prominent individuals. At least this time, she had an invitation.

As soon as she arrived, she sought out Emmanuelle. The bride-to-be was resplendent in a shimmering, gold silk and sequin gown that brought out the tawny streaks in her hair and the yellow flecks in her eyes. The model opened her arms, visibly relieved to see her. "Kenzie, I'm glad you could make it."

Kenzie had arrived on time, a no-no at such events, but she often found that being early gave her the opportunity to talk to other early arrivals who were embarrassed to be standing alone. They were more likely to strike up a conversation with a stranger than if she'd arrived when they were surrounded by other, more familiar guests.

"Thanks for inviting me." Kenzie kissed her on both cheeks. "You look gorgeous. Is that Carolina Herrera?"

"Valentino."

"Stunning."

"Thank you. Allow me to introduce you to Nathaniel Lee, my PR Manager." Emmanuelle turned to the striking Asian-American man wearing a high-end custom suit that fit his carefully toned body to perfection.

"Pleasure," he drawled, shaking her hand, but his smile was guarded. "Emmanuelle has told me all about you."

I'm sure, Kenzie thought.

"Only good things, I hope." She flashed him a smile. Emmanuelle turned away to greet another guest, the glass of champagne in her hand untouched. There wasn't even a lipstick mark around the edge.

"Of course." The fake smile almost reached his eyes. "You're with the *Herald*, is that right?"

"It is, yes."

"You're covering the wedding?"

"At the bride's request," she said, her smile wearing thin.

"I understand. I told Emmanuelle it was foolish to trust a reporter, but she insisted on you."

"We've worked together in the past."

"You outed her as Maria Lopez's illegitimate child," he corrected. So this was how it was going to be.

"I didn't. My paper did. I let her know it was happening so she could prepare for the media storm. That's why she trusts me. Funny, I don't recall you being there?"

"I was hired afterwards," he sniffed. "Damage control."

"Ah, well at least you don't have a drug dealing cartel boss to worry about anymore." She turned away and wandered over to the bar. The room was wood paneled with elaborate stenciled ceilings and large windows overlooking Central Park. Filling up now, Kenzie marveled at the array of glamorous guests. She spotted several congressmen, the

Attorney General, a Vogue centerfold of supermodels, and two Hollywood A-listers.

There was a murmur, and the crowd parted like the Red Sea as President Sullivan, flanked by his entourage, walked in. Kenzie had never seen him up close before. He looked in surprisingly good shape for his age, his freshly dyed hair without a hint of gray, and he was sporting an expensive tan. The suit fit almost as well as Nathaniel's. On closer inspection, Kenzie noticed his hands were leathery and his face had a lot more lines in it than was noticeable on television.

The President strode over to his son, shook his hand, and patted him on the shoulder. Kenzie wondered if it was rehearsed, or if the rumors were true and they hadn't seen each other in a while. Warner smiled stiffly. The President's smile looked genuine. Maybe he did miss his son.

They spoke for a while, the two Secret Service officers hovering behind, their heads moving from side to side like homing beacons. Kenzie couldn't hear what was being said, but to those watching, it looked sincere. Several fake smiles and a curt handshake later, they split up. The President went in search of Emmanuelle, while Warner turned to a bunch of friends and accepted a beer.

So far, so good.

Kenzie quickened her step, reaching Emmanuelle just as her father-in-law did. Now it was the President's turn to put on a practiced smile. He didn't approve of his soon-to-be daughter-in-law, that much was obvious. To give Emmanuelle credit, she nodded and said all the right things. The tension was evident in her straight back and stiff neck.

"Have you met Kenzie Gilmore of the *Miami Herald*?" Emmanuelle said, eager to turn the attention toward someone else.

"Ah, the award-winning reporter." He bowed his head. "Good to finally meet you, Miss Gilmore."

"And you, Mr. President." He must have been briefed on all the guests. There's no way he'd have known who she was otherwise. "I'm glad to see you've reconciled with your son."

His gaze turned frosty. "Yes, although you know the press, they always exaggerate everything."

She accepted that statement with a little incline of her head. "Will you be coming to the wedding, sir?"

"Of course." He smiled at Emmanuelle. "I wouldn't miss it for the world."

Great, she had her quote. Keith would be happy.

A thin, spritely man rushed over and took the President's arm. "There's someone you should meet, Mr. President." And the most powerful man in the world glided off without so much as a backwards glance.

"He's always like that," Emmanuelle hunched her shoulders as if she'd been kicked in the gut. Her knuckles around the champagne flute were white. "I'm surprised he even spoke with me. He usually doesn't."

Kenzie gave her a sympathetic grimace. She wondered if the model knew how much like her mother she was. Maria Lopez had also caved in on herself when she'd talked about her past. It was a protective gesture, a defense mechanism to safeguard against vulnerability, and her daughter was doing the same thing now.

Warner sidled up to his fiancée. "You alright, babe?"

"I'm fine." She squeezed his hand. Not for the first time, Kenzie admired the bond between them. They'd been through a lot. First Warner's estrangement from his father, and his refusal to toe the line. Then the news of Emmanuelle's biological mother being the infamous cartel boss, Maria Lopez, and the subsequent media fall out.

Emmanuelle had issued a public statement saying she had never met her biological mother and had no intention of doing so. As far as she was concerned, her parents were the couple who'd raised her in France. Maria had died without meeting her daughter, but somehow, Kenzie didn't think the cartel boss had minded.

I chose this life because I had no other option. She does.

That was the reason Maria had given for not contacting her daughter and letting her know who she was. She'd tried to protect her, and Kenzie respected that.

"Evening, Kenzie."

"Warner." Kenzie shot him a smile. "How are things?"

"Good." His gaze followed his father across the room. "You know, as good as they can be."

"I take it you haven't hugged and made up?"

Warner scoffed. "As long as I have business in the Far East, I'll always be in his bad books. There's nothing he can do about that. The ironic thing is—" Emmanuelle put her hand on his forearm. He stopped talking. "Never mind. It is what it is." He shot Kenzie a wry grin. "Politics."

"Indeed." She wondered what he'd been about to say, or rather, what Emmanuelle had stopped him from saying.

The Edwardian Room filled up and soon it was uncomfortably packed. Kenzie, having got what she came for, decided it was time to leave. Emmanuelle's model friends had arrived, and her attention was diverted. Kenzie was no longer needed.

She messaged Keith to tell him she'd deliver the article by noon tomorrow, then caught a cab back to the hotel. The beautiful ornate clock in the lobby of the Sheraton said it was eleven twenty. Would Reid still be awake? Stepping into the elevator, she hesitated. His room was on the third floor, hers was on the eighth.

She told herself it was because she wanted to see if he'd made any headway with the case. Perhaps the police reports had contained a snippet of evidence they could use to identify the perpetrator.

An elderly couple got in.

"Floor?" The man looked at her expectantly.

"Um—" She wavered. "Eight. Thank you." Probably not. Besides, he'd left Miami early that morning and would be exhausted by now. Tomorrow would be soon enough.

The elevator pinged, and the doors sighed open. Kenzie stepped out feeling strangely bereft. It had been a long day. Wearily, she made her way down the corridor to her room.

17

REID STAYED up late poring over the police reports. He first looked at the two murdered women, Becca Wilson and Margaret Downey. Becca, as he already knew, had been found out back near the dumpster, while Margaret had been discovered in the hotel room by the maid the following morning. Both had been strangled.

The autopsy on Becca showed she'd been raped before being strangled. There were defensive wounds on her arms where she'd fought off her attacker—or tried to. He'd won in the end, though. Reid gazed at her wide-eyed expression in the crime scene photograph. Young, pretty, her whole life ahead of her. How dare the killer do this to her! He'd been brutal too, judging by the purple bruises around her neck. It wouldn't have taken long to squeeze the life out of her. Three minutes, maybe four.

Grinding his jaw, he moved on to the second folder, that of Margaret Downey. The hotel where her body had been found was called the Casa del Frango, also in lower Manhattan, but it had closed down shortly after the murder. He wasn't surprised. It would be hard to keep going after something like that. Malcolm Lord had been lucky in that the body had been found behind his hotel and not in it, otherwise his establishment may not have survived either.

The police report named the proprietor as a man called Rodrigo Ferreira. According to his statement, Rodrigo had heard the maid, a Maria Gonzalez, screaming hysterically, and went to investigate. When he walked into the room, he found the dead girl on the bed. The guest had gone.

The hysterical maid had run out of the hotel and was never seen again. The police hadn't been able to trace her. They eventually discovered that Maria Gonzalez wasn't the maid's real name. She was an unauthorized immigrant who'd either gone back to her native country or adopted a different name and continued to work illegally in the United States. Rodrigo had sworn he hadn't known she wasn't registered.

As was his MO, the rapist had paid cash and used a fake name. This time it wasn't Jeff Dooley, but Jackson Reese. Reid wondered if that was a real person too, or if he'd plucked the name out of thin air.

There was a telephone number for Rodrigo Ferreira, but it was the same as the hotel's so was no longer in existence. Reid wondered where Rodrigo was now. The file contained no forwarding address. It looked like the detective in charge, a Rod Mather, had run out of leads and shut it down.

Interestingly, the CSI team had found semen at the scene, which matched that found inside the victim, however, they hadn't managed to match it to anyone on the police database. That might not be the case anymore. It would be worth running it again and comparing it to the rape kit Monica had done privately, if she'd agree.

Margaret's murder wasn't linked to any other sexual assaults or suspicious deaths, and because it had happened before Becca Wilson's murder, there'd been no connection with that crime either. The killer had gotten away with it.

Next, Reid turned to the victims of sexual assault that he'd uncovered. Two in the same year as Gail Winslow, one in the following year. There had been others, but he'd focused on these because they'd occurred around the same time and the circumstances were similar.

All three women had been picked up in the same area. Gail and Silvia had met their perpetrator in Augustine's, a wine bar on the Lower East Side, while Milena and Freya had met their rapist in two separate bars, but within a two-block radius of Augustine's.

That was his hunting ground.

Reid looked up addresses for the three women on the DVLA database. Silvia and Freya still lived in New York, but Milena now resided in Wisconsin. Tomorrow, he'd visit the two local women and place a call to Milena. He could call all three, but in his experience, people were far more likely to talk to a police officer standing on their doorstep than on the phone.

He checked his watch. Nearly midnight. He wondered if Kenzie was back yet. She'd said she would be late, but he wasn't sure what that meant. The glitzy party had been held at The Plaza, a premium New York event venue, from what he could gather.

Resisting the urge to knock on her door to check, he took a shower, climbed into bed, and turned off the light. Maybe tomorrow they'd get some leads as to who the mysterious rapist was. One of the surviving victims must know something, something they could use to identify him.

Kenzie awoke to her phone beeping. Groggily, she squinted at the screen. A text message from Reid.

Meet you downstairs for breakfast? 8am?

Breakfast? What time was it?

Her phone said seven forty-five. Groaning, she got out of bed and stumbled to the bathroom, but not before she replied, *See you there.*

"How was the party?" Reid asked as she sat down. The dining room was full of eager tourists chattering away merrily. The noise level was inordinately loud.

"Good, thanks."

Coffee! She needed coffee. After Reid's text, she'd taken the world's fastest shower, pulled on jeans and a fresh shirt, and raced down to the dining room where breakfast was being served. It was just after eight o'clock.

"I spoke to the President." She ran a hand through her still damp hair, airing it out.

"Really? What's he like in person?"

"Aloof," she replied. "But I got a quote for my article, so mission accomplished."

"Did you speak with the bride and groom?"

"Yep, both of them. Emmanuelle is not the President's favorite person, as you can imagine. He's barely civil to her. Relations between Warner and his father were chilly, but they seem to have buried the hatchet for now."

Reid rubbed his chin. Kenzie noticed he'd shaved, which made him look younger. "When is the wedding?"

"Saturday. I have to admit, I'll be glad when this is over. Then I can focus on finding Gail's rapist and the man who strangled those two girls." A waiter came over with a pot of black coffee and she sighed in delight. Once he'd poured, and she'd taken a satisfying gulp, she asked, "What did you find out?"

She listened while Reid told her how he'd re-read the police reports and was hoping to speak with all three rape victims today. "They might remember something we can use to find this guy."

Kenzie gave a small nod. "I'm sorry I can't come with you, I've got to write this article for Keith."

"I know." Was that disappointment in his voice? "I'll keep you posted throughout the day. How about we meet for supper and a debrief?"

"Sounds great." She hesitated, biting her lip.

"What is it?"

I nearly came to your room last night.

He watched her, his gaze probing. "Is something wrong?"

"No, nothing's wrong." Stop acting weird, she told herself sternly. "I just wanted to say thanks for being here. It would have been difficult doing this by myself. It means a lot."

"You're welcome." He looked away. "I couldn't leave you to bring down a killer by yourself."

"I called Liesl's editor at the New York Times yesterday, while I was at the salon," she said, changing the subject.

"Oh, yeah?"

"He was even more unhelpful than Keith, if that's possible."

Reid gave a wry grin. "Does that surprise you?"

"Not really. We wouldn't give away a story to the competition either, even if our reporter had passed away."

"Did he say anything about it?"

"Only that it was of a sensitive nature, but that could be true of any story, depending on how you look at it."

"No clues there, then?"

Kenzie shook her head. "Do you think we're looking at this all wrong, Reid?"

"What do you mean?"

"Maybe her death had nothing to do with the rapist."

He sighed. "It's another line of inquiry. If I had a team working on this, I'd assign officers to both, but since it's just us, we'll have to rule one hypothesis out before we go onto the next."

"Let's hope Sergeant Randal is more forthcoming today."

Reid gave a nod. "I'll keep you posted."

They finished breakfast and were about to leave the dining room when Kenzie's phone buzzed.

"Sebastian's calling," she told Reid. "I hope everything's okay." She'd taken in the Cuban teenager after his mother had been killed in a botched human trafficking operation last year. It was a temporary arrangement, but she'd become attached to the boy.

"Hi Seb. Is everything alright?"

"Yes, but Kenzie, a package arrived for you last night," he told her. "The postmark is New York. I thought you'd want to know."

"New York?" She frowned. "Does it say who it's from?"

"No, there's no return address." He paused, and she heard paper crinkling. "I think it's a laptop."

Kenzie glanced at Reid.

It couldn't be Liesl's... Could it?

"Can you open it?" she asked, breathless.

"Sure, hang on."

They heard rustling in the background, and Seb came back on the line. "Yeah, it is a laptop. Not new, though. It looks quite old. Who'd send you this, Kenzie?"

"I don't know." But she could hope. "Can you open it?"

There was a pause as he lifted the lid. "The login address is bernsteinl@nytimes.com."

"Holy crap," Kenzie murmured.

Seb's voice. "You know who this is from?"

Reid was watching her intently. "It's hers, isn't it?"

Kenzie nodded. "She must have known she was in danger, so she sent it to me for safekeeping."

"We need to see what's on it," Reid said urgently.

"Kenzie, are you still there?" Seb was waiting on the line.

"Yes, sorry. I'm here." She hesitated, then said, "Seb, I need you to do me a favor."

18

Silvia Ferri lived in a neat, clapboard house on Long Island. Everything about it was tidy, from the freshly trimmed borders to the welcoming yellow front door and shuttered windows.

Reid rang the gleaming gold buzzer and waited while a classical tune played inside the house. He heard running footsteps, and then the front door swung open. A child of about fourteen stood there, a wide smile on his face. In the background, Reid could hear whistling.

The smile disappeared when he didn't recognize the man at the door. "Mom, it's for you." The boy turned and ran off before Reid could even say hello.

"I'm so sorry," called a voice from inside, and a middle-aged woman appeared in the hallway. She wore an apron and had a smudge of flour on her cheek. "He's waiting for a friend."

Reid nodded. "No problem. Are you Sylvia Ferri?"

"Yes. How can I help you?" She looked him up and down, her gaze open and friendly. Reid liked her.

"Mrs. Ferri, I'm a detective working with the NYPD on a cold case. We're looking for a man you might know. Can I come in and talk to you about it?"

She hesitated. "You've caught me in the middle of my weekly baking session. I make cupcakes for my son's school every Friday."

"That's okay. I don't mind if you don't."

She relented, beckoning him in. "Okay, come in."

He followed her into the hall and down a short corridor to the kitchen. It was bright and airy, with daisy patterned blinds over large windows that let in lots of light. The delectable smell of baking cupcakes filled the air. Reid's stomach rumbled.

"Are you hungry, detective?" she asked.

He reddened. "No, ma'am. I'm okay. It smells great, though."

She gave a knowing smile. "The boys love them. I'll let you have one when they're done." She glanced at a large timer on the countertop. "Five more minutes."

Mrs. Ferri wouldn't be so keen to feed him cupcakes once she heard what he wanted to talk to her about. She seemed in such a good mood, he was reluctant to ruin it. He put her age at about forty-five, give or take.

"Please sit down." He sat on a small chair at the kitchen table. A vase of brightly colored tulips nodded at him. "Now, who was it you wanted to ask me about?"

"Well, it's a little delicate," he began, "and I'm sorry to have to bring it up after all these years."

Her shoulders stiffened. "You mean—?"

He nodded. "I'm sorry." Reid found himself apologizing to this woman who'd obviously managed to move on with her life. She glanced at the door, but the kid was nowhere to be seen. Wiping her hands on her apron, she sat down at the table opposite him.

"Detective—?" she hesitated.

"Garrett, ma'am."

"Detective Garrett, I was a young girl when that awful incident occurred. I don't remember much about it."

"I understand, but the thing is, that man who sexually assaulted you, he's still active." Reid watched her eyes widen. "And he's killed two women that we know of."

"Killed?"

"As in strangled."

"Oh, my gosh." Her hand flew to her mouth. "I don't understand. How do you know it's the same man?"

"Because the body of one of the women was found in the same hotel as one of his rape victims. Rohypnol was also found in her system, as it was with all his victims."

Sylvia paled, clenching her hands in her lap. There was a brief pause. Reid waited, sensing she was going to talk.

"He picked me up in a bar," she began, her voice wobbly. "I was there with some friends. He bought me a drink and stupidly, I accepted. I was seventeen."

Reid winced. "Can you describe the man?"

"Yes, I remember him well. He was tall with sandy colored hair and a good physique. Attractive. You'd never expect someone like him to... well, you know?"

Reid nodded. "Can you tell me what happened?"

"I don't remember much after that, until I woke up the next morning. He was gone, and I was alone in the hotel room."

"He was gone?" Reid was surprised. That differed from what had happened to Gail and what Kenzie had told him had happened to Monica.

"He'd taken his stuff and cleared out. I felt sick to my stomach, and I remember puking in the bathroom." Probably a reaction to the drug.

"Then I got dressed and left. I was embarrassed by what had happened, but I confided in a girlfriend, and she made me call the police and report it."

"Did they test you for DNA?" Reid asked gently.

She shook her head. "No, I didn't want that. I didn't want to know what he'd done to me, or how often. I just wanted to forget it had ever happened."

All the women had dealt with their trauma in different ways. Gail had spurned affection, Monica had lashed out and was now in a same sex relationship. Silvia had blocked the episode out and moved on.

"I can understand that." He leaned forward. "Silvia, we're trying to find this man. Did he give any indication as to his real identity?"

"He said his name was Steve, and he was in sales. That's all I remember."

Steve. That was a new one.

"Did he say what kind of sales?"

She grimaced. "I don't think so. Sorry. Like I said, it was a long time ago. Over twenty years now."

"I know, and I'm sorry to make you dredge it up. Could I ask you a couple more questions?"

She gave a soft sigh. "Sure."

"Did you notice a tattoo on his left arm?"

Her eyes widened. "I'd forgotten about that. Yes, he did have one. A creepy thing. Skull and crossbones or something like that."

Reid exhaled. Definitely the same guy. "He didn't say where he'd got it, or why?"

"I don't think so, but I didn't ask."

"Okay, thank you." Reid got up to leave. "Oh, one last thing. Why do you think he left you alone in the hotel room?"

She shrugged. "Maybe he had to go? I don't know. I'm just grateful that he wasn't there when I woke up."

Reid thanked her again and saw himself out. The house felt colder than it had when he'd arrived, and he regretted that.

Sergeant Randal was about to go on his lunch break when Reid strode into the department. "Mind if I join you?" he asked, when Randal tried to palm him off on someone else.

Much to the New York detective's disdain, Reid accompanied him to the sandwich bar where he got a tuna sandwich and a black coffee.

"Talk to me about the burglary," Reid said, taking a seat next to him on a park bench.

Randal shot him a sideways look. "It's an open investigation."

"Yeah, and I'm working the cold case for the department."

"We don't know the two are linked yet," Randal said, eyeing his sandwich.

"We won't know until we share information and rule it out," Reid countered.

Randal sighed. "Okay, but you didn't hear it from me."

"Fine."

Reid sipped his coffee and waited for the lanky cop to speak. "The place was clean. No DNA, no prints, nothing. Whoever turned over that apartment was a pro."

"You found nothing?"

Randal set his lunch down on his lap. "The door had been expertly picked, the apartment methodically searched, and they didn't touch anything they didn't have to. Even the smudged boot print in the kitchen was inconclusive, like the guy had been wearing foot coverings, or something."

"What does that mean?" asked Reid.

"It means they knew what they were doing."

"Do you think they found what they were looking for?" Reid thought about the laptop that Liesl had sent to Kenzie in Miami.

"I don't know. They either found it and left, or they didn't find it and abandoned the search."

"Do you think they were disturbed?" Reid asked.

Randal shrugged. "I don't see how. No one was there apart from Miss Gilmore, and she found the apartment door ajar. Whoever had searched the joint was long gone before she arrived."

"Hmm..." Reid thought for a moment. A pro job. No fingerprints, no DNA. Nothing taken. It didn't sound like their rapist. Their perp left DNA inside his victims. He didn't wear a condom. He forgot to check under the bed for shoes. He was either arrogant or careless. Possibly both.

"Have you asked the other residents if they saw anything?"

"Of course. I have done this before, you know."

"I'm sorry. What did they say?"

"Nothing." Randal picked up his sandwich. "Nobody heard a goddamn thing."

19

KENZIE SPENT the morning writing her article. Keith was delighted with the quote. "Great work, Kenzie," he gushed, after she'd called him to let him know it was in his inbox. "No one else has gotten near to the President, let alone managed to get his views on the wedding."

No sooner had she hung up than Raoul called. "Kenzie, I've got the laptop."

"Great! Anything on it?"

"Tons. What are we looking for?"

"I need to know what Liesl was working on before she died," Kenzie replied.

"I'll take a look at the time stamps," Raoul told her, "and send you everything she accessed in the last week. Will that do?"

"That's perfect," Kenzie said. "And Raoul, this requires absolute discretion. Do not tell Keith what you're working on."

A pause. "What if he asks?"

"Just say you're doing research for me. He'll assume it's about the wedding."

"Okay, fine." He hesitated. "Are you any closer to finding out who the rapist is?"

"Not yet, but we're getting there."

"We?"

"Reid is here with me. He flew up to help with the investigation."

"Oh, I see." She heard the gentle teasing in his tone.

"It's not like that. He's on leave and—" She petered off. Why was she making excuses? So what if Reid had come to New York to help her? So what if something *was* happening between them? Something was always happening between them... The problem was, she just didn't know what. "You know what? Never mind. Just get back to me as soon as you can."

"Sure thing." The researcher chuckled quietly as he hung up.

Kenzie took an elastic band out of her pocket and pulled her hair up into it. Speaking of Reid, she wondered how he was doing. Used to doing her own legwork, it felt weird leaving the investigating up to someone else. But this was Reid. She trusted him. They made a good team. He wouldn't freeze her out. Together, they'd figure out who this killer rapist was and bring him in. Since Reid had made a connection with the NYPD, they were better placed to do that. It made sense to let him take the lead on this one, for now.

Over the next few hours, Raoul sent through multiple emails containing word documents, PDFs, and web links Liesl had either been working on or looking at. Kenzie asked the hotel office to print them out —for a small fee, of course. By the time Reid got back, she was sitting in the lounge, wired from too many cups of coffee, and bleary-eyed from reading all afternoon.

"What is that?" he asked, coming over. He looked weary, his shirt crumpled and his hair messy. The clean-shaven chin was now sporting the beginnings of a five o'clock shadow.

"That is the contents of Liesl's laptop." She nodded to the scattered mess around her. "Raoul sent it through."

Reid moved a pile of paper off the armchair and placed it on the table, then he sat down. "Find anything interesting?"

"Yes, but first fill me in on what Detective Randal said."

"You want a drink?" She shook her head. "I've been mainlining caffeine all day."

He grinned, then flagged down a waiter and ordered a beer. Leaning back in the armchair, he said, "The CSI team didn't find anything. The apartment was clean."

"What? It was a mess. I saw it."

"They didn't leave any prints or DNA. Randal says whoever searched it was a pro."

Kenzie pursed her lips. "Now, that is interesting."

"None of the neighbors heard anything," Reid continued. "And the concierge swore he didn't see anyone come in or go out before you arrived."

"Except for the dark-haired guy," Kenzie said, thoughtfully.

"What?" Reid sat upright.

"There was a dark-haired man who rushed out as I was going in. We collided. Literally. He elbowed me in the ribs. Then he left without apologizing."

"Would you recognize him if you saw him again?" Reid was frowning.

"Yes, I think so. You think he's the one who searched her apartment?"

"Could be, yeah. You said he was in a rush?"

"It looked like it."

"Was he carrying anything?"

Kenzie tried to remember. Her leg was jittering under the table. Damn coffee. "I don't think so, although I can't be sure. I wasn't paying much attention." She shook her head. "I wish I had now. I don't think he was carrying anything because he elbowed me. He had bony elbows."

"Don't beat yourself up about it," Reid told her.

A waiter delivered Reid's beer and took away Kenzie's empty coffee cup. "I'll never sleep tonight," she moaned. "Anyway, that's not important. Tell me what else you discovered."

"I spoke with one of the earlier victims, Sylvia Ferri. She was sexually assaulted the same year as Gail."

"Any leads?" Kenzie asked, hopefully.

"Not as such. Her attacker told her his name was Steve, and he was a salesman."

"Steve?"

"I know. He's got quite the collection of aliases."

"Real person?"

Reid shrugged. "Who knows? But it's him alright. He had the same tattoo Gail described. The same one you saw on the surveillance image at Windsor Heights."

Kenzie sucked in a breath. "I knew it. What about the others?"

"Freya Andersen wasn't home. Apparently, she works in the city, but her husband said he'd get her to call me. And I haven't called Milena Kownacki yet."

"Okay, good. Now it's my turn." Kenzie gave him a knowing grin. "Wait until you hear this."

Reid sipped his beer, his gaze locked on her face.

She leaned across the wide coffee table over which the printouts were scattered and picked up a stapled wad. "These are Liesl's notes. You'll never guess who she was investigating."

"Tell me. I don't have the energy to guess."

"Warner Sullivan."

Reid balked. "*The* Warner Sullivan? The same guy who's marrying Emmanuelle Lenoir the day after tomorrow at The Plaza?"

"The very same. From what I can gather, Liesl was looking into his ties to the Middle East."

"I don't know what to say to that," Reid said after a long beat. "Why was she looking into him? What does it mean?"

Kenzie wrinkled her forehead. "Maybe nothing. Maybe something. I think that's why she wanted to meet me the day I arrived. She was going to tell me about this."

"But why?" Reid reiterated. "Did she find something shifty?"

"Well, it appears Warner was more involved with the Chinese than he let on. He's on the board of a Chinese bank, we know that much, but did you know that bank is almost entirely owned by the Chinese government? The same government whose semiconductor market our President is trying to stifle with his export ban."

Reid blinked several times. He did that when he was trying to wrap his head around something. Kenzie found it endearing. "Okay, so he's involved with the Chinese government. I can see how that would be a conflict of interest with the President's policies, but Warner is not the President. He's an entrepreneur and minor politician."

"I'm not sure that matters," Kenzie pointed out. "He's still his son. But wait, there's more." She paused for dramatic effect. "According to Liesl's notes, Warner Sullivan has been receiving backhand payments to broker deals between the Chinese and his father."

"Is that proven?" Reid asked.

"I don't know." Kenzie shrugged. "I haven't got that far yet. There's a lot of stuff here to get through." She glanced up at him. "If it's true, though, it's potentially career-ending."

"For Warner or the President?" Reid murmured.

"Both."

There was a small pause as her words sunk in, then Reid took a sharp breath. "This is going to sound crazy, but I'm going to say it anyway. Do you think Warner Sullivan had Liesl silenced because she was going to blow the whistle on his backhanded deal with the Chinese?"

Kenzie met his gaze. "I don't know. I hope not, but it's possible, I suppose. It depends how far he'd go to keep it out of the press."

"He's about to get married," Reid pointed out.

"And his father is up for reelection," Kenzie added. "It's not a good time for this to come out."

Reid dropped his voice. "Are we saying the President of the United States is involved?"

Kenzie swallowed. "I don't know."

The possibility hung heavily in the air. Reid's phone buzzed, breaking the tension.

"It's Randal," he mouthed, before answering it. Kenzie watched as his face turned pale beneath his tan.

"What?" she mouthed back.

He listened for a moment, then said, "Thanks for letting me know."

Kenzie leaned forward. "Reid, what was that about?"

"Randal called to tell me they traced that number on Liesl's phone."

"Yes?"

"It belongs to Warner Sullivan."

20

"What's Warner Sullivan doing calling Liesl?" asked Reid.

Kenzie looked as shell-shocked as he felt. "We know Liesl was looking into him, but that was a missed call on her phone. *He* was trying to get ahold of *her*."

"To persuade her to let it go?" Reid's head was spinning.

Kenzie stared at him. "And when she didn't...?"

Reid shook his head. "We shouldn't jump to conclusions. Just because he called her doesn't mean he killed her."

Kenzie arched an eyebrow. "It wouldn't be the first time a public figure went to extreme measures to cover something up. He could have hired a hitman to take her out at the intersection."

"What about her apartment?" Reid tried to piece it together.

"He could have searched it, hoping to find incriminating evidence. Like a laptop or phone." Kenzie exhaled. "Tell me I'm wrong?"

"It's one theory," Reid said cautiously. "That phone call might also be harmless. Warner may have simply been returning one of Liesl's calls."

"True." Kenzie shook her head as if to clear it. "You're right. Sorry, my brain is flipping out from all this caffeine. This doesn't mean Warner's involved in her murder."

They sat in silence, shocked by what they'd discovered. Eventually, Reid's stomach gave a loud rumble. "Let's eat. We're not achieving anything sitting here."

They walked across the lobby to the hotel restaurant and took a seat by the window. Outside, the sidewalk was as busy as the middle of the day. The city that never sleeps.

Reid ordered a burger and fries, and Kenzie a Caesar salad. Neither of them wanted anything complicated. Their minds were too busy processing what they'd learned. "Perhaps we've got this all wrong," Kenzie said, once their food had come. Reid dug in, aware that Kenzie was just picking at hers. "Jeff Dooley, or whoever was posing as him, may have nothing to do with Liesl's death."

Reid acknowledged that fact with a stiff nod. "It's beginning to look like that."

Sensing her frustration, he said, "After dinner, we'll go back to the room and call the other two victims. Maybe they can shed some light. Whoever this bastard is, regardless of whether he's involved in Liesl's death or not, we have to stop him before he sexually assaults—or worse—someone else."

"Agreed," Kenzie said with a rallying nod. "We need to take him down."

"Your place or mine?" asked Reid once they'd finished eating.

"Yours is closer." Kenzie seemed miles away.

They rode the elevator in silence. Kenzie stared into the middle distance, chewing on her lower lip, which meant she was thinking. Reid didn't interrupt.

The elevator pinged, and they got out. Housekeeping had been by, and Reid's room was spotless. He'd barely been in it since he arrived.

"I'll call Milena," he said, taking out his phone and scrolling to her number. "We'll give Freya Andersen another hour or so to call me. She might not be home from work yet."

Kenzie got out her phone too. "I'll give Mrs. Dooley a ring. She was going to look through some old photographs for me."

Reid moved to the window and placed the call. A tired-sounding woman picked up. "Hello?"

"Good evening. Is this Mrs. Kownacki?"

"Yes, who's calling?"

"My name is Detective Reid Garrett from the New York Police Department. I'm working on a homicide case, and I think you might be able to help."

There was a pause. "Why do you think I can help? I don't know anything about a homicide."

"It involves two women. I know you weren't involved, but I think you might have met the man responsible."

"I don't think so."

"Mrs. Kownacki, we think the murders were committed by the same man who sexually assaulted you back in 1989."

A much longer pause.

When she spoke, her voice was brittle. "I don't know what you mean."

"Freya—May I call you that?"

No answer.

"Freya," he pressed on. "We know you reported it to the police, then later redacted your statement."

"I—I changed my mind. I didn't want anyone to know."

"I understand, and that's not going to change. I just need to ask you some questions about your... about the man who assaulted you."

A heavy sigh. "I haven't thought about Jake in over a decade."

"Jake?"

"That's what he said his name was."

Jeff. Steve. Jake. The list went on.

"Did he give a last name?"

"No, and I'm ashamed to say I didn't ask."

"That's okay." It wouldn't be real anyway. "Do you mind if I ask where you met him?"

"At a bar, downtown. It was called Augustine's."

Bingo.

"And what happened?"

He heard her take a ragged breath. "The whole thing was a nightmare. I was waiting for a friend to show up, but she was running late. I was sitting by the bar when this man approached me. He seemed nice. Polite, well mannered. He was good looking too."

"Could you describe him?"

"Tall, fair, athletic build."

Same guy.

"And then what happened?"

"He bought me a drink. We talked. He was knowledgeable."

"What about?" Reid cut in.

"The war in Afghanistan. I worked for a newspaper, and he had a lot to say on the topic."

"He did?"

"Yeah, I thought perhaps he'd been in the military at some point, but when I asked, he denied it."

Now that was very interesting.

"I don't suppose you remember if he had a tattoo on his left arm?" He found he was holding his breath.

"Why, yes. I think he did. I do recall a tattoo, now that you mention it."

"Can you remember what it was?"

"Oh, no. I'm sorry. It was too long ago."

"A skull, maybe?"

"That's it! A skull and crossbones. I didn't like it." He almost heard her trembling down the line. The rest of Freya's story was similar to the others. He'd spiked her drink, taken her to a motel room—she didn't know which one. When she woke up, stark naked on the bed, he was gone.

.   .   .

Reid hung up, his pulse elevated. Kenzie was still on the phone with Mrs. Dooley, so he waited for her to finish. "Could you send me a photo of those pictures you found? Yes, that's right. Just snap a photograph with your phone and message them to me. That would be great. Thank you so much, Mrs. Dooley."

Flushed, she ended the call. "She's got something. It might be nothing, but she's found a couple of photographs of her husband back in '89. He's with friends and work colleagues."

"You never know." Reid slid his phone into his back pocket.

"What did you find out?"

"It looks like our guy might have been in the military."

Kenzie's eyes widened. "What makes you say that?"

"Freya Kownacki remembers talking to him about the war in Afghanistan. He seemed pretty knowledgeable. So much so, she asked him if he'd been in the forces. He denied it, of course."

"But he could have been lying," Kenzie breathed.

"He wouldn't have wanted to give away too much about himself," Reid agreed.

Kenzie swiped at a stray hair. "Unfortunately, until we have some point of reference, we can't look up any military records. We don't even know what year he served, if he really did."

"Freya was picked up in the same bar as Gail." Reid sat down on the bed.

"He's territorial," Kenzie surmised. "Two bars in the same strip."

"The motels he takes them to are all in the vicinity too," Reid added. "He must have lived around there."

"Usually, I don't like jumping to conclusions, but I'd say that's likely."

Reid looked up at her. "Are we getting anywhere? I mean, is this helping?"

"We know it's the same man," she pointed out. "Gail, Monica, Freya, the dead women. It's his MO."

Reid sighed. "I know. I feel like the list of women he's assaulted is growing, but no one knows anything that will help us catch the bastard."

"Every victim gives us a little more information," she said. "Slowly, we're building up a picture of the guy. Sooner or later, we'll find something we can use."

Reid hoped she was right.

Kenzie's phone beeped. Glancing down, she gave a wry smile. "Mrs. Dooley's figured out how to use WhatsApp."

There was a continuous stream of pings, before her phone finally fell silent.

Kenzie sat beside Reid. She surveyed the photographs, studying each one before moving on to the next one. Five photographs in, she paused.

"What?" He studied the image on her screen but couldn't see anything unusual.

She frowned. "I don't know. Do you have a magnifying glass?"

"Not on me, no. Can't you zoom in?"

"It's blurry. I need to read that sign in the background." She handed the phone to him. Reid took a look, squinting at the photograph. Jeff Dooley, the leather worker, stood next to two other men. They were in a street, cars in the background. The styles were old, definitely 8os. On the other side of the road was a narrow, brick building with a red awning over the door. Stenciled on the awning was a name.

Reid didn't need a magnifying glass to read it. He recognized the building. The awning wasn't there anymore, and the door had faded and peeled, but it was the same place.

"That," he said. "Is the Formosa Hotel."

Kenzie gasped. "I knew it looked familiar, but I couldn't place it. What on earth is Jeff Dooley doing outside the Formosa?"

"It's a link," Reid hissed, under his breath. "It doesn't matter what he was doing there. What matters is that he *was* there."

Kenzie stared at him. "I don't get it. I mean, I know the killer used Dooley's name when he took Gail there, but this doesn't tell us who he was. It just shows us Dooley went there too."

When he didn't reply, she asked, "Am I missing something?"

"Hang on." Thoughts tumbled through his head like an unstoppable avalanche.

I found her body around the back near the dumpsters...

A creepy thing. Skull and crossbones...

The war in Afghanistan.

Jeff Dooley. Jackson Reese. Steve, the salesman.

He felt like his head was about to explode.

"Reid, what's going on?" Kenzie got to her feet. "You've gone white."

"I have to check something," he muttered, heading for the door. "I'll be right back."

Kenzie grabbed his arm. "Reid, talk to me."

His eyes bore into hers. "I can't be sure, Kenz, but I think I know who the killer is."

21

KENZIE STARED AFTER HIM. Did Reid know who the killer was? For real? If so, how? And why was she so far behind?

Frustrated, she went back to her room and took a long, hot shower. Tomorrow was her final interview with Emmanuelle. The last one before the wedding. They were meeting in Emmanuelle's suite at The Plaza, as it was deemed too risky for her to be out and about on the eve of her wedding.

"I want the inside scoop," Keith had told her on the phone earlier that day. "If she's got the wedding jitters, I want to know. If she's been given the cold shoulder by the President, find out how she feels about that. How her fiancé feels about it."

"I know how to do my job, Keith," Kenzie had retorted.

"I know." He'd sighed. "I've got the networks lined up, which always makes me nervous." Keith got performance anxiety when they had an exclusive. The syndication was worth a lot of money.

"It'll be fine," she told him soothingly. "I've got this."

"Okay, Kenzie. I expect copy by end of play tomorrow."

"Understood."

. . .

Fed up with pacing up and down her hotel room, Kenzie went downstairs to the bar. Reid still hadn't appeared. What was he doing? She texted him but annoyingly, got no reply. Sipping her wine, she racked her brain to figure out what it was she'd missed. Something in the photograph. Jeff Dooley at the Formosa.

Had Reid recognized someone else in the photograph? The two men weren't familiar, although one did bear a passing resemblance to Leonardo Vittore. It wasn't him, though. She was certain of that.

An hour passed, then two. It was getting late. Kenzie got up, stretched, and walked into the lobby. At that point, Reid rushed in. One look at his face and she knew...

"Who is it?"

He didn't answer. Instead, he countered with one of his own. "Kenz, I need to ask you something."

"What?"

"Did you speak with Malcolm Lord at the Formosa Hotel?"

"No, only his assistant. I think she was a temp."

"Okay, good." He nodded, out of breath.

"What on earth is going on? Is it Malcolm Lord? Is he the rapist?" In her frustration, she'd raised her voice and a couple of tourists walking past gave her a worried look. She lowered her voice. "I thought you said he was a cripple."

"He is, or rather, I thought he was."

She frowned. "Are you saying he's not?"

"I don't know." He ran a hand through his hair. It was damp with perspiration.

Kenzie shook her head. "Come over here." They moved to the side of the lobby where they couldn't be overheard. "Tell me where you've been."

"I went back to the hotel. The temp was there. She let me take a peek at the computer system."

Kenzie rubbed her temple. "Okay, are you going to tell me why you wanted to look at the guest register?"

"I was looking for the aliases. Jeff Dooley. Jackson Reese. Jake

Cantor." He took hold of her shoulders. "They were all there, Kenz. Every one of those people has stayed at the hotel at some point over the last twenty years."

Kenzie was stunned.

"But... So, they weren't aliases?" she stammered, beginning to join the dots.

"They were real guests. Whoever stole their names, got them off that database."

Kenzie's brain went into overdrive. "Who has access to that system? Malcolm Lord and his assistant?"

"Correct. And his assistant is a four-foot seven female."

"Which leaves Malcolm Lord."

Reid gave a triumphant nod.

"You think he's faking his disability?" It sounded plausible, but was it? She hadn't even met the man. Had it been Malcolm Lord all this time?

"He must be. At a glance, his foot looks crippled, but he could be putting it on. And he's not bad looking if you take away the stained shirt, the dirty cap and the beard. He hunches over, but that could be an act. At his full height, he'd probably be close to six feet."

"What about that tattoo? Has he ever been in the military?"

"I didn't see a tattoo, but he was wearing a long-sleeved shirt last time I spoke with him. But I checked, he was in the military. He did two tours in Afghanistan in the early eighties."

"Holy crap." Kenzie stared at him. "It is him."

"Looks like it."

"Should we tell Sergeant Randal? Perhaps he can bring him in?"

"For what? Questioning? There isn't a shred of evidence on Lord."

"One woman was raped and another murdered in his hotel," she reminded him.

"Twenty-one years apart. That's a hell of a gap."

"Wasn't there semen found at the scene of the second murder? Margaret Downey?"

"Yeah, but she wasn't murdered at his hotel."

"So what? If it's his DNA, we've got him. We also have the rape kit Monica Stoller did."

Reid nodded. "Okay, I'll talk to Randal."

"I'll wait in the bar."

He didn't take long. "Randal said Malcolm Lord was never a suspect in the Becca Wilson case."

"Why not? He found the body."

"The hotel room was booked in the name of Jeff Dooley, which was obviously a fake name. The girl's shoes, which they found under the bed, did not contain his DNA. There wasn't any forensic evidence to place him inside that room. No hair on the bed, no semen, nothing. There was plenty of other DNA, but none belonging to Malcolm Lord."

Kenzie pursed her lips. "And they're sure that's where she was murdered?"

"Apparently so."

She fell silent.

"What are you thinking?" Reid asked.

"He could have strangled her in any of the rooms," she said quietly. "If you're right, and it is him, he could have raped and strangled her in a different room, dumped her body out back, then planted her shoes in that room to make it look like she'd been killed there."

"Diverting suspicion from himself," Reid finished.

"Exactly. That's why it seemed sloppy. It was deliberate. He staged the crime scene. I'll bet he even put some of her DNA on the bed."

Reid was nodding. "It works."

Kenzie gazed up at him. "What are we going to do?"

"We need another way to catch him. Even if we somehow manage to get some of his DNA and it matches Margaret's and Monica's, it isn't admissible. The judge will throw it out of course. We need a warrant for that."

"I have an idea," Kenzie said. "But you're not going to like it."

He frowned.

"He's still active, right? So why don't we dangle some bait?"

Reid stared at her. "I don't understand."

"You spoke with the temp, and she told you Malcolm's got his weekly bowling game tonight."

"Yeah, so?"

She spread her arms. "We know where he's going to be, and we know he likes blondes in their twenties and thirties."

Reid began shaking his head. "No, Kenzie. Absolutely not."

"You haven't heard my plan yet."

"I know what you're going to say, and the answer is no."

"You said yourself we needed another way to catch him."

"I didn't mean send you into the lion's den."

"I'm used to it. Entrapment, I mean. We use it all the time in investigative journalism." She smiled at him. "We don't have the same rules to abide by."

He scowled at her.

"Besides, I'll be perfectly safe. I'll get his attention, start chatting him up and see what happens. If he slips something into my drink, we know it's him."

Reid looked horrified. "You're not planning on drinking it, are you?"

"No, silly." She patted his arm. "I'll go to the restroom, give you the drink, take the glass back and pretend I've drunk it. He'll take me back to the hotel."

"Jesus, Kenz. I can't believe you're suggesting this."

"Hear me out."

He clenched his jaw, his gaze piercing.

"You'll be right behind me. He'll take me up to a room, check in under some other guest's name, because that's what he does, and he'll assume I'm ripe for the plucking."

Reid glared at her.

"I'll scream. You run in and we catch him in the act."

"You're crazy. There are too many variables. What if it's not him? What if he's not at the bowling club? How is he going to spike your drink? He may not have any Rohypnol or whatever he uses nowadays on him."

"Then nothing will happen, and you can relax."

Reid exhaled noisily.

Kenzie checked the time. "It's nearly eight o'clock. If we're going to do this, we have to move quickly."

Reid shook his head. "We're not going to do this."

Kenzie leaned forward until his face was inches from hers. "Reid, think about it. When will the circumstances be so perfect? Are we going to wait until next week to catch him? We know where he is right now, at this moment in time."

Reid said nothing.

"It's worth a shot, isn't it?" She pleaded with him. "It might be our only shot."

He moved back, his face expressionless. "Okay, you've made your point. We'll do this, but we're going to do it my way."

22

KENZIE SAUNTERED into the bowling club, her three-inch heels clacking on the wooden floorboards. Reid was already there, sitting at the bar, nursing a bourbon, a sour expression on his face.

Kenzie gasped and rushed over. "Oh God, babe. I'm sorry I'm late. Traffic was awful."

Reid scowled. "I've been waiting half an hour."

It had been Reid's idea to play this game. He'd doubt a woman would go to a bowling alley alone, not unless she was deliberately trying to get picked up, and that wasn't how their rapist operated. He liked them fresh, with a hint of innocence. Kenzie hoped she looked fresh enough.

She'd taken care with her makeup, applying only a smudge of blusher and mascara. Her lips were liberally laced with gloss, however, and right now they were protruding in a sulky pout. "Don't be like that, babe." She rested her hand on his arm. He flinched, but she wasn't sure if it was deliberate or not. Eyes were on them, in particular the bartender's.

"What are you having?"

"Double vodka lime." She smiled sweetly at him.

"Make it a single," Reid cut in.

Her face fell. "Don't be like that."

"You can't play when you're drunk. Let's at least try to have a nice time tonight."

Kenzie rolled her eyes at the bartender. "Okay, a single."

He shrugged and poured the drink. Kenzie shimmied onto the bar stool beside Reid. They talked in low voices, Kenzie giggling every so often at something he said.

"Is he here?" Kenzie looked around the club from beneath her lashes.

"Alley 7. I'm going to go now. I'll be outside, waiting. He knows me, so I can't risk staying any longer. The game will be over soon. They're on their last frame."

"Okay."

Reid threw some money on the counter. "This was a bad idea. I'm outta here."

"What? You're dumping me?" Her voice rose sharply. A few heads turned. The bowlers didn't hear, they were out of earshot.

"'Fraid so, sweetheart. I changed my mind. You're not my type." He turned and stalked out of the bar.

Kenzie dropped her head in her hands.

"Don't worry about him," the bartender said. "He's an idiot."

She sniffed and gave him a wobbly smile. "Thanks."

"Want that double now?"

She nodded. "Yeah, that'd be good."

The team in aisle 7 finished their game and came over to the bar. Kenzie sat still, staring into her glass. In her peripheral vision, she noticed a tall, sandy-haired man checking her out. Slowly. Like he was sizing her up.

That's it. You know you want to.

He sauntered over.

Yes!

Kenzie's heart skipped a beat. They were in play.

Eyes on her drink, she let a tear slip down her face.

"You okay, darlin'?"

"Not really." She sniffed without looking up. "My boyfriend just dumped me."

"That's too bad. You're too pretty to be sitting here all by yourself. Can I buy you a drink?"

She looked up as if seeing him for the first time. A smile wobbled on her lips. "You're sweet, but I'm not in the mood for talking."

"No problem, honey." He met her misty blue eyes. "I'd still like to buy you a drink, if that's okay?"

She hesitated, just long enough. "No, thanks. I'm good. I should really be getting home."

"Why?" He spread his arms. She caught a whiff of sweat and after-shave. "The night is young. A drink and some friendly conversation is just what you need to put that douchebag out of your mind."

She bit her lip, grazing it with her teeth. His gaze dropped to her mouth. It was almost too easy. "Okay, but just the one."

"Excellent." He gestured to the bartender. "Jake, get this girl a..."

"Another double?" Jake asked her.

She nodded.

"Ah, I see you've met."

"Yes, earlier." Kenzie sniffed and whipped at her eyes. "I'm sorry, I must look a mess."

"Don't apologize. You look fine."

A wavering smile. "Thanks." There was a slight pause. "How did your game go?"

"We won." He grinned. "We usually do."

"You friends with those guys?" She wondered how he was going to spike her drink in front of his buddies.

"Yeah, kind of. We meet here once a week. It's a bar league."

She gave a distracted nod.

"How about you? You from New York?"

"Miami, originally." Just in case he was good with dialects. She once knew a guy who could tell which part of America you were from after only a short conversation. "I've been here a few years now."

"You live locally?"

"I've got an apartment in Manhattan." It had to be far enough so she couldn't get home by herself. "I'm sorry, I don't know your name." She laughed, embarrassed.

"Pete. Pete Doherty. Pleased to meet you."

"Hi, Pete." That hesitant smile. "You know what? I'm going to go to the ladies' room and freshen up. You don't mind, do you?"

He grinned. "Nope. I'll be right here."

Kenzie scampered off, teetering slightly on her heels. She hadn't touched the drink he'd bought her, but it was sitting on the bar, exposed. If he was going to spike it, it would be now.

When she got back, her glass was in exactly the same position. Had he done it? She stared at the clear liquid but couldn't see any difference. "You know, I wouldn't mind a soda to chase it down," she said. "I'm feeling a little woozy."

"Sure." He ordered her a soda and she gratefully took a long gulp.

"You're not going to leave this, are you?" He pushed the vodka closer to her.

Yeah, he'd done it.

"No, I'm just pacing myself." Kenzie picked up the vodka and took a sip, then she picked up the soda bottle and spat the alcohol into it. A trick she'd learned when tending bars at college. No one will ever know you're not drinking it.

It worked like a charm. Soon the vodka glass was empty, the soda bottle full. Her head was a little foggy, but she put that down to the single and double she'd had before he arrived. The slight dizziness helped her perfect her role. She laid it on, slurring her words and gripping his arm. "I'm not feeling so good. I need some air."

"I'll take you outside." Pete wrapped his arm around her.

"You okay, miss?" The bartender asked. He was a nice guy. What would he say if he knew what was really going on?

"I'm fine. Just a little woozy. I'm going home now."

He nodded as Pete led her out of the bar. She noticed he didn't stop to say goodbye to his friends. Nor did they look up as he passed. Clearly, they weren't that close.

"That vodka's gone straight to my head," she groaned. "I'm going to walk home."

"I'll call you a cab." He held out a hand and whistled. A taxi stopped. She wondered what Reid would do, being on foot. Luckily, they'd shared their location with each other in anticipation of something going wrong. That way he'd always be able to find her. She wasn't worried.

The cab drove two blocks down the street and dropped them outside the Formosa Hotel.

"I don't live here," she slurred, looking up. Pretending the world was spinning, she squeezed her eyes shut.

"Easy now." Pete paid the cab driver and escorted her into the hotel. "It's upstairs."

"What is?" Her head lolling against his shoulder.

"Your room. You can sleep it off here."

"Okay." She pretended to be too drunk to care. He half-dragged her up the stairs to the first-floor landing, then he picked her up and carried her down the corridor to the room at the end. She pretended to pass out, while he opened the door.

"What's happening?" she murmured, as he lay her on the bed.

"Don't worry. You'll be fine. You just need to sleep it off."

Kenzie tried to raise her head, failed, and flopped back down again. It was a convincing performance. One of her best.

She lay still, bracing herself for what Pete would do next. Hopefully, he wouldn't hear her heart thumping.

The mattress creaked where he climbed onto it. Kenzie felt his hot breath as he leaned over her.

"I want to look at you," he murmured. She felt her skin crawl.

Without warning, he ripped her shirt apart. She gasped but managed to turn it into a moan.

He ran his rough hand over her stomach. Forcing herself not to react, she lay still, listening to his breath quickening. He was enjoying it. It was terrifying being at the mercy of this man and not being able to look. Not being able to react, or to protect herself.

God, she hoped Reid was outside. If she screamed now, he'd come barging in and it would all be over. But they still wouldn't have him. All he'd done was drug her and bring her back here. He'd deny spiking her drink and claim he was going to let her sleep it off.

They needed more.

Warm hands undid the button on her jeans. The zipper came down. Soon, he was peeling them off. Inch by inch. His breathing became more erratic, and she knew he was getting turned on.

Trying not to flinch, she lay still and let him remove her jeans.

Still not enough.

Come on...

There was a rustle as he took off his clothing. A soft thud as an item dropped to the floor. The swish of a shirt. Hot body odor and that cloying aftershave.

The bed creaked again.

Kenzie's heart thumped as he slid on beside her. God, no. His fingers looped into the waistband of her panties, and it took every ounce of self-control that she possessed not to flinch.

Keep calm. Do. Not. Move.

His touch made her skin crawl. She thought of the poor women who'd ended up in this position for real. Drugged. Scared. Paralyzed. They'd asked for none of this. He'd abused them, exploited their vulnerability, assaulted them in the worst possible way and destroyed their lives.

Right now, in this moment, she completely understood why Gail hadn't let another man touch her. The revulsion was overwhelming. Yet she forced herself to remain calm. A few more seconds, that's all. Then she would scream.

When her panties were almost at her knees, he straddled her.

That was enough. Opening her mouth, she screamed as loud as she could.

"What the—?" Her attacker sat upright, startled.

Nothing happened. The door didn't open. Nobody came running in.

Where the hell was Reid?

Momentarily confused, Pete stared at her, then he sprang into action.

"Shut up, bitch!"

Leaning forward, he pinned her down, forcing her hands above her head. His body weight made it hard to breathe. "Struggle all you want." His voice in her ear made her skin prickle. "I like it."

Monica Stoller had fought back, but only the next morning. Had Margaret? Becca? Is that why they were dead?

She bucked, trying to throw him off, but he was stronger than her. It was futile. She screamed again, and he let go of one of her arms to cover her mouth. "Shut up, you fool."

Muffled moans, that's all she could utter. Tears of frustration streamed down her face. She fought down a rising tide of panic. What the fuck had happened to Reid?

Using her free arm, she clawed at Pete's face, pushing him away. He smacked her. Hard. A black film descended, and she had to blink to clear it. He hit her again and she saw stars.

Don't pass out.

Was that how he was going to do it? The Rohypnol hadn't worked, so he was going to beat her unconscious first, then rape her? A surge of adrenaline kicked in.

Over my dead body.

She kicked and thrashed from side to side. When he lifted his hand from her mouth, she yelled again. "Reid!"

The door crashed in.

"Get off her!" roared a voice.

Thank God.

He was here.

The weight lifted and her attacker was thrown to the floor. She heard a yell and realized it was Pete. Reid was laying into him, pounding him with his fists.

"Reid, no!"

She lurched off the bed, toward him.

Shit, she was practically naked. Pulling up her panties and closing her shirt, she stumbled off the bed toward Reid. Pete was cowering on the floor, his face a bloody mess.

"Reid. Stop it. You'll kill him." She grabbed his arm, and he turned to look at her. The haunted expression on his face made her gut wrench.

"Reid, I'm okay. He didn't hurt me."

23

Reid blinked at Kenzie. She was alright. Conscious. Unharmed. The red mist began to lift. Her words filtered through the brain fog.

I'm okay. He didn't hurt me.

Thank God.

He dropped his arm. "I thought ... I thought he'd ..." He couldn't get the words out.

"I'm fine. I swear. He didn't hurt me."

A deep red hand mark was imprinted on the side of her face. She saw where he was looking and said, "It's nothing. Honestly, I'm fine."

He wanted so badly to take her into his arms and hold her until the awful feeling passed, but he couldn't. Not here. Not now. The raping scumbag was still lying on the floor, groaning. What a wimp. Reid hadn't even hit him that hard. Had he?

With a grimace, he realized the guy's nose was broken. Blood streamed from both nostrils and one eye was swollen shut.

"I'm going to call Randal," Kenzie said.

"Okay." There was nothing for it, he'd have to take the blame. How had he lost control like that? But he knew.

Kenzie.

He'd taken one look at the naked man straddling Kenzie, who was also barely dressed, and assumed the worst. Somehow, he'd managed to subdue her.

"I'll cuff him." Reid read him his rights and put the cuffs on him. Kenzie spoke with Randal, gave him their location, and then got dressed.

"I'll get you for this," Lord snarled. "I'll have your badge."

Reid leaned over him. "You're going down for multiple cases of rape and two murders," he growled. "We have your DNA, you rapist pig. Mind what you say about me because I can make life a whole lot more difficult on the inside, you know what I'm saying? They don't like rapists in prison."

Lord paled under the blood.

Reid stood up, gave him one last withering look, then strode to the bathroom to wash the prick's blood off his hands.

"Holy Smoke!" Detective Randal exploded as he walked into the hotel room. "What the hell happened here?"

"I can explain," Kenzie said.

"I freakin' hope so." Randal stared at the guy in cuffs on the floor. "This your guy?"

"That's him," Reid said.

"What'd you do to him?" Randal looked from the suspect to Reid and back again. "He looks like he'd gone a few rounds with Anthony Joshua."

"He was sexually assaulting me." Kenzie turned her bruised cheek toward the NYPD detective. It had turned an impressive shade of purple. Her lip, also swollen, was cracked at the side. "I couldn't fight him off. I screamed for help, and Reid barged in. He saved me."

Randal gave something that resembled a grunt mixed with an uh-huh. Another officer came in and lifted Lord up off the floor.

"I've read him his rights," Reid muttered. "You can book him."

"He'll have to be cleaned up first, Sarge," the officer said.

Randal waved his hand. "I want to see you two down at the station first thing tomorrow," Randal told them.

"We can come now, if you like," Kenzie offered.

"Nope. Right now, I'm going home to my wife and family. Tomorrow is soon enough."

Reid shook his hand. "Thanks for coming through."

"I won't say you're welcome, but I am glad you caught him."

Kenzie was shivering uncontrollably by the time Reid got her back to the hotel. The dramatic events of the evening were taking their toll. Even though she insisted she was fine, he knew her well enough to know she was going into shock.

The receptionist gave them a strange look as they walked in. Kenzie, in his oversized shirt—as hers had been ripped—and he, in turn, bare chested under his jacket. Hardly the Sheraton's normal, well-heeled clientele. Ignoring her, Reid guided Kenzie to the elevator, and put his arm around her as they rode up to the eighth floor. She didn't complain. In fact, she snuggled closer, wanting his warmth and comfort.

"I'm going to take a shower," she said, as soon as they got inside her hotel room. He could understand why. She wanted to wash off her attacker's touch. Rid herself of the memory of that bastard's hands on her body.

"I'll go."

She hesitated, then shook her head. "No, stay for a while. I don't want to be alone."

"Sure."

Reid could have done with a shower too, but it could wait. He'd already washed Lord's blood off his hands, which were now bruised from the beating he'd administered. Staring at them, he couldn't believe he'd lost control like that, but when he'd heard Kenzie scream, then found her lying on the bed ... He'd assumed the worst.

Reid shook his head. In hindsight, he may have overreacted. Kenzie was fine, albeit a little shocked, and the rapist hadn't done any serious damage, although he did deserve a smack for hitting Kenzie in the face and splitting her lip.

Still, he wasn't going to beat himself up about it. The guy was a pig. After all the women he'd hurt, the lives he'd destroyed, he deserved everything that was coming to him.

Steam began to seep beneath the bathroom door. Kenzie had been in there for at least ten minutes. "You okay, Kenz?" he called, getting up.

"Yeah, just finishing up. I'll be out in a sec."

He shrugged off his heavy leather jacket. Kenzie had taken his shirt into the bathroom with her, so bare-chested, he sat back down on the bed.

A moment later, Kenzie emerged in a puff of steam, wrapped in a toweling robe. With wet hair dripping over her shoulders and flushed, glistening skin, she looked like a beautiful water nymph.

"Feel better?"

"Much."

She sat down next to him. "Reid..."

"Yeah?"

"I thought you were going to kill him."

"I wanted to."

"What happened? Why did you lose it?"

He shook his head. "I don't know. When I saw you stumble into the taxi, I got worried. I thought maybe you'd ingested the Rohypnol or whatever it was he put in your drink. Then the car drove off, and I panicked. Looking at the app, I knew you'd gone to the Formosa, so I ran there as fast as I could, but didn't see you go inside. I didn't know what room you were in. It took me a while to figure it out."

"How did you?"

"Kicked in every door on the first floor."

She chuckled. It was good to see her get some of her sparkle back.

"Is that why you were late?"

"Yeah. Sorry about that."

She nodded. "I thought you weren't coming, that something had gone wrong. I thought ..." She broke off, then cleared her throat. "I thought he was going to rape me."

Reid felt the familiar rage gurgle up inside him. "I wouldn't have let that happen."

"I know." She looked at him. "Thank you. I mean it. That was a close call."

He gave a wry grin. "And you've had a few."

She scoffed, but it didn't reach her eyes. Grabbing the remote, Reid settled back on the bed. "Wanna watch something? Take your mind off that scumbag?"

She nodded, and climbed under the covers next to him, still in the robe. He could smell lavender shampoo and minty toothpaste. He put on the comedy channel, even though neither of them was in the mood for laughing. Still, it was better than anything else he could find.

Kenzie snuggled up next to him, dropping her head on his shoulder. He wrapped his arm around her and let her absorb his warmth. Soon, he felt her stop trembling and shortly after that, her breathing became deep and rhythmic. She'd fallen asleep.

Reid changed the channel and watched an action movie. It was pretty good, but by the end, his eyes were closing too. He ought to go back to his room, but Kenzie hadn't moved, and he didn't want to wake her.

Shutting his eyes, he decided to take a nap. Just half an hour, then when she moved off him, he'd leave and go back to his room. Except she didn't, so he didn't. The next time he opened his eyes, it was morning.

24

KENZIE WOKE up in exactly the same position she'd fallen asleep. On Reid's bare chest. For a minute, she didn't move. His arm was wrapped around her, holding her close, and she'd snuggled into him. She felt warm, snug, and safe, which was a miracle after what had happened last night.

Last night.

Oh, God. She bolted upright, then groaned as her face began to throb. Touching her cheek, she gently pressed the tender skin. Her lip felt swollen too, and there was a metallic taste in her mouth.

"You okay?" Reid shot her a concerned look. She noticed with a twinge of guilt that he was still wearing his jeans from the day before and lay on top of the bedspread. He hadn't moved all night.

"Yeah, I think so." She turned to him. "How do I look?"

He gave a soft chuckle. "You've got a shiner."

"Crap. I've got the interview today!" Flinging back the covers, she got up. Padding over to the mirror, she braced herself for the catastrophe, but it wasn't as bad as she'd imagined. Her cheek had turned a lovely shade of magenta, but she could cover that with make-up. Her lip would be harder to disguise, but hopefully with lipstick on, it wouldn't be too noticeable.

"What interview?" he asked, getting up and stretching.

"I'm spending the afternoon with the bride-to-be," she explained, trying not to stare. She could have sworn he'd got more toned since she'd last seen him without a shirt on. It must be a result of the manual labor he'd been doing on his cabin in the Glades. Warmth spread through her as she thought about how they'd spent the night. Her, snuggled into him, his arm around her. Intimate. Protective. Comforting. "I can't miss it."

"What time do you have to be there?"

"Two o'clock." She glanced disparagingly back at the mirror. "I only hope I can cover this bruise up."

"Mind if I use the bathroom?"

"Oh, sure." The poor guy hadn't even done that. As he walked barefoot across the room, she reached out and took his arm. "Thanks for staying last night."

"You asked me to."

She smiled at the simplicity of his statement. She'd asked and he'd stayed, with little or no thought for his own needs. "Yes, I did, but I want you to know that I appreciate it."

The warmth in his gaze made her catch her breath. "Glad I could help."

Kenzie got dressed while Reid freshened up, and when he emerged, she was sitting cross legged on the bed, Liesl's notes arranged in piles in front of her. "You know, I don't think Malcolm Lord had anything to do with Liesl's death. Apart from that initial meeting with him, she's made no reference to him at all."

"I'd have to agree with you there. Lord isn't the type to arrange a hit on a journalist. Too stupid."

"To think that all this time he was using names from the guest register to check into his own hotel, and before he owned the hotel, he was using names of people he knew."

Reid's eyes hardened.

"What I don't understand," Kenzie said. "Is why check in at all? It's his hotel."

"I'm guessing so the rooms aren't allocated to anyone else. The weekends are his busiest times, believe it or not, and those kinds of places do get walk-ins. The temp on duty would look to see which are available if a guest walks in without booking."

"Yeah, of course." Her brain wasn't working today. God only knew how she was going to conduct an interview.

"Why don't you order some breakfast, and I'll go take a shower, then we'll head to the police station and give our statements."

"Okay." She'd forgotten they still had to do that.

"I'll meet you downstairs in an hour."

Before they left for the police department, Kenzie placed a call to Monica Stoller. "Hi Monica, it's Kenzie. I thought you'd like to know we got him."

"You did?" The incredulity in her voice made Kenzie smile.

"Yeah, he's in police custody. He was apprehended last night attempting to assault another woman." Monica needn't know the details.

"Oh, God. Really?"

"Yes, but the police got to him before he did any real damage."

"Thank God." There was a shaky pause. "Thank you, Kenzie. Thanks for letting me know."

"You're welcome."

"I won't need to come forward, will I?"

"Not unless you want to. The police have DNA from his other victims, so the choice is yours."

She hesitated. "I should, shouldn't I?"

"There is no pressure," Kenzie replied. "He'll be going away for first degree murder as well as on multiple rape charges, so if you don't want to add to his rap sheet, that's your decision."

"I'll think about it," she whispered.

Gail Peters was less controlled. She broke into a flood of tears when Kenzie told her. "You got him? Is it really over?"

"Yes, we got him. It's over, Gail. He's going away for a long time."

The sobs continued, the relief evident in every gasp. Kenzie realized just how much trauma Gail had been carrying with her over the last twenty-four years.

"Thank you," she sniffed, through her tears. "Thank you."

Kenzie smiled as she hung up. Now, perhaps, Gail could start to heal.

The Plaza had rolled out the red carpet. That hadn't been there on her last visit. The hotel was pulling out all the stops for this wedding. Kenzie felt like royalty as she walked into the lobby and was enjoying the opulence of the moment when she saw Nathaniel Lee sashaying toward her.

"Kenzie, how *are* you?"

Heavens, she'd forgotten Emmanuelle had hired him as her PR manager. This would make the afternoon even more tedious. She plastered a smile on her face, ignored the sting in her lip and said, "Nathaniel, how nice to see you."

He gave her a strange look. "What happened to your face?"

So much for the full coverage foundation. "Oh, nothing. I slipped getting out of the swimming pool."

"Ouch. It looks painful."

"Thanks." They began walking. "How is the bride this morning?"

"Emmanuelle is always fine." He tossed his head back. "She's the most composed client I've ever had. Being a model, you'd think she'd be more highly strung... They usually are, you know?"

She did.

"You wouldn't think she's about to marry the President's youngest son," he continued. "I'd be a bundle of nerves if it was me." He pressed the elevator button. "Now, we have a photographer coming today too. Pre-wedding shots, you know."

"Yes, I do know." She'd been told the *Herald* was using them to accompany her feature. "Has he been vetted by the Secret Service?"

Nathaniel's eyebrows shot up. It was clear that was the first time he'd considered any risk. "I certainly hope so."

They walked down the plush corridor to the penthouse suite. A bulky Secret Service agent in an oversized suit stood outside the door. He nodded to Nathaniel, then asked Kenzie for ID. She showed him her press pass and he said, "Wait here. Take a step back, please."

Kenzie did as he said and waited while he poked his head around the door and spoke with someone inside. A moment later, he gave her another nod and held the door open so she could enter. Nathaniel followed. "Kenzie's here," he announced, unnecessarily.

Emmanuelle, standing in the center of the room, held out a hand. Kenzie took it and kissed her on both cheeks. "How are you holding up?"

"I'm good. It's everyone around me who is stressed." She flittered a hand at Nathaniel and the other agent hulking by the window.

"Is Warner here?"

"He's in the bedroom on a call. They've reserved another room for him. Apparently, it's bad luck for a bride to sleep with her lover the night before the wedding." She gave a very French shrug. It wasn't something Kenzie had ever thought about.

"Let's talk about the preparations." Kenzie took a seat.

Nathaniel joined them. "I can tell you all about those."

"Nathaniel's been handling that." Emmanuelle reached over and squeezed her PR manager's hand. "He's been amazing."

Nathaniel flushed smugly. "Just doing my job."

They ran through the details, Nathaniel doing most of the talking, with Emmanuelle commenting between sips of jasmine green tea. Today she wore skintight jeans that made her legs go on forever, coupled with a thin, designer T-shirt that showed off her pale arms. Her boots cost more than Kenzie's annual salary, and her hair was freshly blow-dried, no doubt for the photographer who was apparently running late but should be here any minute. As usual, she looked stunning.

Kenzie had just started asking Emmanuelle about how she felt now that the big day was almost here, when a fire alarm pierced through the building. The two agents in the room sprang into action. One checked the window, the other spoke urgently into his earpiece.

The bedroom door swung open, and another agent appeared, followed by a frowning Warner Sullivan. Kenzie had forgotten he was here. Had he been on the phone all this time?

"What's going on?" he barked.

No one answered. The operative was still muttering into his earpiece.

"Is it for real?" Nathaniel clutched his clipboard to his chest.

"I think so." Kenzie got to her feet. "We might have to evacuate the building."

Emmanuelle put down her tea. "Is that really necessary? It's probably just someone smoking in their room."

Kenzie glanced at the lead agent who'd opened the door. He gave a curt nod, his finger to his ear. "Okay, we're heading out," he said.

"What? Why?" Nathaniel looked from one to the other.

"Apparently there is smoke coming from one of the kitchens," the lead agent said. "We have to move."

Warner's agent opened the door, peeked out and then beckoned for him to follow. Warner took Emmanuelle's hand and stepped into the corridor. The other two agents were right behind her. Kenzie followed, while Nathaniel was still freaking out. "We'd better go," she told him, taking his arm.

They followed the engaged couple and their bodyguards into the corridor. The group moved swiftly toward the emergency stairs, situated on the opposite side of the corridor to the elevators. They were almost there when two masked men appeared in front of them and threw something small and tubular at their feet.

"Get back!" Kenzie yelled, recognizing the device as a stun

grenade. She'd seen them once when reporting from a prison where there was a riot. Grabbing Nathaniel, she hauled him back toward the room.

"What—?" He didn't have time to finish his sentence before there was a loud explosion and a blinding flash of light. The shockwave sent both her and the PR manager stumbling to their knees. Smoke filled the corridor.

Through the haze, they heard Emmanuelle screaming.

"Get down," yelled an agent.

Kenzie crawled back into the room as shots rang out.

25

"ARE WE UNDER ATTACK?" Nathaniel scampered inside behind her. He'd lost his clipboard in the mayhem.

"Not us," she corrected. "Them."

His eyes were huge. "Shit. What are we going to do?"

"Nothing. Stay down and get behind something. We're not the target." Nathaniel dropped to his knees and crawled behind the sofa. Smoke wafted through the open door. Outside, there was a volley of gunshots, followed by multiple male voices, all yelling at the same time.

Kenzie backed into a corner, her heart pounding. This was a professional job. A kidnapping, rather than an assassination, although she couldn't be sure. The flashbangs, the masked men, the rapid bursts of gunfire. Designed to confuse and discombobulate the Secret Service agents and their charges.

"In here," cried a voice she didn't recognize. To her horror, the two gunmen in balaclavas ducked into the room. Where were the agents? Probably focused on getting their principals out of the hotel. One shut the door and secured the chain.

They were trapped.

Nathaniel cowered behind the sofa, quaking like a terrified puppy, while Kenzie huddled in the corner of the room, trying to make herself as inconspicuous as possible. It was only a matter of time before the first gunman saw her.

"Who are you?" he growled, aiming his weapon at her.

"Reporter," she said meekly.

"Wedding planner," whimpered Nathaniel, poking his head above the sofa.

The gunman grunted as his sidekick sent him a questioning look. "Leave 'em."

Kenzie exhaled softly. They were going to be fine. She watched as the assailants headed for the balcony door. They were pretty high up. Emmanuelle and Warner's suite was the penthouse. She didn't rate their chances if they went out that way.

The first gunman opened the sliding door and stepped out onto the balcony. He looked down at the sidewalk twenty-one floors below, while holstering his firearm. "It's doable."

The other guy joined him and to Kenzie's astonishment, they climbed over the railing.

"They're going to jump," Nathaniel whispered, his hand over his mouth.

"Not all the way down." Kenzie realized what they were doing. They watched as the men, standing on the narrow ledge, dropped into a crouch, grabbed the bottom bar of the railing and swung off.

"Holy shit," Nathaniel stage whispered. "I can't watch."

As they disappeared over the edge, Kenzie jumped up and ran outside. She got there in time to see them land on the balcony below. It took balls, but it wasn't a particularly difficult maneuver. She, herself, had done it a couple of years back in a hotel in Miami. Not voluntarily, mind you—she'd had a gun pointed at her head—but she'd managed. Right now, the gunmen would be charging down the corridor below to the service elevator, after which they'd make their way to an exit.

"They're gone," she called.

Nathaniel, whiter than the interior wall paint, stepped out onto the balcony.

"Don't touch the railing," she barked, as he put his hand out. He snatched it back.

"Where'd they go?" Leaning over, he peered down, expecting to see their broken bodies on the road below.

"They made it to the floor below."

He shook his head. "They're crazy."

"Or desperate."

Kenzie walked back through the suite, took the chain off the door, and peered out into the corridor. It was empty. Emmanuelle and Warner, along with their Secret Service agents, had gone.

"Where's everyone?" Nathaniel ventured out and picked up his clipboard.

"The agents must have taken them downstairs," Kenzie guessed. The air was still hazy with explosives, but she could see fine.

"Let me call her." Nathaniel took out his phone and dialed Emmanuelle's number. "Voicemail," he said, disgruntled. Kenzie wasn't surprised. The couple would have been told not to take any calls. In fact, they may have turned their phones off completely. Phones could be traced.

Kenzie went back into the hotel suite. Soon, this place would be crawling with law enforcement officers. Secret Service, FBI, NYPD, anti-terrorism. They'd all be summoned to make sense of what had happened.

An attempt had been made on the President's son's life. The crime scene would be processed, the stun grenades analyzed, fingerprints taken from the balcony. Had the perpetrators been wearing gloves? She couldn't remember.

"What are you doing?" Nathaniel asked.

"Taking a quick look around. Don't touch anything." She hurried toward the bedroom. There was a hotel issue notepad lying on the table by the window, presumably where Warner had been sitting before the alarm sounded. There were indents on it, as if someone had been writing on the sheet above.

The alarm. Had that been a ploy to get them out of the room?

Using a tissue from a box on the bed stand, Kenzie tore off the top sheet of the notepad and stuffed it into her suit jacket pocket. She had no idea if it was important or not.

"They're coming!" Nathaniel hissed.

Kenzie darted back into the lounge moments before the door swung open and a barrage of law enforcement officers swarmed in. "Get down," they yelled. "Put your hands on your head."

Kenzie already had her hands in the air, but Nathaniel stared at them, shocked. A brutal hand shoved him to his knees and jerked his hands behind his back. The clipboard went flying again.

"Ouch! I'm the PR manager," he cried.

"He is," Kenzie agreed, as her hands were also wrenched behind her back. "Hey, take it easy."

"Who are you?" a surly officer asked.

"I'm a reporter. I was doing an interview with Emmanuelle Lenoir when the fire alarm sounded." She nodded at a trembling Nathaniel. "This man is her PR agent."

"Why are you still here?" the officer growled.

"We hid in the room. There was gunfire in the corridor."

"They went over the balcony," Nathaniel stammered.

"What?"

"The gunmen," Kenzie clarified. "They ran through the suite and climbed over the balcony. They jumped down to the floor below."

The man nodded to one of the other officers who looked over the balcony. "Clear."

"Are you sure?" the growly officer asked.

"Of course. We were right here."

Nathaniel nodded, backing her up.

More people swarmed in. Suited, neatly dressed, shiny shoes. FBI, or perhaps Secret Service agents. One of them was Sergeant Randal. Kenzie sighed in relief.

The NYPD detective took one look at her and rolled his eyes. "Not you again."

"You know this woman?" Growly asked.

"Yeah, unfortunately. You can let her go."

The officer holding her gave a stiff nod and undid her handcuffs. "Thank you," she retorted.

Randal stormed up to her. "Now, do you want to tell me what the hell went down here?"

"What about me?" squeaked Nathaniel.

"He's Emmanuelle's PR manager," Kenzie told Randal. "He's been vetted."

Randal nodded to the officer securing the wide-eyed public relations manager, and Nathaniel was freed. He rubbed his wrists, then sank down into the armchair Emmanuelle had vacated. Her cold cup of herbal tea sat unfinished on the table next to him.

Kenzie explained what had happened, finishing with the gunmen hopping over the balcony and getting away.

"Did you see their faces?" asked a man who'd come over during her explanation. Sleek, fit and disciplined. He wore an earpiece in his left ear.

"No, they were wearing balaclavas."

"Special Agent Gordon," he said, curtly.

She nodded a greeting.

"Get a CSI team in here," Randal barked, and one of his officers pulled out his phone and strode into the corridor to make the call.

"Did anyone get hurt?" Nathaniel squeaked. "We heard gunshots."

"No, thankfully," Gordon replied. "My agents managed to get Sullivan and his fiancée to safety." They'd be in a safe house somewhere in the New York area, Kenzie surmised. Out of reach and off the grid until things settled down.

"But... but what about the wedding?" Nathaniel whimpered.

"I don't know about that," Gordon replied. It wasn't his problem.

"It's unlikely it's going to happen now," Kenzie told the PR expert. This place would be locked down for a couple of days with police crawling all over it. It would be deemed way too risky to have it here, and the President certainly wouldn't be coming.

"Oh, God." Nathaniel dropped his head in his hands. "I'll have to cancel everything. We'll lose our deposits." Poor Nathaniel, but to be honest, that was the least of their problems.

"Was this an attempt on Warner Sullivan's life?" she asked Special Agent Gordon.

"I can't talk about what happened, ma'am."

"So much gunfire," Nathaniel murmured. "I was certain they were going to shoot us."

"Thankfully, no one was hurt, and the President's son and his fiancée are safe."

They may be safe, but the shooters were still out there. They'd gotten away, and nobody seemed to know who they were. The thought made her distinctly uneasy.

26

REID COULDN'T BELIEVE what he was hearing. "The shooter actually pointed a gun at you?" He'd gone up to her room as soon as she'd called and told him what had happened.

"Yes, but we weren't the targets, obviously." Kenzie sat at the table by the window, a glass and a vodka bottle from the minibar in front of her.

"Still, Kenz..." A shiver ran through him. "You could have been shot, killed even."

"They were after Warner Sullivan, not me. At least that's the current theory."

"Was anyone injured?"

"Not according to the Secret Service agent. Shots were fired, but somehow, no one got hit."

Reid raised his eyebrows. "That's lucky."

"I know. Both Warner and Emmanuelle were in the corridor, along with three Secret Service agents. It would have been a bloodbath."

"Maybe the agents shot first?"

"That's all I can think of. There was a lot of smoke from the flash-bangs, so visibility was limited."

"The intruders threw the flashbangs?"

"Yeah, I recognized them. That's why I ran back into the room."

He nodded. "Good. Well done. Except why did they use stun grenades if their aim was to take out Warner Sullivan?"

"I don't know. Maybe they wanted to scare him, not hurt him."

He frowned. Something didn't add up.

"I don't know," Kenzie continued. "It could be they wanted to blackmail the President. Prove they could get to his son. Something like that?"

Reid wasn't convinced. "I guess. What did the Secret Service agent say?"

"Special Agent Gordon wouldn't talk about it. He did say nobody was hurt, though."

Reid leaned back and gave a low whistle. "Well, this wedding just got a whole lot more interesting."

"The wedding's off." Kenzie drained the rest of the vodka in her glass. "The White House issued a statement half an hour ago. Postponed until the threat against the President's son has been eradicated."

"Not surprising." Kenzie ran a hand through her disheveled hair. Her clothes were crumpled, the one side of her face was showing up blue under the makeup. She looked like she'd been through the ringer, but her eyes were sparkling. "Where does that leave you?"

"Well, I was on the scene during the firefight, with the scoop of the season." She chuckled, then grimaced. "Ow. It hurts to laugh."

He frowned sympathetically. "How are you feeling?"

"Bruised and battered, but I'll live." He admired her spirit. "How did it go this morning?"

After Kenzie had left him at the police station, he'd watched Malcolm Lord's interrogation on a computer in Randal's office. Part of him wanted to see the man confess, to make sure justice was being served. Another, less ethical part, wanted to make sure the bastard wasn't going to hit him with an assault charge.

"Interesting. The custody officer who booked Malcolm Lord took a DNA swab. It's been fast-tracked through the system."

"Hopefully it'll prove he raped Margaret Downey," Kenzie said.

"No need. He confessed."

At her surprised look, he elaborated. "Randal tricked him. Hinted that the DNA had come back already, linking him to both murders. He was too dumb to realize you can't get DNA back in under twenty-four hours. Forty-eight if you're lucky." He snorted.

"He admitted killing Becca and Margaret?" Kenzie stared at him.

"Yeah, and multiple rapes going back decades. That scumbag is going to spend the rest of his life in prison."

Not once did he complain about Reid's treatment of him.

"That's great news." Kenzie closed her eyes. "I'm glad that's over."

"And now the wedding has been postponed." He looked at her. "What happens next? Is it time to go home?" A big part of him didn't want to leave New York. Last night had made him realize that. Even though Kenzie had been in shock and needed him, he felt they'd grown closer because of it. He didn't want that feeling to end.

"I'd like to stay a while." Kenzie tapped the table thoughtfully with her fingernails. "My gut is telling me this isn't over."

That made him refocus. "You think whoever attacked Warner Sullivan will try again?"

"Yeah." She hesitated, then pursed her lips. "I'm not convinced it was an attempt to get to the President."

Warning bells went off in his head. Kenzie's instinct for a story was uncanny. He'd learned to take it seriously. "What do you think it's about?"

She shook her head. "The China issue? I don't know. But according to Liesl's notes, Warner Sullivan's record is far from squeaky clean."

Reid thought back to what she'd said before. "You think the Chinese are sending him a message?"

She shrugged. "All I know is that they want to use Warner to broker a deal with the President. That's what they're paying for."

"What if Warner reneged on the deal? Told them his father isn't interested."

"They'd be angry," Kenzie replied. "Very angry."

"Angry enough to kill?"

She sighed. "Probably not. The shooters weren't Chinese."

"You saw them?"

"Only their eyes, and I heard them speak. American accents."

"Could be a local assassin."

"True." She touched her split lip. "I mean, it could be internal. We know the President wants Warner to sever his ties with the Far East. That's why they fell out."

"The President would never put out a hit on his own son." Even Reid, who knew the depraved lengths to which people would go, couldn't believe that.

"No, but what about his staunch supporters? Other government agencies? People who have invested in the Presidential campaign and don't want to see it fail?"

Reid contemplated this. Eventually, he said, "If this was politically motivated, it's way out of our league. It's way out of the NYPD's league."

"But not the Secret Service," she murmured, meeting his gaze.

"The Secret Service isn't going to let you anywhere near this investigation."

"No, but Emmanuelle might. If I can get ahold of her, she might let me talk to Warner. Maybe I can find out what's going on."

"It's risky, Kenzie. Whoever did this is dangerous and, from what you've told me, professional."

"I'll dig a little from the sidelines. I'm not going to put myself at risk."

"I've heard that before."

At his arched look, she added, "I promise."

Reid knew there was no stopping her. "Okay, but we proceed with caution. This is not our jurisdiction, and the Secret Service won't appreciate our involvement."

"I'll see if I can get in touch with Emmanuelle."

"They'll be offline until things quieten down."

"She'll still have her phone with her," Kenzie said. "Even if it's not on right now. I bet she'll check it when she can. She's got two million Instagram followers who want to know why the wedding's off."

Reid chuckled. Staying longer was fine with him. He wasn't ready for their adventure to end just yet.

Kenzie sent a text message to Warner Sullivan's fiancée, and then frowned, thoughtfully. "There's something bugging me about the way those gunmen escaped over the balcony."

"Oh, yeah?"

"Remember in Miami at the Ritz-Carlton, when the same thing happened?"

"How could I forget? Maria Lopez forced you to go with them." He'd been worried sick. Come to think about it, he spent a great deal of time worrying about Kenzie.

"Exactly. And the men who came for Warner Sullivan did the same thing."

Reid studied her. "Kenzie, what are you saying?"

"I don't know, but it's bothering me. Why would they have thought to do that? I mean, out of all the ways they could have escaped—the stairwell, the work elevator—what made them head for the balcony?"

"Maybe it was their planned escape route? The Secret Service was crawling all over the building."

"I don't think so. The first shooter looked down and said, 'It's doable.' Those were his exact words. Then, they leaped over and disappeared."

"Like they'd done it before?"

"Exactly." Her eyes met his. "You don't think...?"

He shook his head. "Surely not."

"It could be." Her voice was breathless. "The Morales Cartel."

Reid stared at her. "You realize what that would mean, don't you?"

She nodded. "That Warner Sullivan wasn't the target. Emmanuelle was."

27

"IF EMMANUELLE WAS THE TARGET, then it's even more important that I speak with her." Kenzie stared across the table at Reid. Outside, the sun had sunk behind the buildings and the hotel room had grown dark. "Her life could be in danger."

Reid got up and switched on the light. "Would the cartel really come after her now, before her wedding?"

Kenzie took a thoughtful breath. "They might. Who knows what they're thinking? I mean, she's Maria Lopez's biological daughter. The next in line, so to speak."

"Yeah, but she doesn't want anything to do with the cartel," Reid reminded her. "When you broke the story about her mother, she publicly renounced the woman."

"Still, she is a threat to Matteo Lopez, Maria's son."

"Her brother?"

"Half-brother. He's being groomed to take over by Romeo Herrera, head of the Californian branch of the cartel." Kenzie had studied the cartel when preparing to interview Maria Lopez in prison. She knew who all the key players were. Reid, while he'd read police reports, wasn't as familiar with them.

"Wasn't he part of Maria's inner circle?" Reid asked. "One of the few people that knew her husband was dead, and she was running the show."

"That's right. He's also Emmanuelle's biological father." Kenzie gave him a pointed look.

Reid nodded slowly. "So—?"

Kenzie stretched her neck. "So, how's this for a theory? Romeo Herrera finds out he has a daughter. A beautiful supermodel engaged to marry the President's son. He'd be stupid not to see that as an opportunity, so he tries to contact her, bring her into the fold."

"Emmanuelle tried to distance herself from the cartel," Reid pointed out.

"Wait." Kenzie held up a finger. "It doesn't matter whether he contacted her or not. Matteo Lopez would still consider her a threat."

Reid's eyes narrowed. "You think he arranged to take her out?"

She spread her hands. "Maybe. I mean this is all conjecture. I don't know anything for sure. I could be way off base here."

Reid massaged his temples. "You *are* basing all this on how the men fled over the balcony."

"It is their MO. Not so unrealistic when you think about it."

Reid was silent. She could see the cogs in his detective brain turning. "How are we going to prove any of this? We need evidence."

Kenzie pursed her lips. "What about the shooting? A crime scene investigation team was called in to process the hotel room and corridor. They may have found fingerprints or DNA."

"There'd be a ballistics report too," Reid added. "The shooters would have left shell casings in the corridor."

Kenzie cocked her head to the side. "Can we get a copy of those reports?"

"It won't be for a few days," Reid said. "And that's if they expedite it."

"It is the President's son," Kenzie reminded him. "I think they'll expedite."

He grunted in agreement.

She smiled at him. "Maybe it's time you paid Sergeant Randal another visit. He's much more likely to talk to you."

Reid folded his arms across his chest. "I can, but this isn't his case. The Secret Service will be running it."

"But Randal could get access to those reports, right?"

Reid shrugged. "Maybe. Unless they're redacted."

"It's worth a shot. We could also talk to Special Agent Gordon."

Reid looked skeptical. "Why would he talk to us?"

"He'd talk to you; you're law enforcement. We could tell him our theory."

"He'd laugh at us."

"Okay, then we'll present him with a different hypothesis. We could tell him about Liesl's research into Warner Sullivan, and the Chinese bribes."

"Hmm..." Reid rubbed his stubbly chin. "It might be a way to find out what's going on."

"It's worth a shot," Kenzie said. "In the meantime, I'll message Emmanuelle again."

Reid stood up and began pacing. "I feel like we need something else, something concrete."

Kenzie snapped her fingers. "Raoul has a contact at Miami International. He might be able to look at the passenger lists of flights into JFK. All the airports use the same database. We could check if any cartel members have flown in."

"He can do that?"

"Yeah, he's very resourceful."

"Hmm..." Reid didn't like Raoul's dubious research tactics. "Matteo Lopez isn't the type to pull the trigger himself. He'd send his thugs to do that."

"True." Kenzie fell silent, thinking.

"I'll contact the drug squad in L.A. They'll know the key players. Once we get a list of names, we can cross-check them with the passenger lists."

Kenzie felt an ache in her stomach and realized she couldn't remember the last time she ate. "Can we order room service? I'm starved."

"Good idea."

They listened to the news channel while they waited for it to arrive. Kenzie found she was quite happy to have Reid hang out in her room. She was getting used to his presence. A first for her.

"I know I'm right, Reid," she said, once their food had arrived. They'd ordered two pizzas and a salad to share. Kenzie placed the boxes on the table and the salad in the middle. "It's finally starting to make sense."

Reid took a slice of pizza. "Until we have proof, it's best not to jump to any conclusions."

"I know. But the timing fits. When Emmanuelle marries Warner Sullivan, she's got access to the White House. That puts her in a very powerful position."

"A good connection for the cartel."

"Exactly. You can understand why Romeo Herrera would want her on their side."

"And why Matteo Lopez wouldn't."

"Yep." Kenzie bit into her pizza.

Reid didn't stay with her that night, but then she didn't ask him to. After they'd eaten, he went back to his room, and hers had felt emptier because of it. Kenzie didn't want to analyze why that was. Not now. She had more important things on her mind.

Sleep didn't come easily, and she was plagued by dreams of car crashes and shootouts. The morning couldn't come soon enough.

At seven o'clock, she texted Reid to make sure he was up. "Can I come over? We've got work to do."

"Sure, I'm up."

He opened the door, his hair still damp from the shower. "I've spoken with my contact in the L.A. drug squad," he told her, before she'd even said hello. Clearly, he'd been obsessing about their new theory too. "She's sending through an up-to-date list of the cartel members and their known associates. If we cross-check that with passenger lists of airlines flying into New York City in the last week or so, we might have something."

"She?" Kenzie had expected a man.

He blinked, thrown by the question. "Yeah, Chantelle transferred to L.A. from Miami a couple of years back. We used to work together."

Kenzie gave a quick nod. "Okay, great. I've sent Emmanuelle another text, asking to meet. I mentioned I had some important information for her."

"Do you?"

"I think it's time she found out who her real father is, don't you?"

His eyes widened. "She doesn't know?"

"No, only you and I know. I haven't told anyone else in case it got out."

"You think now is a good time?"

"Why not? Maria's dead. Emmanuelle has a right to know if a relative is trying to kill her. Besides, I need a reason to see her. She won't agree otherwise."

"What about Warner? We can't be a hundred percent sure this isn't about him."

"As soon as we cross-check that list, we'll know."

Reid's contact was true to her word and less than an hour later, they received a spreadsheet containing the names of the Morales cartel members, their families, and known associates.

"That is quite a list," Kenzie murmured. "I thought I knew most of the members, but I don't recognize half of these."

"These are just the ones they know of," Reid said grimly. "There'll be a whole lot more flying under the radar."

"I've spoken with Raoul," she told him. "He's agreed to run a search for us."

"I won't ask how he does that."

"Probably for the best," Kenzie muttered. "Why don't you forward that list to me, and I'll send it to Raoul."

Reid did as she asked, and seconds later, the list of names was being fed into a computer program at the Herald's offices in downtown Miami.

"I'll let you know when I have something," Raoul had texted. "Stand by..."

While Raoul was doing his thing, Kenzie and Reid took a cab to the NYPD building where Randal was based. As expected, the detective nodded at Kenzie when she walked into the squad room. "What is it now?"

"Nice to see you too, Sergeant."

Randal gave a snort, then straightened up as Reid walked in behind her. A respectful nod. "Lieutenant."

Reid returned the gesture. "Sergeant, we were hoping to ask you some questions about the shooting at The Plaza yesterday."

"That's not my case. You'll have to speak to Special Agent Gordon."

"I know, but just out of curiosity, did the shell casings found at the scene give any indication who the shooters were?"

"The ballistics report hasn't come back yet."

"You were there, right?"

Randal nodded.

"What's your professional opinion?"

The detective puffed out his chest. He liked being asked his opinion. "They were 7.62mm slugs."

Reid gave a knowing nod. "Kalashnikov?"

"Looks like it."

"Who would use that sort of firepower?" Kenzie asked.

"Any number of organizations," Randal replied. "Armed forces, as well as irregular forces and insurgents."

"But not the US military?" Kenzie asked.

"No." He shook his head. "Not the military."

"What about the cartels?" asked Kenzie, glancing at Reid.

"It's possible. We do find the gangbangers using them," Randal added. "They usually come in from Central and South America."

Kenzie raised her eyebrows.

"On a different note, forensics got some DNA from the car that ran your friend over," Randal turned to Kenzie. "We think it belongs to the driver."

"Really? That's great news."

"Unfortunately, he's not in the database."

"He?" Reid questioned.

"A witness saw a man emerge from the car and walk away."

"Can they describe him?" Kenzie asked, leaning forward.

Randal shrugged. "Average height. Dark hair. Slim build. Nothing definitive."

"Damn." She bit her lip, then winced. It was still painful.

Reid frowned. "He was walking, not running? The witness is sure about that?"

"Yeah, why?"

"The perp didn't want to draw attention to himself. Running would mean it was an accident and he panicked. Didn't want to be found with the stolen car. Walking means it was deliberate. He was a pro."

Kenzie gave a sharp intake of breath. "What now?"

Randal shrugged. "That's it for now. If he's ever been arrested, we'll get a match, but until then, there's nothing we can do." The phone on his desk rang. The detective picked it up, listened for a moment, and said, "I'll be right there."

Kenzie got up. That was their cue to leave.

"Appreciate the help." Reid extended his hand.

Randal shook it. "Sorry it's not better news."

"The large rounds, the 7.62mm casings. That's one more piece of evidence in favor of the cartel theory," Kenzie said as they walked back to the hotel. It was a beautiful day in the city, the sky cloudless and very blue above the silver skyscrapers. If she wasn't so tense, she might enjoy it. They were getting closer to the truth. She could feel it.

"I agree it's suspicious, but it's not definitive," Reid replied as they crossed a busy street. "We have to be careful not to skew the evidence to fit our narrative."

"Is that what we're doing?" She side-stepped a gaggle of map-reading tourists.

"You want everything to fall in line with your theory, and while I admit it isn't outside the realm of possibility, we have to look at the evidence in isolation. Analyze it on its own merit."

She remembered that from her police training at the academy, before she'd had the accident that had ended her career in law enforcement. It was far too easy to see links where none existed. The hotel shooting might have nothing to do with the cartel. There was nothing to base it on other than some circumstantial evidence and her gut instinct.

Her phone buzzed. It was Raoul. Putting it to her ear, she tried to ignore the background noise. "Raoul, did you find anything?"

She listened while he spoke, feeling Reid's eyes on her.

The moment she hung up, Reid said, "What?"

Her pulse was racing. "Three people on the cartel list were also on the passenger lists," she told him. "Different flights, though. Raoul's sending me the names now."

On cue, her phone beeped. They both leaned over her phone as she opened the message. Three names.

Matteo Lopez.

Luis Hernandez.

Joaquín Nieto.

Kenzie turned to look at Reid. "That definitive enough for you?"

28

"LET'S SIT DOWN. I need to think about this." Reid pointed to a small park across the road. They walked in and took a seat on a bench. A dog played with a ball on the grass in front of them. It pushed it around with its nose, trying to get a grip, but it was too big and kept rolling away. Kind of like them and this damn case.

Reid tried to make sense of what they'd learned. "Two known associates of the Morales cartel fly into JFK airport in New York two days before two armed men attempt to shoot the President's son and his fiancée at The Plaza."

"Luis Hernandez and Joaquín Nieto," Kenzie supplied.

"And the very next day, Matteo Lopez himself arrives."

"Hell of a coincidence," Kenzie said.

"Do you recognize them from the hotel?" Reid nodded to the mug shots Raoul had sent of the three men. Her researcher was thorough, he'd give him that much.

Kenzie shook her head. "The gunmen wore face coverings and were dressed in black. It was impossible to make out any features. They were fairly heavyset, but that's all I got."

Reid thought for a moment, then said, "Talk me through it again. Everything you can remember of the attack."

Kenzie took a deep breath. "Okay. I arrived and Nathaniel, that's the PR guy, took me up to the suite. The penthouse. I showed my ID at the door, and a Secret Service agent let us in. Emmanuelle was inside, waiting, along with another agent who was standing by the window." She paused to think.

"Where was Warner Sullivan?"

"In the bedroom on a call. There was another agent with him."

"Okay, so how did it all kick off?"

"The fire alarm sounded. At first, I thought it was a drill, but then we were told to evacuate the building."

"By whom?"

"The Secret Service agent by the window. He spoke into his earpiece and told us to move out."

Reid gave a thoughtful nod. "Then what?"

"Warner and his bodyguard came out of the bedroom. They were first out the door."

Reid held up a hand. "Wait. Warner Sullivan and his SS agent went into the corridor first?"

"That's right." Kenzie gasped. "That's why the gunmen didn't open fire, because *he* was in the way."

"Warner Sullivan?"

"Yes, they were there to kill Emmanuelle."

Reid warmed to the theory. "It makes sense. They didn't want to injure the President's son. Imagine the fallout."

Kenzie jumped off the bench. "When the Secret Service agents opened fire, the gunmen retreated into the stairwell."

"How did the agents get Warner and Emmanuelle out of the building?" Reid asked.

"The emergency stairs, at the other end of the corridor."

"So how did the gunmen end up in the hotel suite?"

"Because by that time, the alarm had been raised. Agents were storming up both sets of stairs. The elevators were out of order because of the fire alarm. They were trapped. They had nowhere else to go but the hotel room."

"Where they made their escape over the balcony?" Reid finished.

"Exactly."

They looked at each other, breathless. The dog managed to get its teeth into the plastic ball, which deflated with a loud hiss. A child ran up, crying, followed by an aggrieved parent.

"I have to warn her," Kenzie murmured, gazing at the distraught child.

"Has she responded to your text messages?" Reid stood up. It was time to leave. The kid was screaming his head off, pointing to the sorry-looking ball. The dog panted up at its owner, tail wagging, as if to say, 'Look what I did!'

Kenzie checked her phone. "No response. I wonder where they've been taken?"

"A safe house, probably. Once the coast is clear, they'll take them home, but they'll ramp up their security. The natural conclusion is this attack was aimed at Warner Sullivan to get to his father."

"Which we believe to be incorrect," Kenzie said.

Reid gave a somber nod. "It certainly looks that way."

Kenzie had just reached her room when her phone rang. Heart pounding, she glanced at the caller.

Emmanuelle.

"Hello, Emmanuelle. Thanks for calling me back."

"Hello Kenzie. Sorry for the dramatic end to our interview. Are you and Nathaniel okay?"

"Yes, we're both fine, thank you."

"Thank God. I was worried." But not enough to call.

"Listen, there's something I need to speak with you about," Kenzie said in a hushed tone.

"Can it wait? I'm not allowed to see anyone right now." Kenzie heard the frustration in the model's voice. It couldn't be easy, living under armed guard.

"I'm afraid it can't, no." Kenzie hesitated, aware that the line might be compromised. "I think I know who was responsible for yesterday's attack."

"Really? Shouldn't you talk to Agent Gordon? He's in charge of the investigation."

"It pertains to you."

"Me? I don't understand."

"I think they were after you," Kenzie whispered.

The model's voice dropped. "But why? I mean, who would want to hurt me?"

Kenzie hesitated. Emmanuelle had no idea who her father was. Finding out he was also connected to the cartel would come as a shock. It was something Kenzie would prefer to tell Emmanuelle in person. Face to face. "I'd rather not talk on the phone. Can we meet?"

A soft sigh. "It'll be difficult. I'll have to clear it with the Secret Service."

"Can you do that? I have been vetted, and they know I'm not a threat. It's imperative I speak with you."

There was a slight pause.

"Okay, Kenzie. I'll see what I can do."

29

"I'LL SEE YOU LATER," Kenzie said, as a nondescript black SUV swooped to a stop outside the hotel.

"I wish I was coming with you," Reid growled. "I have a bad feeling about this."

"Don't worry, I'll be fine. I'm only going to talk to her. Besides, you can track me, remember?" They still had the GPS set up on each other's phones. Neither had suggested removing it. Normally, Kenzie didn't like someone knowing her every movement, but she had to admit, it was reassuring knowing Reid could get to her if she needed him and vice versa.

Reid grunted. "Call me as soon as you're done."

"They're bringing me back to the hotel, so I'll tell you all about it later."

"Okay." He fidgeted on the top step, a lone figure silhouetted against the backlighting of the hotel entrance. She resisted the urge to bound back up the stairs and hug him.

"Ready?" asked the Secret Service agent in the passenger seat. She nodded, and they glided away, the tires barely making a sound on the tarmac.

The drive took a little over an hour. Kenzie gazed out of the window, but she didn't know New York very well, and after a while, the streets all began to look the same. Soon they were in an industrial area. The buildings were more spaced out, more rundown.

The agent glanced in the rearview mirror. "This is not where they're staying," he said, which she'd ascertained by now. They wouldn't take her to the safe house itself in broad daylight without a blindfold.

The SUV glided to a halt outside a dreary prefab office block. It appeared deserted. There were no other warehouses or buildings within a hundred yards, which was a good thing from a defensive perspective. The agents surrounding it would be able to see if a threat was approaching.

All this so that she could speak with Emmanuelle.

Kenzie climbed out of the SUV, her feet crunching on the loose gravel.

"This way." An agent took her arm and led her quickly into the prefab. Inside was a small area that would have originally been the reception. It smelled musty, like it hadn't been used in a while. Kenzie tried to figure out what had been here before. Shipping company, maybe? Logistics? There was an old print of a fleet of trucks leaning against the wall. Forgotten when they packed up and left. No desk, no chairs, no equipment. It was the only evidence that someone had actually worked here.

"This way."

Kenzie followed him down a short corridor, into a darkened office. Emmanuelle stood in the center, away from the closed windows. The blinds were drawn, the light off. "You have ten minutes."

"Very dramatic," Kenzie said, once he'd left.

Emmanuelle spread her arms. "This is my life now."

"How do you feel about that?" Kenzie asked.

A shrug. "It's not what I expected, but I hope it will be temporary. Once they catch whoever is responsible for the shooting, things will return to normal."

"You know there are always going to be threats," Kenzie pointed out.

"I know, but hopefully not toward me." Her perfectly plucked eyebrow rose. "Now, what is all this about, Kenzie?"

If only there was somewhere they could sit down. Standing made her feel awkward. Yet, that wasn't a possibility. She just had to spit it out.

"I know who was responsible for the attack."

Emmanuelle craned her long, slender neck forward. She reminded Kenzie of a praying mantis. "Who, Kenzie? Who did this?"

"I think it was your half-brother, Matteo Lopez."

Emmanuelle stared at her, uncomprehending. She blinked several times, then swallowed. "I have a half-brother?"

That had been the reaction Kenzie was expecting. The fact Emmanuelle had family out there she didn't know about would override any sense of shock that they were out to kill her.

"Yes, you do. I'm sorry to break it to you this way. Your biological father is a man named Romeo Herrera. He was part of your mother's inner circle. Her confidant."

"He's still alive?" Her face was so pale it was almost luminous in the dark interior.

Kenzie nodded. "He lives in California. L.A., to be precise. I'm sorry, Emmanuelle, but he's not a good guy. He runs the Californian branch of the Morales Cartel."

Emmanuelle wavered, and for a moment, Kenzie thought she might sink to the floor, but she pulled herself together, took a shaky breath, and fixed her beautiful, oval eyes on Kenzie. "How do you know this?"

"I've been investigating the cartel for years, ever since I first met your mother."

"Why didn't you tell me?"

"Your mother asked me not to." It was a simple answer, but a truthful one. "She wanted to keep you away from the cartel. Give you a chance at a normal life."

Emmanuelle stiffened. "That wasn't her decision to make. I have a right to know who my father is."

"You renounced any relationship with your mother and the cartel," Kenzie reminded her.

There was a long moment while Emmanuelle just breathed. Kenzie watched her wrestle with her emotions. Then she gave a stiff nod. "You're right. I don't want to know. In fact, I don't want anything to do with them."

"Unfortunately, they don't feel the same way." Kenzie said softly. "You see, Maria's son, Matteo, is being groomed to take over the cartel, and he sees you as a threat."

Emmanuelle laughed. "That's preposterous."

"I know, but it doesn't change the fact that he wants to eliminate you."

Her eyes widened. "He sent those men to kill me?"

"Yes."

"So, why didn't they?"

Kenzie sighed. "Their orders were to kill you, not Warner. The cartel doesn't want to be responsible for taking out the President's son. Imagine the backlash. They'd be the most hunted organization in the world."

"But it's alright to take me out?"

"No offense, but you're not as valuable to the President as his son is."

She rolled her eyes. "That is true. He wouldn't care if I died. In fact, he'd probably be relieved. He certainly wouldn't pay a ransom for me." That was a bit harsh, but Kenzie knew what she meant. She'd sensed the frostiness between them at the soiree.

Emmanuelle was quiet for a moment. The agent knocked on the door. "Time's up. Let's move out."

"How sure are you about this?" Emmanuelle clutched Kenzie's hands. "Do you have proof?"

"Quite sure. Matteo flew into New York a day before the shooting.

And two of his henchmen arrived the day before that. We think they were the ones who came after you."

"You have their names?"

Kenzie nodded. "Do you want me to give them to Special Agent Gordon?"

Emmanuelle thought about this. "Let's keep this between ourselves for now."

At Kenzie's puzzled look, she elaborated, "They won't believe us. They're convinced it's Warner who was the target. Besides, I don't want anything to derail the wedding. If the President thinks I'm putting his son at risk, he'll hate me even more. He might even try to stop us getting married."

Kenzie nodded. She'd seen the bond between Warner and Emmanuelle. They depended on each other. They were each other's port in the storm of their lives. The elements raged around them, but as long as they had each other, they were fine.

Kind of how she felt about Reid.

The door opened and an agent marched in. "Miss Lenoir, we have to go."

"You're sure?" Kenzie called, as he led Emmanuelle from the room.

"Yes, but thank you, Kenzie. I mean it."

Kenzie was left alone in the office. It was eerily quiet. A moment later, her driver appeared. "I'll take you back to the hotel now, Miss Gilmore."

She gave a grateful nod and followed him out. As she climbed into the SUV, she saw a man striding toward the entrance of the abandoned prefab. From the back, he seemed vaguely familiar, but she couldn't place him. Then he turned and stared straight at her.

It was the man who'd bumped into her at Liesl's apartment.

30

REID STOOD UP, his hands on his hips. "You're sure? You're absolutely sure it was the same man?" Kenzie had just returned and come straight up to his room. Flushed cheeks, flashing eyes, chest heaving, she was obviously perturbed by what had happened.

"A hundred percent. I looked straight at him. He was the man who elbowed me in the ribs at Liesl's apartment block."

"Did he recognize you?"

Her voice was a whisper. "I think so."

There was a pause as the implication of this set in.

"How did he react?" Reid needed to know every detail if he was to try to make sense of this.

"I don't know. It was a split-second, and then the driver closed the car door."

Reid rubbed his forehead. "It doesn't make sense. What was a SS agent doing at your friend's apartment?"

"Searching it," Kenzie replied. "Randal said it was a professional job. No forced entry, the place was methodically searched. He knew where to look. It makes perfect sense."

Reid exhaled. "You know what this means? If it was the Secret

Service who searched her apartment, it stands to reason—" He broke off, unwilling to vocalize what they were both thinking.

Kenzie sank onto the bed. "That they killed her too?"

He gave a curt nod.

"But why?" Kenzie pushed her palms into her closed eyes as if trying to banish the unwelcome thoughts in her head. The bruising on her cheek was still visible, but a blotchy yellow now, rather than blue. "The Secret Service doesn't go around murdering innocent civilians."

"I know. They're trained to save lives, not take them."

"Okay, let's think about this rationally." Kenzie took a deep breath. "Maybe they were trying to prevent Liesl's article from coming out, so when they discovered she'd died, they searched her apartment to get rid of any incriminating evidence."

Reid was nodding. "That makes more sense. They were worried it might end up in the wrong hands."

"Like her editor." Kenzie warmed to the idea. "Although they didn't find what they were looking for."

"That being her laptop."

"Because she'd sent it to me."

Reid, aware they were finishing each other's sentences, said, "I have to admit, that was a genius move on her part. It shows she must have known she was under surveillance."

"Or she feared for her life," Kenzie said soberly.

"Either way, she didn't want the Secret Service to get ahold of it."

Kenzie let out a measured breath. "That still doesn't explain why she was killed. If it wasn't the Secret Service, then who was it?"

"Maybe it *was* just a tragic accident." Reid turned and looked out of the window. The sun, on its downward trajectory, hovered behind the skyscrapers and shot fiery orange beams between the buildings.

"You don't really believe that?"

He turned back. "Not really, no."

"Warner Sullivan is the person with the most to hide," Kenzie said. "The question is, would he murder a reporter about to expose him?"

"He might," Reid shot her a pointed look. "And now you're in that same boat."

"*We're*," she corrected. "You're involved too."

He nodded.

"But would the President's son be embroiled in an assassination plot?"

Kenzie shrugged. "He's got a lot to lose."

They fell silent.

Eventually, Kenzie asked, "What are we going to do, Reid?"

"We could talk to Special Agent Gordon about it."

She shook her head. "We can't just ask him if one of his agents was involved in a murder. He'll think we're crazy. Besides, he might be involved."

"You think so?"

"I'm not sure. We can't trust anybody."

Reid ran a hand through his hair. "There is one way of checking whether that agent you saw at the apartment ran down Liesl."

Kenzie brightened. "The DNA in the vehicle?"

"Exactly. If we can compare the two, we'd know if it was the same perpetrator."

"He'll never agree to that," Kenzie argued. "Neither will Special Agent Gordon. But—" She fixed her gaze on him.

"What?"

"We have to assume that whoever that guy was at the meeting this afternoon, he saw me. It won't take much for him to find out who I am or where I'm staying."

"You think he's going to come after you?" Reid asked.

"I think he might."

That was something Reid hadn't anticipated. He should have, but he wasn't sure of the extent of it until now. He got to his feet. "Then we must change hotels."

"Or—" Kenzie hesitated. "We stay here and let him come to us."

"I am not using you as bait," Reid stated flatly. After last time, he wasn't prepared to put her at risk again. "It's out of the question."

"You wouldn't be," she argued. "I won't be in the room. We'll just set it up to look like I am."

He relaxed, but only slightly.

"We've done it before. Remember a couple of years back, when Ingleman's men were after me and we staged that motel room to make it look like I was there?"

"Yeees." He drew out the vowel. That had been one close call.

"Well, we can do that again. I know someone who can get us a mannequin and a wig. The light will be off. It'll look like I'm in bed, asleep."

Okay, maybe it wasn't such a bad idea. "How do you know he'll come?"

He didn't like her smile. "Because I'm going to give him an added incentive."

At his arched look, she elaborated. "I'm going to give Special Agent Gordon a call and tell him I have information on Warner. It might speed things up a little."

"We don't know he's involved."

"True, but he'll discuss it with the other agents. He's their team leader."

"You'd be making yourself a target," Reid warned.

"I probably am already. If they think I've got Liesl's laptop, and they know I'm a reporter, you can bet they're going to come for me too."

"Shit, Kenz." His gut tightened. Kenzie didn't look overly concerned. In fact, quite the opposite. "Please tell me you're not enjoying this?"

"Of course not. But if we can catch Liesl's killer ... If the mysterious agent's DNA matches that from the vehicle that mowed her down, we have something to take to Randal."

She was right. He didn't like it, but it could work.

"What choice do we have?" Kenzie stared straight at him, her eyes blazing. "He'll come for me either way. We may as well take advantage of it."

"Okay, you've made your point. We'll do it, but just so we're clear, you're not going anywhere near your room. You're going to stay here, where I can keep an eye on you. That's the deal."

Her eyes crinkled. "Fine, if that's what you want."

"Yes." He nodded firmly. "It's what I want."

Kenzie couldn't take her eyes off the grainy image of her hotel room. Reid had installed the mini surveillance camera a couple of hours ago, when they'd set the scene. They'd tucked the blonde mannequin under the duvet and turned off the lights. Taking one last look from the door, Kenzie shivered. To an intruder, it would appear she was asleep under the covers.

Earlier that day, Nathaniel had rushed over with a store mannequin and a blonde wig in a hairstyle similar to Kenzie's. He'd been more than happy to help them out after Kenzie's cool headedness at The Plaza. "What's it for?" he'd gushed.

"A crime reenactment."

It was close enough to the truth to be believable.

True to her word, she'd called Special Agent Gordon and asked if he could meet her. When he'd inquired what it was about, she'd replied that it had to do with Warner Sullivan, and might be a reason why he was targeted the other night.

He'd listened, then asked where she was staying. Once Kenzie told him her room number at The Sheraton, she'd hung up and looked at Reid. "He said he'd send someone over in the morning."

"How did he sound? Do you think he's involved?"

"I don't know, but we'll find out soon enough."

Kenzie lay on the bed, while Reid sat upright in a chair, his eyes glued to his laptop. He didn't say much, but she could tell he was tense. He wasn't comfortable with the sting operation, particularly because it was outside of any police jurisdiction. Going rogue wasn't his style.

When she'd met him a little over two years ago now, he'd quit the force and was living off the grid in an isolated cabin in the Glades. After the case that had restored his reputation, he'd taken over as Lieutenant at Sweetwater PD southwest of Miami. Back then, the backwater department had a reputation for being corrupt and ineffective. A place cops went when they'd outlived their usefulness. Now, thanks to his leadership, it was one of the finest police departments in the county, with young graduates requesting to be posted there.

Reid had built quite a team at Sweetwater, and he'd come to rely on them. This idea of hers took him way out of his comfort zone. No plan. No protocol. No backup.

She, on the other hand, had never had anyone to back her up. Not until she'd met Reid. It had always just been her. If she wanted the story, she had to go and get it. If something required undercover work, she was on her own. Not even her editor, Keith, knew half of the things she'd done to get where she was in her career. That's just how it was.

But not anymore. She glanced fondly at him.

Time ticked by. Still no movement in the room above.

At nine o'clock, they called room service and ordered something to eat, not that either of them was particularly hungry, but it was something to fill the time. Yawning, Kenzie murmured, "I hope this isn't all for nothing."

Reid gave a grunt of agreement.

"How's your house coming along?" she asked to make conversation. Ever since he'd gotten here, they'd talked about nothing but her and this case. Not once had she asked about what was happening in his life.

"It's getting there."

"How long to go?"

"Another couple of months." He stretched his neck. "Can't come soon enough."

"You still staying at the Gator Inn?"

"Yeah, for my sins."

She smiled. The motel in the Glades wasn't known for its five-star hospitality. Kenzie was about to sympathize when a movement on the screen caught her eye. She sucked in a breath and pointed to the screen. "Reid, look!"

The door to her hotel room was opening.

31

REID LEAPT off the chair and raced out the door, pulling his gun from his holster as he did so. Taking the stairs, he bounded up them two at a time until he reached the eighth floor. Breathing heavily, he peeked around the corner into the hallway. Almost a minute had passed since they'd seen the intruder on the camera. Would he still be there?

Reid crept down the corridor, his feet soundless on the plush carpeting. The recessed spot lighting in the ceiling offered no shadows in which to hide, but then he didn't really want to hide. Firearm in his hand, he approached Kenzie's open door.

He was mere yards away when he heard a gun discharge. The sound was muted, but loud enough to hear from outside the room, especially if you knew what it was. The shooter had a suppressor attached.

Rage clutched at his gut. If Kenzie had been sleeping in that bed, she'd be dead right now. He stood in the doorway, silent as the night, weapon pointed at the stranger.

The black figure dropped his arm and began backing out of the room. Turning around, he jumped when he saw Reid standing there. He lifted his gun, but Reid was ready for him. "Don't even think about it."

Unfortunately, the man didn't listen. Reid saw his finger curl around the trigger and knew he only had seconds until the gun spat again. He fired. The sound deafening in the confined space.

Point blank range.

The shooter went down.

Reid kicked the gun out of his hand and stared down at him. The hole in his chest was leaking blood all over the carpet. It wouldn't be long before the man lost consciousness. "Who are you?" Heavy-set features, a square jaw, stocky physique. Reid didn't recognize the guy.

The man groaned, clutching his chest. Unfortunately, Reid had hit him center mass. There was no coming back from this one.

"Who do you work for?" Reid repeated, bending over the shooter.

The man shook his head, gurgled something incoherent, then fell limp.

Fuck.

A door opened, and a woman in a hotel bathrobe stuck her head out into the corridor. She saw Reid holding his gun and screamed.

"Police officer, ma'am. Get back into your room."

A couple of other doors opened. Reid held up his badge. "Go back inside, please. This is police business."

Booted footsteps could be heard thundering up the stairs. The stair-well door flew open and four armed hotel security guards charged towards him, weapons drawn. He held up his hands, still clutching his gun and badge.

"Lieutenant Garrett," he called out. "I've just shot an intruder."

They looked at the body on the carpet, then back at him, unsure whether to believe him or not. The closest guard, a surly, dark-haired man in his late thirties leaned in and studied his badge. "You not NYPD?" He had an Eastern European accent. Serbian or Czech maybe.

"No, I'm from Miami."

The guard holstered his weapon and ran a hand through his thick, curly hair. The others didn't. They were waiting for word from their boss. "What happened here?"

Reid put his gun away too. "This man broke into the room in order to shoot and kill one of the hotel guests."

The man's eyes widened. "Are they okay?"

He gave a stiff nod. "She wasn't in there."

There was a murmur amongst the other guards, and the surly one nodded to them to check it out. They stepped over the body and entered the room. Reid grimaced at the blatant disregard for crime scene protocol, but let it slide. Preservation of life came first, and they were just doing their job.

"Call Sergeant Randal at the NYPD." Reid said. "He's familiar with the case."

That was a lie. Randal had no idea what he and Kenzie were up to, but he'd be the best person to straighten this out.

While they waited, Reid set up a temporary cordon around the body. The night manager, distraught at the turn of events, found two screens which they used to block the view of the dead man from the lurking hotel guests. Every time a head poked out of a room, they were told to stay inside.

"Great, everybody's going to check out in the morning," the night manager grumbled. "A shooting at the Sheraton. Who would have thought it?"

Reid rolled his eyes. It couldn't be helped. "Call it an accident," he suggested. "A gun went off accidentally. There's no perceived threat that way."

The manager gave a relieved nod. "Can I do that?"

"You can do what you like," Reid retorted as Sergeant Randal strode along the corridor.

"What the hell, Garrett? What is it with you two? You come to my town and all hell breaks loose."

"Sorry, Sergeant." He handed Randal his Glock. "You'd better take this."

The police officer nodded and took it in a gloved hand. His sidekick took out a plastic evidence bag, and he dropped the service weapon inside.

"I'm going to need that back," Reid muttered.

"That's not up to me," Randal said. "There's going to be an inquiry."

"I know." Reid gave a sour nod. It wasn't the first time he'd had to take a life. He was confident the camera they'd installed in Kenzie's room would have picked up the action, along with the CCTV in the corridor. The shooting was justified. The intruder had been about to pull the trigger. It was shoot or be shot. Simple as that.

Reid glanced down at the dead man and absorbed the hollow sense of regret. Shooting someone was never easy. Ever since he'd discharged his weapon, he'd felt slightly nauseous. The acrid taste in his mouth wouldn't go away. That would last a couple of hours, until his brain had processed what he'd done and come to terms with it.

"Okay, talk me through it," Randal said.

Reid told him what had happened, beginning with Kenzie's meeting with Emmanuelle Lenoir. Randal balked when he mentioned the man she'd seen inside the apartment block.

"You'll have him on CCTV leaving Liesl Bernstein's building," Reid said.

"She's sure it was the same guy?"

"Absolutely. He was one of the Secret Service agents assigned to the President's son and his fiancée."

Randal shook his head. "I don't like this at all."

"Me either," Reid agreed. "I don't want to accuse the Service of anything, but the same day that Kenzie recognizes the guy from the apartment, a man breaks into her hotel room and tries to kill her."

Randal stared at the dead man. "Do we know who he is?"

"Hired merc, I'd say. Military background."

"How'd you figure that?"

"The way he moved. Tattoo on his right hand. Scar next to his left eye. That's a shrapnel wound, I'd swear it."

Randal nodded, impressed.

"I'm sure if you run his prints, you'll find him in some DoD database."

"American?"

"I think so. Isn't that an 82nd Airborne Division tattoo? I recognize the patch."

"You serve?"

"Nope, but I know people who did."

Randal gave a somber nod. "Whose room is this?"

Reid swallowed. "Kenzie's." The detective's eyebrows shot up.

"She's not in there," Reid said quickly. "We were expecting this." He hesitated. "There's a dummy in there with a couple of bullet holes in it, and a mini surveillance camera that caught the whole thing."

Randal frowned. "You knew he'd come after her?"

"We suspected he might. Whatever Liesl Bernstein was working on, it was dangerous enough to get her killed. We figured Kenzie was in the same position, especially since they think she's got Liesl's laptop."

"Does she?" Randal frowned.

Reid sighed. "Why don't you come back to my room and we'll fill you in? There's a lot you need to hear."

"Do not let anyone past this tape," Randal ordered the police officers who'd taken control of the scene. The hotel security officers were still around, but on the periphery. They'd been relegated to keeping guests away from the crime scene.

Then he looked at Reid. "Lead the way. I'm right behind you."

Reid led Randal back to his room on the third floor where Kenzie was waiting, pale-faced and breathless. He'd told her to stay where she was and not come back up to her room. They didn't need more confusion at the crime scene.

She jumped up as they walked in. For a moment, he thought she was going to hug him, but then she saw Sergeant Randal and stopped. "Thank God you're okay." Her voice was shaky. "For a moment there, I thought he was going to shoot you."

He gave her what he hoped was a reassuring smile. "I pulled first."

He didn't want to think how close he'd come to eating a bullet. Nothing good ever came of dwelling on that.

"Who was he?" Kenzie asked. "I didn't recognize him."

"Must have been a hired hit," Reid said. "But he came for you, Kenzie. Unloaded a couple of rounds into the mannequin. He wanted to make sure you were out of the picture."

Kenzie gulped.

"We'll find out soon enough." Randal looked at Kenzie. "What on earth was on that laptop?"

Kenzie gathered up the papers and handed them to him. "It's all there. She was investigating a bribery scandal involving Warner Sullivan."

The NYPD detective gazed at her, momentarily lost for words. When he spoke, his voice was hoarse. "Please tell me you're not suggesting Warner Sullivan killed your friend?"

She shrugged. "I'm not suggesting anything. All I'm saying is that's what Liesl was investigating. I started looking into it, and tonight someone tried to kill me. You can draw your own conclusions."

Randal stared down at the papers in his hand. "Sweet Jesus."

Reid nodded in agreement. "Why don't you take a seat, and we'll run you through it."

White faced, the detective sat down.

After they'd finished, Randal shook his head. "What am I supposed to do with this?"

"You could ask Special Agent Gordon for a meeting?" Kenzie suggested. "He'd know who the dark-haired man at Liesl's apartment was."

Randal shifted uncomfortably. "This is the Secret Service. They're not going to cooperate."

"No one is above the law," Kenzie said firmly.

Randal sighed. "Okay, well, we've got a dead body upstairs, so we'll start with that." He nodded at Reid. "You'll have to come in and give a statement."

Reid knew the drill. "Will do. Take the camera footage from

Kenzie's room, along with the dummy in the bed. It's evidence of attempted murder."

"I'm aware. A crime scene photographer is there now. We'll be bagging everything and taking it with us, don't worry." Wearily, he got to his feet. "Don't take this the wrong way, but I'll be glad to see the back of you two."

32

THE SUN WAS PEEKING its head between the skyscrapers as Kenzie and Reid walked into the police station to give their statements. Reid had said very little on the way there, a sure sign he was worried. "It was self-defense," she told him, as they sat in Sergeant Randal's office. "You had no choice. If you hadn't shot him, you'd be dead right now."

"I know." It didn't change the fact there'd be an investigation. Until then, Reid wouldn't be allowed to use his service weapon. If he wasn't on leave, he'd be put on light duties.

"Stay where you are," Captain Perez had said, when Reid had called to tell him what had happened. "Let the dust settle."

Captain Perez, formerly Lieutenant Perez of the Miami PD, had been promoted to Police Captain of Miami-Dade County. Kenzie had liked him the few times she'd met him and thought the promotion well deserved.

"I feel naked without my Glock," Reid muttered irritably. Kenzie knew it was also being told to stay away that was irking him. It was one thing being here by choice, but not being able to go back to work when he wanted was pissing him off.

Randal took Kenzie's statement, which didn't include anything she hadn't already told him. It needed to be officially recorded though. Reid had been taken to an interrogation room to do his. Every word would be captured on camera. She didn't envy him.

"I've watched the camera footage," Randal told Reid, once they were back in his office. "I'm confident you'll be cleared of any wrongdoing. The shooting was lawful."

Kenzie's attempted murderer was now in the morgue, awaiting his autopsy. "We identified him as Aldo Burke," Randall said. "You were right, he served in the 82nd before he was dishonorably discharged following a court martial in 2012."

"What was the court martial for?" Reid asked.

Randal's voice lowered. "Killing an unarmed civilian. Apparently, he was becoming increasingly violent and unstable. 'A liability,' his commanding officer called him."

Reid arched an eyebrow. "And now he's working for... who? The Secret Service? Warner Sullivan?"

"Probably a private contractor," Kenzie guessed.

Randal nodded. "I know guys like this. The military is their life. They don't have any other skills. Most of them join a private security company and get sent straight back to the war zones they've just left."

"How's the investigation coming on?" Reid asked.

"I'm meeting with Special Agent Gordon this afternoon," Randal told them. "I'll see what he has to say for himself."

"Will you keep us posted?" Kenzie asked.

He gave a curt nod.

"I think we better change hotels." Reid looked over at her.

Kenzie frowned. "Do you think they'll try again?"

"They might."

"Probably not a bad idea," Randal agreed. "Until we can prove Burke was hired by Sullivan or the Secret Service, there's not much we can do." The look he exchanged with Reid told her neither of them held out much hope of that happening.

Kenzie shivered as an icy chill swept over her. They weren't out of the woods yet. "Okay, let's go back to the Sheraton and pack."

It was a little after midday when they got back to the hotel. A car backfired as they walked in, making her jump. She couldn't stop looking over her shoulder as they crossed the lobby.

"Relax," Reid said, pushing the elevator button. "I've got your back."

"Thanks." She managed a small smile. He'd proven that countless times, and now, because of her, he was under investigation for killing a man. "I'm sorry I got you into this."

"It's okay. None of this is your fault."

"I know, but if it wasn't for me, you wouldn't be here. Wouldn't be on suspension."

"And you'd probably be dead."

The elevator pinged, making her jump. Boy, she was on edge. This case had gotten to her in a big way.

"It's going to be alright," Reid said, looking at her. She could tell he was concerned. It wasn't like her to be so... needy.

A nod was all she could manage.

"Hey, come here." He held out his arms and in the privacy of the elevator, she went into them. Hot tears burned her eyes, so she closed them to stop them from falling. An image of Liesl lying dead in the road flashed before her eyes.

The car came out of nowhere.

Malcolm Lord's hands ripping her blouse.

Struggle all you want. I like it.

The shooting in the hotel room.

He came for you, Kenzie.

She stifled a sob. Reid held her close, enveloping her. Kenzie clung to him like her life depended on it. She didn't want the elevator ride to end.

When the doors opened on the third floor, she sniffed, and moved away.

"You okay?"

Get a grip, she told herself firmly. You can't fall apart. Not now. "Yeah, thanks. I needed that."

He shot her a worried look. "I mean it. It's going to be okay. We're going to get these guys."

"I know."

She sat on his bed, unable to relax, while he booked them into another hotel. "This one is off the beaten track," he told her, texting her the details. "No one will find us there."

Earlier this morning, the officer on duty outside her room had allowed her access to pack her things. She'd stayed in Reid's room last night. There'd been no discussion about getting another room. Exhausted, she'd fallen asleep almost immediately, and when she awoke, Reid was taking a shower. Had he slept at all? She had no idea.

Reid threw his stuff into his hold-all. "Once I'm finished packing, I'll go down to reception and check us out. I'll message you when the cab's here. Don't leave the room before that."

"Okay."

Kenzie tried to concentrate on work. Cases were piling up. Keith wanted a follow-up on the wedding. The exclusive had gone out, but not the way he'd imagined. It was far better. Now all the networks were clamoring for more.

Should she write about the attempt on her life? Publicize the threat? Would that lessen it or make it worse? The spotlight would shift to the Secret Service then, and Warner Sullivan's sneaky Chinese backhander. It would implicate the President. The President and his son's newfound reconciliation would be questioned. Alibis would be strengthened, defenses mounted. It could end up being a media shitstorm.

Kenzie sighed. It was best left alone for now. Perhaps in time, perhaps if they caught whoever had tried to kill her. Not if. When.

She shuddered, took a shaky breath, and checked her phone. No message from Reid. What was taking so long?

Looking out the window, she gazed down at the congested roads with their Lego vehicles sitting in back-to-back traffic. Tiny yellow taxi cabs. One of those would whisk her and Reid away to a new hotel. Somewhere they'd be safe until they could figure this out.

Another fifteen minutes passed. Where was he?

She fired off a text.

Should I come down?

Scowling, she stared at her phone. One tick. He hadn't even seen it. She waited another ten minutes, then called him. No answer. Eventually, it diverted to voicemail.

This is Lieutenant Garrett, please leave a message, and I'll get back to you.

Damn.

She opened the Find My iPhone app and took a look.

What the hell?

Reid was moving away from the hotel at a slow, but steady pace. She called him again, desperation making her hands tremble.

Reid, pick up!

But he didn't. Instead, his phone died.

She looked at the app again, but it was still the last location. No update.

Shit.

Panic made her pulse race. Ignoring the threat, she raced down the three floors into the lobby. The checkout desk was busy, so she sprinted outside and grabbed the doorman's arm. He looked at her in surprise. "Did you see a man get into a car?"

"I'm sorry?"

She fumbled to bring up a photograph of Reid. "This man? Did you see what happened to him?"

The doorman studied the photograph, then gave a nod. "Yeah, he got into a black SUV."

"Was there anyone with him?"

"Lady, I can't remember everyone who leaves this hotel."

"Please, think. It's important."

"Yeah, I think there were a couple of guys with him."

Her heart dropped.

"What did they look like?"

He shook his head. "I don't know, lady. I wasn't paying that much attention." She wanted to yell at him, to ask him why he wasn't paying attention. Wasn't that his job?

"Did you get the plate number of the SUV?"

His look said, 'are you crazy?'

"Never mind." The panic rose, threatening to choke her. Why was he moving away from the hotel? They didn't know anyone with a black SUV.

She could think of only one reason: Reid had been abducted.

It was confirmed, when her phone beeped a few seconds later.

Greenpoint Terminal Warehouse, Brooklyn. 4pm. No cops. Come alone. Or he dies.

33

KENZIE STOOD outside the hotel watching the vehicles pass in a hazy motion blur. It felt like someone had pressed the slo-mo button on the remote. Even the sound was reduced to a dull hum.

Come alone. Or he dies.

They were using Reid to get to her. *She* was the one they wanted. Her first thought was to call Sergeant Randal, but they'd said no cops. What would Randal do anyway? She didn't even know who had taken Reid. Was it the Secret Service? A few individuals loyal to Warner? Or hired mercenaries tasked with retrieving Liesl's laptop and making sure the information on it wasn't disseminated?

Kenzie didn't kid herself that they'd let Reid go. Once they had her, they'd kill him. They'd kill them both. The sidewalk tilted and she grabbed onto the railing. Panic threatened to choke her. Oh, God. She'd really done it this time.

"You alright, lady?"

Barely acknowledging the doorman, she stumbled back into the hotel.

Think.

Her mind was blank. All she heard was the pounding of her heart.

This was Reid, for God's sake. The man who'd always been there for her. He was in trouble, and she didn't know what to do.

Come on! Forcing herself to take slow, steady breaths, she stumbled into the hotel bar. This was not the time to have an anxiety attack. Reid needed her. She had to do something. Ordering a stiff drink, she took a vacant seat and tried to pull herself together. There must be something she could do.

Randal was out of the question. She didn't know who'd taken Reid, had no plate number, not even a make of car. Sure, there was hotel CCTV outside the front entrance, but the kidnappers had warned her not to involve the police. They'd see Randal and a SWAT team coming a mile away.

Going to the meeting by herself was foolish. If she arrived alone, it was game over. Of that, she was certain. She needed a plan. A good one.

The alcohol hit her system and she felt slightly more in control. There *was* someone she could call. Someone who was used to brokering deals.

Carlisle.

Whether he would help her or not, she had no idea—but she'd run out of options. Her mysterious source. A self-serving enigma of a man who negotiated deals on behalf of the rich and powerful. A sizable donation for a seat on the board. A corporate investment in exchange for mining rights in Africa. A mansion in Dubai to fund a small army.

Kenzie would never admit to the things she'd found out about Carlisle. Or thought she'd found out. As with everything he did, there was an air of secrecy around him, and absolutely no proof. Nothing that could link back to him.

Still, he knew people. But Carlisle didn't work for free. Luckily, she had a big carrot to dangle in front of him.

Taking out her phone, she called the number of the burner that he'd given her. As usual, it went straight to voicemail. She left a hurried message.

With nothing more to do than wait, she looked up the location the kidnappers had given her. An abandoned storage and distribution center in Brooklyn. It was huge, the size of a whole city block. She googled it. Partially destroyed by fire. Pollutants contaminating the surrounding area. Plans were afoot for redevelopment, but nothing had happened yet. Going there alone would be insane.

It was just after two o'clock. Two hours until she had to meet the kidnappers.

Carlisle, please call me back.

Kenzie finished her drink, then remembered Reid had been in the process of checking them out. Where was his luggage?

She went back into the lobby and looked around. Reid's hold-all was nowhere to be seen. "Excuse me," she asked a smiling receptionist. "Did my friend leave his luggage here earlier?"

"We did find a lost bag," she said. "It's in the luggage store."

"Does it say Reid Garrett on it?" she asked.

"One moment, I'll check." The woman clattered into the back on her two-inch heels and returned a short time later. "That's it," she said with a nod. "Do you want it?"

Kenzie's heart sank. He'd been accosted in the lobby. Had they put a gun to his back? Somehow, they'd coerced him into leaving the building and getting into the black SUV? If only she could see the camera footage in the lobby, but the Sheraton would never show it to her. She wasn't law enforcement.

Anyway, it didn't matter. These guys wouldn't have a plate that was traceable. They were pros.

Reid was gone. That was all she could think about. And it was up to her to get him back.

An hour and twenty minutes later, Kenzie's phone rang. She nearly fell off the bed in her haste to reach it. "Hello?"

"Kenzie, darling. How are you?"

"Carlisle, thank God."

"Not good then?" As always, his voice was measured, controlled. Unlike hers.

"Not really. Reid's been taken."

There was a pause.

"Taken? Where?"

"I don't know." Calm down, she told herself. Carlisle didn't do emotion. To him, everything was a transaction. If she wanted his help, she'd have to shelve her anxiety and talk to him in a language he understood.

"We're in New York," she began. "A reporter friend of mine was killed. She was investigating Warner Sullivan."

"*The* Warner Sullivan?"

"That's right. Remember I did that piece last year about Emmanuelle Len—"

"I remember." His voice was quiet. "Maria Lopez's illegitimate love child."

"Well, Liesl, my friend, uncovered some information that Warner Sullivan would rather not get out. She was killed for it, they came for me, but—"

"They got Reid?"

She exhaled shakily. "They shot up my hotel room. Now they've kidnapped Reid."

"And what exactly is this information?" His tone was measured, but she knew that's what he really wanted to know. That was what he dealt in. Information. No price was too high. No topic off limits.

"I can't tell you on the phone."

"This line is secure."

"Carlisle. They're going to kill him. If I don't get to the rendezvous—"

"They've contacted you?" Sharp, abrasive. He knew how these things worked.

"Yes, I'm supposed to meet them at four and to bring the laptop with me."

"Your friend's laptop?"

"Yes, although I don't have it."

"I'm confused."

"She sent it to my apartment in Miami."

"So how do you know what's on it?" He broke off. "Oh, yes. Your brilliant researcher."

"That's right. Raoul emailed me the relevant info."

"Kenzie. If you want my help, you're going to have to tell me everything. From the beginning."

She took a breath. "I'm not sure we've got time for that."

"Start with how you got involved in this investigation."

A short while later, after she'd told him the whole story, leaving nothing out, he said, "Do not go to this meeting."

"But Reid—"

"You know they'll kill you both? This is not an exchange of information. It's a one-way street. What you know could destroy Warner Sullivan. Could destroy the Presidential campaign."

She swallowed. "But what can I do? I can't just leave him."

"You'll have to. For now. Reid's a big boy. He'll be okay for a while. He's their bargaining chip."

Carlisle was right. She knew he was, so why did it feel so wrong leaving Reid at their mercy?

"Okay," she gulped. "What do you suggest?"

"Don't worry. I have a plan, but I'm going to want something in return."

"Of course." She knew Carlisle.

"We can talk about that later. First, let's get your man back."

34

THE NEXT FORTY minutes were the longest of her life. Kenzie paced up and down her new hotel room, an insignificant establishment several blocks from Times Square, wondering what was happening to Reid. Did he think she'd deserted him? Or would he know she'd come up with a plan?

He must know she wouldn't turn up at four o'clock. Agreeing to meet was the most foolish thing she could do, and she wasn't a fool. But then, he also knew how she felt about him.

Or did he?

She stifled a sob. Maybe Reid didn't know how crazy she was about him. She'd never actually said the words. All she'd done was keep him at an arm's length. As soon as things got heated between them, she backed away. The wall went up.

After all they'd been through ... Kenzie shook her head. If they ever got out of this. If she ever got Reid back. She'd tell him. Make sure that he knew.

Four o'clock came and went.

Kenzie stared at her phone, daring it to ring. Carlisle had been firm. Don't message them. They'll call you when you don't show up.

Five past four. Ten past.

It rang.

Heart leaping, she answered it. "Hello?"

"You're not here."

"No. I'm sorry. I've been held up. The police came to the hotel to question me. They've only just left. I was going to let you know, but—"

"The police? I warned you what would happen if you went to the cops."

"I didn't tell them anything," she said quickly. "It was about the shooting in the hotel room. They've gone now." She'd followed Carlisle's advance. Would they buy it?

The voice was silent.

Kenzie noted how he'd said, *I warned you.* Not we. Was the perpetrator acting alone? Or was he the boss? The one who made the decisions?

"You have one hour."

"It's not enough," she stammered, following Carlisle's script. Buy us some time. As long as possible. I can assemble some men, but I'm going to need a couple of hours.

"I've... I've had to move hotels. The cab is on its way."

"You have the laptop?"

"I do," she lied. Of course, she wasn't about to give it to him, but he didn't know that.

"Six o'clock. And I'll text you a new location. If you're even one minute late, he eats a bullet."

The line went dead.

Kenzie exhaled shakily. She'd bought them some time. When Carlisle called, she relayed the information.

"Well done," he replied. "I'm going to send some of my people to get Reid back, but they're going to want to see you there, to make the exchange."

"I told you, I don't have her laptop."

"Take yours. It doesn't matter. The exchange is not going to take place."

"What do you mean? What are you going to do, Carlisle?"

"Kenzie, do you want my help or not?"

She hesitated, but not for long. It was Reid. She'd do whatever it took to get him back. "Yes."

"Then don't question my methods. Just text me the new address when you have it. I'll send a driver. He'll take you to the exchange. Go through the motions. Pretend you're there to hand over the computer. When the time is right, my men will take over."

That was the part that worried her. Still, she had no choice. She had to trust Carlisle.

"Kenzie, I do this for a living."

"I know, and I appreciate your help. I'll be there."

The kidnapper texted her the new address. With a lump in her throat, she forwarded it on to Carlisle. At five thirty, a dark blue sedan pulled up outside her hotel. It was exactly the type of car she'd have hired if she'd ordered one herself.

Carrying her own laptop, which she'd backed up and wiped clean of data, Kenzie ran down the stairs and jumped inside. Her driver was a rugged man in his late thirties. Hooded eyes under a black cap looked up at her. "You'll drive when we get closer to the location."

Kenzie nodded. "Okay." The kidnapper had been clear. Come alone.

They set off. The driver's gloved hands rested easy on the wheel, and he drove with a skillful confidence that told her he'd done this sort of thing before.

Her heart hammered all the way to Brooklyn. Trying to distract herself, Kenzie gazed out the window at the massive stone towers and steel cables of the iconic bridge, the deceptively tranquil waters of the East River, and as they got closer to the waterfront, the Manhattan skyline across the water.

Under normal circumstances, the view would be stunning, but tonight, with the cloud cover overhead and a gloomy, charcoal haze hanging over the city, it was less than spectacular. A sign that the light had literally gone out of her life.

The sedan exited the expressway and came to a stop next to a small park. Children played on the playground, while rowdy teens whooped and yelled in the skatepark. Cherry blossoms bent over the sidewalk, nodding in the breeze that had kicked up since they'd left the hotel.

Her driver got out of the car. "Your turn. I'll direct you."

"Where will you be?" she asked.

"Hunkering down in the back. Don't worry, they won't see me, but I'll have eyes on you the whole time."

Her gut twisted in anticipation. She got behind the wheel and set off. Greenpoint Terminal warehouse was only four or five blocks away, and it didn't take long to get there. Too soon, she pulled up outside a large, fenced-off property. Behind the barbed wire, she made out a derelict, rusting metal and brick structure, scorched in places and falling down in others.

Keep out! it seemed to shout. Yet here they were, about to enter.

"Is this it?"

"Yeah. There's a gate on the west side. It should be open."

Kenzie wondered how he knew that, then figured one of his teammates must have told him. Presumably, they were already here, lying in wait. Nerves made her grip the steering wheel extra hard until her knuckles turned white. "There's the gate."

It was indeed open just wide enough for a car to pass through.

"Go in," he ordered. "Then turn around so we're facing the open gate." The hairs on the back of her neck stood up. That would be for a quick getaway in case they needed one. Kenzie did what he said, then turned off the engine.

"Keep it running," he barked, so she turned it on again.

Kenzie checked the time on the dash. Five minutes.

Please let him be okay.

With two minutes to go, a black SUV slid through the gates, its headlights on. "They're here," she breathed.

"Okay, keep calm."

She was grateful for the man in the back. His calm instructions helped her keep it together. Had she been alone, she may well have spun into a panic.

They faced off with the black SUV. Kenzie could barely think over the thumping of her heart.

"Now what?"

"Wait for their signal, then proceed with the exchange."

She frowned. Carlisle had said the exchange wasn't going to happen. "What about Reid?"

"Ask to see him before you hand it over. We need proof of life."

Proof of life.

The way he said it, so casually, like it was just a passing comment. Reid was a real person. A human being. Someone she loved. Not a pawn in whatever twisted game they were playing. She reached over and picked up the laptop.

The moments seemed to drag out. Eventually, the headlights flashed, and a man got out of the SUV. It was him. The man from Liesl's apartment.

He beckoned for her to come over.

"Slowly," warned her driver from the back. "Keep to the right, out of my line of sight."

Nervously, Kenzie opened the car door and stepped out onto the asphalt. The parking lot, if you could call it that, was deserted. More of an open space that may once have been a trading area.

Every movement was strained. Every sound magnified. Squinting, Kenzie tried to make out Reid, but with the opposing car's lights on, it was impossible to see beyond the glare.

Kenzie walked toward him, then came to a stop. "What's wrong?" The man asked. "Bring us the laptop."

"I want to see Reid," she called. "I mean Detective Garrett."

There was a pause, then the man gave a stiff nod. The back door of the SUV opened, and an enormous man got out. He was holding a gun and pointing it at the person in the car. Slowly, Reid climbed out.

Despite herself, Kenzie let out a loud sob. He was alive. His arms were tied behind his back, and he leaned a little to one side as if in pain, but he was alive.

"Hello, Kenzie." He smiled sadly at her. Disappointment. Fear. Acceptance. She heard it all in his voice. He thought they were going to die.

She knew differently.

35

Reid watched Kenzie approach, his heart constricting painfully. Why did she come? She ought to know better. This was a foolish plan. These guys wouldn't let them live. They couldn't. Not given what they knew.

He'd figured out who they were. An offshoot of the Secret Service. A renegade crew, loyal to Warner Sullivan, operating outside the law. Their leader was the man Kenzie had seen outside Liesl's apartment. The others called him Phillips. It could be his real name.

Phillips and Warner were close. There was a bond there. He couldn't quite work out what it was, but there was a misplaced loyalty on Phillips's part. He didn't think it was money. It went deeper than that.

Reid strained his eyes to see inside the sedan Kenzie had come in, but it looked empty. Had she hired it? Or had Randal somehow organized it for Kenzie? If so, he was placing her at risk. If these guys thought she'd gone to the cops, things were going to get ugly fast.

"You come alone?" Phillips called, as she walked toward him.

"You told me to."

Phillips gave an approving nod. Reid tensed, and the big guy with the gun trained on him, flinched too. "Easy."

There were two more agents inside the vehicle, both armed. One was their driver, a lean, nervous man called Mannie, and another heavy hitter, a sniper who'd downed an Iraqi soldier from half a mile away in strong wind. Reid had heard him bragging to Mannie.

As Kenzie got closer, Reid could see how frightened she was. It was in every hesitant step, every micro-expression on her face. His heart went out to her. So brave. So strong willed. Except this time, it was going to get her killed. Get them killed.

Then he noticed something else. A hesitancy. She was moving slowly, yes, but each step was deliberate, calculated. She was also off center, veering slightly to the right. Nothing immediately noticeable, but she was leaving a clear line of sight from the sedan to Phillips.

Again, he stared at her vehicle, but couldn't detect any movement. The agents hadn't thought to check the trunk or the back seat, assuming she'd come alone. A mistake on their part.

Glancing behind him, Reid scanned the mass of dark, foreboding buildings, but didn't spot anything obvious. No glint of a scope, no dark shadowy figure lurking on a rooftop. If Kenzie had backup, they were well hidden.

"You okay?" she called.

He gave a quick nod. "You shouldn't have come."

"I had to."

"The laptop. Now!" Phillips gestured with his handgun for her to come closer. He was running out of patience. Gritting her teeth, Kenzie held out the device.

A desperate plan began forming in Reid's mind, one that had almost zero chance of success. He'd charge Phillips, hands tied behind his back, and try to knock him off his feet before he could shoot Kenzie. That was, if the big guy or one of the others in the SUV didn't take him out first.

Phillips took the laptop, keeping his gun trained on Kenzie.

"Let Reid go." Her voice was hollow, but firm. Reid almost smiled at her naivety. She couldn't possibly think they'd make the exchange, and all go on their merry ways. Not Kenzie. She was as cynical as he was. Something wasn't right here. Once again, his gaze flickered to the sedan, but it was in darkness.

Suddenly, the two front doors of the SUV opened, and the driver and the sniper climbed out. Both aimed their weapons at Kenzie. With a gasp, she put her hands up in the air. "What's happening?"

"You didn't think we were going to let you go, did you?" Phillips shot her a condescending look.

Kenzie met Reid's gaze. He held it, trying to read her, but couldn't. She was nervous, sure, but not terrified. He'd seen her way worse than this, and she currently had three weapons pointed at her. He got a feeling something was about to go down.

Phillips tossed the laptop into the SUV, then took a step forward and grabbed Kenzie around the neck. She cried out as his gun pressed hard against her temple. Reid saw her look hopefully at the sedan, but there was no shot. No flash of light. No outward spray of glass fragments.

"Bring him over here," Phillips demanded.

Reid's throat went dry. This was it. They were going to execute them right here on the abandoned grounds. His eyes flew to the sedan. Whoever was in there, if he was in there, was holding his nerve.

"Move!" the big man ordered.

Slowly, Reid repositioned himself beside Kenzie. Her face was pale, but he sensed a strength in her. "What's going on?" he murmured.

"No talking. Hands up, Miss Gilmore."

Kenzie lifted her arms.

Reid had just about given up hope of anything happening, when two shots rang out. Bang. Bang. In quick succession.

At first, he didn't know where they had come from. Not the sedan. Then he realized the big guy was falling to the ground, a .50 caliber hole in his forehead, another in his chest. Classic double-tap. Whoever was out there was a pro.

He looked at Kenzie, who stared at the dead guy, stunned. Phillips and the driver returned fire, while the sniper aimed his weapon. "Get down!" Reid yelled, and threw himself into her, knocking her off her feet.

A firefight ensued. Phillips and his men fired randomly into the building, unsure where the shots were coming from. There was a cry as the big guy took one in the head and collapsed. Two down, two to go.

Phillips was crouching behind the door of the SUV, firing indiscriminately at the building, while the sniper, leaning on the hood, was taking more calculated shots, trying to work out where the incoming shots were being fired from.

He yelled as a bullet hit his rifle, sending it tumbling to the ground. He dived into the SUV. "Let's get out of here!"

Phillips nodded, but he was on the wrong side of the car. He had to get around to the driver's side. Reid, powerless to do anything with his hands behind his back, watched helplessly as the two men prepared to get away.

"Not this time," Kenzie said, crawling out from under him and picking up the big guy's handgun. She aimed it at Phillips. "Freeze!"

Phillips turned, a snarl on his face. "You think you can shoot faster than me, little girl?"

"I'm happy to find out," she retorted.

Brave, but she didn't stand a chance against the seasoned soldier.

"Kenzie, no!" he yelped.

A shot rang out. Reid closed his eyes.

Please, no.

He heard Phillips gasp and opened them again, just in time to see the Secret Service agent sink to the ground, a look of surprise on his face.

"Kenzie?" But she looked as shocked as Phillips.

That's when a black figure appeared from behind Kenzie's sedan. He walked toward them, gun in hand, still pointed at Phillips, but the rogue leader wasn't moving.

The sniper, still inside the SUV, grabbed his handgun and fired through the windshield at the stranger. It exploded in a spray of glass segments. Like shattered pixels, they bounced over the tarmac, dancing in the headlights. The sniper hadn't gotten off more than two shots when his head exploded in a cloud of red mist, and he fell back against the car seat.

Kenzie stared at her driver. Reid looked at Kenzie. "I hope he's with you?"

She gulped and gave a small nod.

"You guys okay?" The man in black pulled Reid up off the ground and cut through his ties.

"Are they dead?" Kenzie moved in a daze toward the pockmarked SUV. None of the four men were moving.

"Don't go near it," barked her driver.

She halted.

"DNA transfer," he explained in a clipped tone. Clearly, he was a man of few words. Typical ex-special forces, thought Reid. The shooters from the abandoned building stayed hidden. Nameless, faceless warriors. Used to working in the shadows. He was dying to ask Kenzie where she'd found these guys.

"But my laptop..."

He grimaced, then marched forward to retrieve it. Reid noticed he wore army boots, a tight cap holding back his hair, and black gloves. This guy wouldn't leave a trace.

The man in black retrieved the laptop and handed it to Kenzie. He cast an experienced eye over the crime scene, then turned back to the sedan. "Let's get out of here before the cops arrive."

36

KENZIE HELPED a limping Reid to the car. Her driver slipped in behind the wheel and took off before they'd even closed the door. Like a racing driver, he floored it down the straight, the sedan's engine screaming as it slipped through the gears.

Kenzie helped Reid with his seatbelt, then secured hers. Her driver screeched around the corner, bounced across a central median, and merged with the evening traffic. Not a moment too soon. Seconds later, they passed three police vehicles speeding in the opposite direction. Someone had reported the shootout.

Kenzie glanced across at Reid. He looked pale and wore a pinched expression that told her he was in pain. Taking his hand, she asked, "You're hurt?"

"Nothing that won't heal." Flashing her a tight smile, he gave her hand a squeeze.

"You sure? Do you need a hospital?"

"No hospitals," barked the driver.

"He's right," Reid agreed. "I'm fine. Just a couple of bruised ribs." If they took Reid to a hospital, his injuries would be on file. The police would be looking out for casualties.

They sat in silence, Reid's hand resting on hers, while Carlisle's man drove them back to the hotel. "What's going to happen now?" Kenzie asked before they got out.

Her driver didn't turn around. "Nothing. It's done. Carlisle will be in touch."

Kenzie nodded.

They climbed out of the car, Reid with some difficulty. Kenzie came around and made him lean on her shoulder. They'd barely closed the door before the sedan sped off again. The bemused doorman didn't say a word as a bedraggled Kenzie led a limping Reid into the hotel and up to their room.

"You contacted Carlisle?" Reid winced as he collapsed on the bed. It was a twin room, with two singles in it. Kenzie knew Reid had been thinking about her when he'd booked it. Separate rooms were too risky. She was safer with him.

Meanwhile, it had been Reid who'd been taken. Reid who needed tending.

"I didn't know what else to do." She perched on the end of his bed. "I couldn't go to the police. Those guys would have seen them coming a mile away."

Reid grunted. "Carlisle is a dangerous man, Kenzie. But I don't have to tell you that."

"I wouldn't have gone to him if I'd had any other option, but there was no time to formulate a plan."

"It's okay. You did what you had to do to get me out." He shot her a weary smile. "Thank you. I owe you."

She scoffed. "Don't be silly. It's me who owes you if we're counting. You've saved my ass more times than I can remember."

He chuckled, but it turned into a grimace.

"Who were those guys? The Secret Service?"

"Phillips, he's the guy you saw at the apartment, led a small team of agents working exclusively for Warner Sullivan. I don't know how it came about, but they were trying to stop the bribery scandal from getting out."

Her eyes narrowed. "Did they kill Liesl?"

"I believe so. The skinny guy had a scar on his forehead that looked like it could have been from a car crash. I'll bet it's his DNA the police have."

"Why didn't it show up in the system?" she asked.

"He doesn't have a record, but if they run it against the DoD database, it might."

She nodded. Hopefully, the cops would get it from the crime scene at the terminal warehouse.

"Seems a shame they turned," she murmured. "I feel bad they're dead." She'd never had anyone's death on her hands before. Now she had four.

"They were going to kill us both, Kenz. Phillips told you," Reid said softly. "You did the right thing."

"Were they?" She needed to hear it. Needed the reassurance that she'd had no choice.

"Definitely. They couldn't afford to let us live. Look what they did to Liesl."

Kenzie gave a stiff nod. That was true. They'd run her friend down in broad daylight. She'd died in the gutter, alone. All to protect a slimy, corrupt politician. The thought made her bristle.

"What's going to happen now?"

"There'll be a police investigation into the shootout at the parking lot. The bodies will be identified, but because they're agents, the Secret Service will take over the case. Depending on how high up this thing goes, there'll be an internal investigation, but I doubt anything will come of it. Warner Sullivan will declare ignorance, and the whole thing will probably be swept under the carpet."

"And the threat to us?"

"I don't know."

"Is it over?" She ran a hand through her hair. God, she was exhausted. "Will Warner Sullivan come after us? We still have the laptop."

"And the police have what was on it." Reid closed his eyes as a spasm hit him.

"Are you sure you're okay? Can I get some ice?"

"Ice might be a good idea," he grunted.

"Can I see?"

She lifted his shirt. The right side of his body was crisscrossed with angry welts. Kenzie gasped. "What did they do to you?"

"I may have tried to escape. They caught me."

She shook her head. "I'm so sorry, Reid."

"It's not your fault."

But she knew it was. Somehow, she had to make this right.

"There is something you can do," Reid said.

"What?" She'd do anything to get Warner Sullivan off their backs. All she wanted to do was go home, back to Miami. With Reid.

"Expose the whole thing. You're a reporter, you can bust the case wide open. Let the world know what Warner Sullivan was up to. That way, there'll be no point in his coming after us."

"I can't," she whispered. "At least, not yet."

He frowned. "Why is that?"

"I promised Carlisle."

He raised his head off the pillow. "What did you promise him?"

"Information. That's his trade, what he deals in. The flow of information."

"He sells information for money." Reid scoffed.

"A lot of money," Kenzie corrected. Carlisle brokered deals worth billions of dollars. It wasn't just a couple of thousand they were talking about here.

"It's the only way to keep us safe," Reid insisted.

"Okay, I'll talk to Carlisle. Maybe we can come to an agreement."

They met in person the very next day. Carlisle glided up to the hotel in a bullet-proof Mercedes Benz with tinted windows. A driver got out and opened the back door. Not the same driver as yesterday. That guy was probably on a plane to Mexico or the Caribbean right about now. Kenzie climbed into the sleek, black vehicle and faced the man who'd come to her aid.

"Carlisle." She smiled brightly. "Thank you."

"You're welcome, Kenzie. Although next time, could you at least give me a day's notice? Amassing a hit squad in under two hours is no mean feat."

"But you did it."

His eyes crinkled. "Yes, I did. I take it your friend is alright?"

"A little bruised, but he'll live."

"I'm glad. Now it's your turn."

She swallowed nervously. "About that."

"You're not going to renege on our deal, are you?" The pale blue eyes turned cold.

"No, of course not. Here is everything you need." She handed him a file. It was Liesl's notes, raw and unfiltered. Everything her friend had on the Warner Sullivan fiasco.

"It's all here?"

"Yes, but there's something else. I, erm, I want to ask a favor." There were very few people who could intimidate her, but Carlisle was one of them.

His gaze narrowed. "You're just about out of favors, my young friend."

"I know, and I owe you big time, but this will never be over until I've exposed him. He'll keep coming after me. You know that." She didn't need to specify who 'he' was.

"You want to do an exposé?"

She nodded.

Carlisle was silent for a moment. Eventually, he gave the tiniest of nods. "I think we can work together on this one, Kenzie."

"We can?" Her heart leaped. Not only would she get a massive scoop, but she'd also be exposing Warner Sullivan, giving him no reason to come after them. They'd be safe.

"I need forty-eight hours," Carlisle said, all business now. "Then you will be contacted about the exposé."

Kenzie had wondered what exactly Carlisle had planned to do with the information. Now, she thought she knew. He was going to use it to alter the political landscape of the United States of America. The opposition—or was it someone else in the ruling party?—would pay plenty for this kind of information.

"I get the story?"

"That will be part of the deal. Kenzie Gilmore gets to write the exposé." He smiled. It reminded her of the way a wolf looked at a sheep before going in for the kill. "This is going to be huge, Kenzie. A fallout unlike anything you've ever seen before. Political heads are going to roll." There was an unnerving gleam in his eye. He loved holding the fate of others in his hands, the power it gave him.

She suppressed a shudder. That was his business, not hers. She didn't have the stomach for it. All she cared about was that Warner Sullivan wouldn't be able to hurt them anymore.

37

Kenzie's article went out two days later in the *New York Times* under a shared byline: *Liesl Bernstein and Kenzie Gilmore.*

It was the last piece Liesl had worked on and the scoop of her career. Carlisle's prediction had been spot on, the fallout was immense. Warner Sullivan was arrested on suspicion of Liesl Bernstein's murder, as well as corruption and accepting bribes, pending an investigation into his dealings with China. The President announced he was not going to run for a second term, leaving his party to put forward an appropriate candidate.

Kenzie wasn't sure what Carlisle stood to benefit from any of this, other than a lucrative payout, but she was sure there'd be something.

The article ran first in the *New York Times,* followed by the *Miami Herald.* The other networks, none of whom were aware of the scandal, struggled to catch up.

"You've done it again, Kenzie." Keith, her editor, had called to congratulate her. "I'm sorry about your friend, but this is career gold."

It was bittersweet. She wouldn't have gotten the exposé if it wasn't for Liesl, but then again, she felt a responsibility to finish what her friend had started. Now that the world knew what Warner

Sullivan had been up to, there was no chance of him coming after them.

The one person Kenzie regretted hurting was Emmanuelle. She hadn't heard a peep from the supermodel since their clandestine meeting in the prefab office. Was it only a week ago? It felt like ages.

She and Reid were still staying in their off-the-grid hotel, preferring to avoid reporters and the news networks. Reid was healing, although it still hurt to move. She liked tending to him. Going out for food, applying arnica to the bruising, helping him walk around the room to stay active. They still couldn't get medical help, in case the police were monitoring the hospitals. One thing they didn't want was to be implicated in the murder of the four Secret Service agents.

Randal hadn't been in touch, thank goodness. They had to get Reid well before they could face off with the savvy sergeant.

"I want to follow up with Emmanuelle Lenoir before I leave," Kenzie told Reid on their second night in the hotel. "I owe her that much."

"Will she want to see you?" Reid asked. "That's twice you've ruined her life."

Kenzie bit her lip.

First, she'd outed Emmanuelle's birth mother as the notorious cartel boss, Maria Lopez, causing untold friction between the model and her fiancé's prestigious family, and now she'd ruined her chances of marrying the President's son.

THE WEDDING'S OFF screamed the tabloids. Some hotshot reporter had obtained a statement from the President who wasn't holding back. It was in his best interest to sever all ties with his estranged son and the woman he was going to marry.

"I have to try," Kenzie told Reid. "I feel bad for her. I think she truly did love him."

He nodded, but his expression was guarded. "I've got to get back to work."

"You're going back to Miami?" Her head shot up. It was too soon. She wasn't ready for this to end. For *them* to end.

"Yeah, I'm thinking of flying back tomorrow afternoon."

"Are you well enough?"

"I think so, yeah. I have that hearing coming up and Perez wants me back." She'd almost forgotten that he'd shot and killed the man in her hotel room. So much had happened since then.

"Okay, sure. If you must."

She'd gotten used to having him around, their in-depth talks, and the way he brushed her fingers with his, or put his hand on her back. Even though they were in two separate beds, she'd never felt closer to another human being.

"It's time, Kenz. We've got to get back to reality."

"I know." She couldn't bring herself to look at him.

"How about you? When do you think you'll be back?"

She forced a smile. "A day or two. I want to talk to Emmanuelle if she'll see me. Then I'll be on the next plane home."

He gave a sardonic smile. "We never did get that date."

"No, we kinda skipped that part and went straight to moving in together."

His face softened. "It's been fun. Not the getting kidnapped part, but everything else. Being with you." The way he was looking at her gave her goosebumps.

"It was," she whispered.

A knock on the door made them jump. No one was supposed to know they were here. Kenzie got up and peered through the peephole.

"It's Sergeant Randal," she mouthed.

Reid got off the bed, straightened his hair, and took a seat at the small table in the corner of the room.

At his nod, Kenzie opened the door. "Sergeant Randal, how nice to see you."

"You've been busy." He walked into the room, glancing around. She saw him take in the two single beds and purse his lips.

"You mean my article?" She flashed him her best smile.

"I couldn't help but read it," he said. "I take it that's why you're hiding out here?"

"We thought it best to keep away from the media," Reid cut in, keeping his back straight. "Until things settle down."

"Uh-huh."

Randal strode over to the table. "Mind if I sit down?"

Reid nodded. "Sure. What's up?"

"I wanted to ask if you knew anything about four dead SS agents?"

Kenzie's phone rang. She glanced down. It was Emmanuelle. "Sorry, I've got to take this," she told the police detective, and went outside into the hallway for some privacy, leaving Reid to fend for himself. They'd discussed this eventuality, and had their alibi down pat. They'd moved to their new hotel room and were so exhausted, they'd gone to bed early.

"Kenzie? Is that you?"

"Yes, hi. Thank you for returning my call. I wasn't sure you would."

A brief pause.

"I thought about it," the model said, "but I just wanted to say I appreciate you leaving me out of this mess."

Kenzie had purposely not mentioned more than a passing word about Emmanuelle in the exposé. She'd done nothing wrong and like Reid had said, she'd already destroyed her life once.

"You're welcome. I'm sorry about Warner."

Not really.

A sniff. "Did he really kill your friend, that reporter?"

Kenzie didn't want to get into it on the phone. "Can we meet?" she asked. "I'll take you through everything then." Emmanuelle deserved that much. If the roles were reversed, she'd want to know.

"That would be good. I'm not going out in public. Can you meet me at this address tomorrow?" Emmanuelle gave Kenzie an address on Wall Street. It shouldn't be hard to find.

"What time?"

"How about noon?"

"Sure. I'll be there."

. . .

The address Emmanuelle had given her was a private members' club on the top floor of a financial office block. She gave her name at reception and was escorted to a table by the window. Sitting down, Kenzie admired the view between the buildings towards the harbor. She could even make out The Plaza from here, where Emmanuelle would have married Warner Sullivan, if all had gone according to plan.

"Did you ever find out who attacked you and Warner in the hotel that day?" Kenzie asked Emmanuelle, as the model sat down. Elegant as always, her dark hair hung loose, framing her exotic features.

With everything that had happened, Kenzie hadn't revisited her theory that it was Emmanuelle's own flesh and blood who'd wanted her out of the way.

Emmanuelle shook her head. "No, I think the service was looking into it, but that investigation got put on hold when the story about Warner broke."

Kenzie grimaced. "I'm sorry," she said, meaning it. "I know you didn't want it to be this way."

"I should be married now," Emmanuelle said, her voice tightening. "Instead, my fiancee is on trial for murder, and I'm public enemy number one. I'm surprised they haven't kicked me out of the country."

"Did you know?" Kenzie asked. "That he was accepting bribes from the Chinese?"

"I knew he was negotiating on their behalf," she admitted. "But I thought it was all above board. I mean, it happens all the time, right? People use their connections, their networks, to make deals, form alliances. That's politics."

Kenzie couldn't fault her logic.

"I feel bad for you, though, Kenzie," Emmanuelle added. "About what happened to your friend." Everybody knew about Liesl, thanks to the article.

"Thank you."

"Warner didn't have anything to do with that, you know?"

Kenzie raised an eyebrow. Seriously?

"I asked him, before they came and took him away. He didn't even know her name."

Kenzie frowned. "Emmanuelle, those agents were loyal to Warner. They were working for him."

Emmanuelle shook her head. "They were working for his father."

Kenzie stared at her. "You think the President hired them to prevent the story from breaking?"

"He had the most to lose."

That was debatable. As it turned out, they both lost everything. Warner more so, since he was facing a lengthy prison sentence.

"I'm sure the authorities will get to the bottom of it." It was out of her hands now. The President was only in office for a couple more months, and then his career was over.

Emmanuelle scoffed. "I think Warner will be... how do you say it? The scapegoat." It was the first time she'd known Emmanuelle to stumble with her English. She could believe that if she wanted to. Reid had heard the agents talking. There was no doubt in her mind it was Warner who'd hired them.

"What will you do now?" Kenzie steered the topic away from Warner.

"I don't know." Emmanuelle tossed her hair over her shoulder. "I'll think of something."

Kenzie gave a sympathetic nod. Her life had changed irrevocably in the last few days. Emmanuelle had lost everything too.

Outside, a helicopter was landing at the heliport next to the club. Kenzie watched, mesmerized as it hovered silently, then touched down not twenty feet from where she was sitting. The soundproof glass meant the patrons inside the club couldn't hear a thing.

"I think I'll take a vacation," Emmanuelle was saying. Kenzie turned back to her.

"That's probably not a bad idea. It's been a very stressful time for you."

"I think you should come with me."

Kenzie did a double take, thinking she'd misheard. "Excuse me?"

Emmanuelle nodded to someone, but before Kenzie could turn around, two strong arms lifted her out of her seat.

"What's going on? Ouch!" A sharp instrument like a needle penetrated the skin in her lower back. What the hell was that?

"Say one word and you die," hissed Emmanuelle, her demeanor changing. The soft oval eyes hardened to flint, the full lips curled back in a snarl, and she looked down her nose at Kenzie. In that instant, she was the spitting image of her mother.

"W–What are you doing?" Kenzie stammered. Had they injected her with something? It wasn't that long ago she'd nearly been poisoned with snake venom. Needles were not her favorite thing.

"There are ten mils of insulin in the syringe currently in your back," Emmanuelle informed her. "That's over a thousand units. If you so much as try to run, or create a scene, Louis will press down on that syringe. You will be dead in forty minutes."

Kenzie felt sick.

How could she have been so stupid? She gritted her teeth in frustration. "I should have known. You're just like her."

Emmanuelle laughed softly. "Always trust your instincts, Kenzie. They'll never steer you wrong. My mother taught me that."

So, they had met. Suddenly, everything made sense. Emmanuelle was taking over the cartel. She'd spoken with Maria before her death. She knew who her biological father was, and now she was making her move.

How could she have missed that?

With Kenzie looking on, the model waltzed towards the revolving doors, out onto the helipad. A bodyguard carried designer luggage out to the waiting helicopter. Kenzie struggled, but the arms gripping her tightened into vices. The needle penetrated deeper, stinging as she moved. She froze.

"Out the door," growled the man who held her life in his hands. Kenzie had no choice but to follow Emmanuelle outside and get into the helicopter.

38

REID SURVEYED the hotel room he'd shared with Kenzie. Her clothes were still hanging in the wardrobe, her toiletries in the bathroom. The room smelled of her deodorant. His stuff was packed into his hold-all, including the shirt she'd worn after Malcolm Lord had torn hers.

It had been a hell of a few weeks.

He'd come to New York to help her hunt down a predator of women and ended up being kidnapped by a rogue branch of the Secret Service and getting the crap beaten out of him.

Sergeant Randal had quizzed him about the four dead agents. Thankfully, the detective had believed him when he'd said they'd been in their hotel room all night. Randal had incorrectly assumed he and Kenzie were having an affair, and Reid had let him believe it. It served their purpose.

In reality, what they had was far more than that. He wasn't going to try to decipher it; he wasn't sure it even mattered. He could feel it.

Randal also told him they'd linked the hitman at the Sheraton with Major Phillips. They'd served in the same unit. That meant Warner was on trial for Kenzie's attempted murder too. She might be called upon to give evidence in the trial. Reid was confident they could handle that.

The muted television was still tuned to the news channel, a habit Kenzie had gotten into when she traveled. Reid picked up the remote to switch it off. His cab would be here in under ten minutes to take him to the airport.

He was about to press the power button when an image caught his eye. The writing at the bottom of the screen said *Los Angeles*. Turning up the volume, the presenter's voice filled the room.

Matteo Lopez, rumored to be the heir to the infamous Morales drug cartel, was shot and killed today at a restaurant in downtown Los Angeles.

Reid watched as a man in a body bag was carried out of a restaurant.

Matteo Lopez was dead?

That was unexpected. Matteo was about to take over the running of the cartel. Who'd want him dead? An adversary? A competing cartel? A man like Matteo Lopez would have lots of enemies.

The reporter went on to say the shooting was most likely a result of a turf war between rival cartels, but the police were keeping an open mind.

That meant they had jack.

Last week, Matteo was here, in New York. He'd arrived the day before the attack on Warner Sullivan and Emmanuelle Lenoir at The Plaza. Kenzie's theory was that the cartel had attempted to take Emmanuelle out, because she was Maria Lopez's biological daughter and a threat to Matteo's leadership. Kenzie had even warned Emmanuelle. That's where she'd spotted Major Phillips.

Reid put down the remote. It was a while before he heard his phone buzzing.

"Yeah?"

It was Raoul, Kenzie's assistant.

"Reid, I've just seen the news. Is Kenzie with you?"

"No, she's... er, unavailable."

"I need to talk to her. There's something she needs to know." He hesitated. "It's bad."

"What is it?" he barked.

"I was going through the flight lists, and I missed something. There was a fourth person who came to New York. I missed it because it was *after* The Plaza attack, not before."

"Oh, yeah? Who was it?" But in his gut, he knew.

"Romeo Herrera."

"Shit, Raoul."

"I'm sorry. I only found out this morning, and I've been trying to get ahold of Kenzie ever since."

"I've gotta go," Reid said, his head spinning. Emmanuelle had reached out to Romeo Herrera, her natural father, while he'd been in New York. They'd hatched a plan to get rid of Matteo, so Emmanuelle could take over as head of the cartel.

It was audacious. It was ruthless. It was something Maria Lopez would do. So why not her daughter?

From what Kenzie had told him of the elegant, mild-mannered model, it didn't seem like something she'd do. Emmanuelle reportedly hated the cartel. Didn't want to be associated with it.

But revenge was a strong motive.

Emmanuelle had played Matteo at his own game. Turned the tables so that she, not him, held the reins? Romeo Herrera was her biological father. That trumped Matteo's relationship with Romeo, which was more of a mentorship. There were no blood ties between them.

"Blood's thicker than water," Reid muttered, getting to his feet. Using the *Find my iPhone* app, he looked up Kenzie's whereabouts.

Wall Street.

Leaving his hold-all in the hotel room, and holding his fractured ribs, he ran downstairs out and the front door. In under a minute, he was in a cab speeding towards New York's financial district.

Kenzie stared in horror at the whirling helicopter blades. "Where are you taking me?" she yelled, but her words were swallowed by the wind.

"Get in," growled the man with the syringe. Every time she moved, she felt the needle twinge.

Kenzie glanced back at the tinted windows out of which diners were gazing in fascination at the helicopter. She wanted to scream at them for help. Why hadn't anyone noticed she was being coerced? That there was a syringe pressing into the small of her back? That she was being forced onto this flying death machine against her will?

If it was a gun, or even a knife, she'd have made a run for it. They wouldn't risk a spectacle. But the syringe was silent and took a while to kill. Emmanuelle had thought this through.

Kenzie would feel weak, woozy. Her legs would give way. Drunk, they'd say. Or unwell. They'd carry her into the helicopter, but it would be too late. Forty minutes. That's all she'd have.

It was noisy and windy on the heliport. Her hair flicked around her face, making it hard to see. Inside, Emmanuelle had fastened her seat belt and put on earphones. In her white Dior suit, she looked like she was taking part in a glamorous photo shoot. Meanwhile, Kenzie was going to her death.

The blades whipped around faster and faster, preparing for take-off. A sob escaped her. For once, Kenzie couldn't think what to do. She was trapped. The only way was forward, onto the chopper.

A shout made her glance around. The needle burned.

Her heart leaped.

Reid!

He was running out onto the helipad.

Emmanuelle said something to the pilot. The chopper began to shake. It was getting ready to lift-off. "Get her on!" shouted Emmanuelle.

The two men shoved her towards the helicopter, one with his hand on the syringe in her back. *Please don't push down,* she prayed.

"Let her go!" Reid continued to charge toward them.

Kenzie felt heat in her lower back. Some of the insulin had gone into her system, she was sure of it. "Don't. I'm getting in! I'm getting in!"

One foot on the skids, a bulky arm reached down and hauled her in. The man behind her let go of the syringe. Was it out? She wasn't sure. Glancing down, she saw it wasn't in his hands. It must still be in her back. She reached around, but the helicopter lifted off the ground and she clutched the sides to keep from tumbling out.

"Kenzie, jump!" yelled Reid.

Jump? Was he crazy?

She looked down to see the helipad shimmering in the mid-afternoon sun. The man on the ground turned and tried to hold Reid back but wasn't prepared for the onslaught. Reid barreled into him, knocking him off his feet.

A member of the helicopter ground control came running out, yelling for them both to get clear of the back rotors. The helicopter was spinning round, the blades dangerously close to the fighting men on the ground.

Kenzie felt the wind in her face. Six feet. Seven feet. It was now or never.

Sending a quick prayer skyward, she leaped from the helicopter. She hit the ground hard, her knees buckling, falling forward onto her hands. Her chin hit the tarmac and blood spurted everywhere.

Reid smashed a fist into the big man's face, and he keeled over, out cold.

"Kenzie!" He ran toward her. "Jesus Christ, what do you think you're doing?"

"You told me to jump!"

"I mean getting onto that helicopter." He helped her up. "Are you okay?"

Blood gushed down her T-shirt and dripped onto the ground. "Reid, I've got a syringe in my back. It's filled with insulin. Can you take it out?" She could hear the panic in her own voice. "Please, take it out, but don't push down."

"What?" He frowned, confused.

Kenzie spun around. "The syringe. Take it out!" She was shouting now.

She pointed to her back, and he glanced down. "Holy shit."

"Careful, don't press it."

"I won't."

There was a sharp tingle as the needle came out. "How much is in it?"

"I don't know."

"Give it to me." She grabbed the syringe and stared at the measurements. "Nearly ten milliliters. Thank God." Her legs felt weak with relief.

"Is that good?"

"Yes, it means he only injected a teeny bit. I should be okay with that."

"Insulin?"

"Yeah, this large a dose would kill me in forty minutes."

"Shit, Kenz."

"I know."

He stared at her. "That's why you got into the chopper."

She nodded. They both stared up into the clear blue sky where the helicopter was getting smaller and smaller. They followed it until it was a tiny speck.

"Where do you think she's going?" Reid asked.

"Mexico. She's going to take over from her father."

"Why was she abducting you?"

"I doubt I'd have made it to Mexico. They would probably have jettisoned me somewhere over the Gulf."

Reid looked so horrified she nearly laughed. "They'd have dosed me up and thrown me out, I'm sure of it."

"Thank God you jumped."

She managed a shaky smile. "Thanks to you."

"Oh, my God. That was insane. Are you alright?" The harassed flight attendant hurried over. "You're bleeding. Shall I call an ambulance?"

"No, I'm fine." Kenzie wiped her chin on the back of her arm. Blood smeared everywhere. It was worse than she'd thought.

"Do you have a first-aid kit?" Reid asked, leading her inside the clubhouse. The man hurried off to fetch it.

Kenzie sat down at a vacant table. The other diners stared at them, having watched the drama unfold from inside.

"Here, let me see." Reid tilted her face upwards. "You're probably going to need a couple of stitches."

She held a napkin to her face to staunch the bleeding. "You'd better call Randal."

The attendant returned with the medical bag. Kenzie excused herself and went to the ladies' room to patch herself up. It was a wide gash, but she didn't think it was that serious. Her hands were worse. Grazed and dirty, they stung like hell. She bathed and treated them too, then went back to talk to Reid.

"Matteo Lopez is dead," Reid said, as soon as she got back.

"What?"

"It's all over the news. He was gunned down coming out of a restaurant in L.A. That's what tipped me off."

"Emmanuelle," Kenzie whispered. "She set it up. It was retaliation for what he tried to do to her at The Plaza."

"Exactly."

Kenzie put her head in her hands. "I warned her it could have been her half-brother. Do you think this is my fault? Did I do this?"

"No, she met with Romeo Herrera a couple of weeks back. Raoul told me."

"Crap, really? I wish we'd known that earlier."

"He only found out this morning. When he couldn't get ahold of you, he called me."

She gave a weak nod. "Reid, I think I'd like to go home."

"Back to Miami?"

She nodded.

"Okay, but first, I'm going to take you to get that gash stitched up. Then I promise I'll book us on the first flight home."

39

KENZIE PULLED up outside Reid's newly rebuilt house in the Glades. He was waiting outside, a wide grin on his face.

"Wow, this looks amazing!" Climbing out of her car, she gazed at the two-story wooden structure. It was much bigger than his original cabin, or rather interconnected cabins, since the previous structure had been owned by an airboat company that had gone bust.

"Let me give you a tour." He looked wind-tousled and tanned, like he'd spent time outdoors. Since they'd returned to Florida, Kenzie had been swept up in the frenzy at the paper, working overtime to keep up with the public's insatiable demand for information about Emmanuelle Lenoir, the model who'd disappeared into the blue after her wedding to Warner Sullivan had been called off, thanks to his arrest and subsequent trial.

She'd known it would happen, and had mentally prepared for it, but that didn't mean she wasn't desperate to see Reid. They'd spoken on the phone a couple of times in the last week, but he'd been caught up with his hearing and other police business that had stacked up since he'd been away.

Reid led her into the hall, and then through to the living room. In typical Reid style, it was sparsely decorated with the essentials, but then he probably hadn't had time to go furniture shopping yet.

The entire front of the house was glass. Kenzie stared out through the open bifold doors onto the swamp. The water was calm and glassy, mirroring the blue sky overhead. A bird of prey circled high above, watching them through its beady eyes.

"This is incredible. I love it."

"No neighbors to worry about."

A wide, polished deck stretched out in front of the house, built on stilts to elevate it above the water. The view was breathtaking. Outside, Reid had put a rustic table and four chairs, along with a brand-new bench upon which to while away the hours. She could sit there and gaze at this view forever.

Leading off the deck, a wooden walkway extended down to a launching dock where an airboat stood tethered to the mooring.

"You got a replacement." She smiled at him.

"Of course. I've missed getting out on the water." She knew he enjoyed the rush of speeding over the water, feeling the wind in his face. He'd told her once how much it helped him unwind.

"I'm sure. Are you going to take me for a spin?"

"Later. First, I thought we'd have lunch."

"Lunch?"

"Yeah, we never did go on that date, remember?"

She chuckled. "I remember."

"Consider this it."

She raised an eyebrow. "Oh? I didn't bring anything."

"Don't worry. I've got everything we need."

What could she say to that? He'd thought of everything. "Well, can I help at least?"

"Yeah, you can make a salad, if you want."

"You got it."

Chopping tomatoes, she asked, "How'd the hearing go?"

"Fine. They ruled in my favor. The shooting was lawful."

"That's great." She could tell by his face he was relieved. It must have been awful having that hanging over his head. "So you're off light duties?"

"Yep, I'm back with a vengeance. There's been a spate of burglaries in South Beach. The latest was at the beachfront mansion of Marcus Bradford. Miami PD's got their hands full, so the Captain asked for our assistance."

"Marcus Bradford? The soccer player?"

"Yeah, Inter Miami."

She pursed her lips. "Did they get away with a lot?"

"They took four hundred thousand dollars' worth of watches, jewelry and other valuables."

"Jeez." Her eyes widened.

"The team's been trying to catch them for weeks, but with no luck. They're a pro-outfit, leave no trace, and no witnesses."

"Sounds like you have your work cut out for you." He was looking forward to getting back, that was obvious. A flicker of doubt gnawed at her. What did that mean for them?

They kept it light. She told him about work, how President Sullivan was now facing an investigation into his dealings with the Chinese. "It appears he's the one who instigated Warner's contact with them in the first place, then, when it got out, he did a one-eighty and denied everything. He left Warner to take the blame."

"Some father," Reid muttered.

They ate outside on the deck, the sun on their backs. Kenzie felt herself relax for the first time since she'd touched down at Miami International after her traumatic adventure at the Wall Street Heliport. The only sounds she could hear were that of the water lapping against the deck, the birds chirruping as they called to each other across the sawgrass, and the occasional grunt or croak from a toadfish.

"It's so peaceful here," she murmured. "I can see why you decided to stay."

"I'm glad you like it." The way he was looking at her made her heart beat a little faster. She put down her knife and fork.

"I'm not good with words, Kenz." His gaze was hesitant. This must be hard for him, but she admired him for broaching the subject. They needed to talk about what was happening between them. Now they were back in Miami, things had already reverted back to how they were before. A rushed phone call, a quick drink, avoiding talking about their feelings. She remembered her promise to herself in New York. When it was over, she was going to tell him how she really felt. Well, she hadn't. Not yet.

Maybe it was time.

"But I don't want things to go back to how they were, you know, before."

"I don't want that either," she whispered. "I really enjoyed our time in New York." She cleared her throat. "Apart from Liesl's death, the sexual assault, your kidnapping, and my helicopter heroics."

He laughed. "It was quite a trip."

Kenzie reached across the table and took his hand. "Seriously, though. I liked being with you."

He gave it a little squeeze. "Would you like to be with me more often?"

"You know I would."

"I don't know. You've never told me."

She bit her lip. Crap, this was terrifying. Taking a deep breath, she said, "Well, I'm telling you now. I want... I want to..." Come on, Kenz. Spit it out. "I want to be with you." There, she'd said it.

A smile played at the corners of his mouth. "How much?"

Now he was just teasing her. "A lot."

"That's good." His eyes were twinkling. "Because I feel the same way."

"You do?" She knew he did. She'd always known it.

In reply, he reached over the table, put his hand around her head, and pulled her gently toward him. For once, she went with it. They'd been through so much. He'd seen her at her absolute worst. He'd rescued her more times than she could count. There was no man on earth she trusted as much as Reid. If that wasn't a good foundation for a relationship, then she didn't know what was.

"We're not going to mess up our friendship, are we?" she whispered, just before his lips came down on hers.

"I think we're way beyond friendship, don't you?"

She laughed. He had a point.

Before she could think of any more reasons why they shouldn't be together, he kissed her. And then she could only think of reasons why they should.

The story continues in Storm Surge, the next Kenzie Gilmore Crime Thriller.

In the eye of the hurricane, lies a deadly secret.

A hurricane blasts the coast of Florida, unleashing mayhem and devastation. Amidst the chaos, a billionaire Miami philanthropist, Salvatore Del Gatto, is suspected of foul play when his yacht washes ashore, containing millions of dollars in stolen diamonds. Investigative reporter, Kenzie Gilmore, is assigned the case.

As the tempest rages on, Lieutenant Reid Garrett's team discovers a corpse in a demolished coastal property. Initially thought to be a natural death, things take a dramatic turn when an uncut blood diamond is found on the victim. When it's revealed the victim died six hours before the hurricane made landfall, Reid knows this was no accident.

As Kenzie and Reid piece together what happened, they uncover a sinister plot involving a network of dangerous criminals who will stop at nothing to keep their illegal activities under wraps. Even if it means murder. Suddenly, they're hurled from the eye of the storm, into the path of the hurricane, as they race against the clock to catch the culprits and bring them to justice.

Pre-Order your copy of *Storm Surge* today!

www.amazon.com/B0BYKBZZMC

Stay up to date with Biba Pearce's new releases:
https://liquidmind.media/biba-pearce-sign-up-1/
You'll receive a **free** copy of *Hard Line: A Kenzie Gilmore Prequel.*

Did you enjoy *Fever Pitch*? Leave a review to let us know your thoughts!

www.amazon.com/B0BP2T9MGZ

ALSO BY BIBA PEARCE

The Kenzie Gilmore Series

Afterburn

Dead Heat

Heatwave

Burnout

Deep Heat

Fever Pitch

Storm Surge (Coming Soon)

Dalton Savage Mystery Series

Savage Grounds

Scorched Earth

Cold Sky

Detective Rob Miller Mysteries

The Thames Path Killer

The West London Murders

The Bisley Wood Murders

The Box Hill Killer

Follow the link for your free **copy of** *Hard Line: A Kenzie Gilmore Prequel.*

https://liquidmind.media/biba-pearce-sign-up-1/

ALSO BY WITHOUT WARRANT

More Thriller Series from Without Warrant Authors

Dana Gray Mysteries by C.J. Cross

Girl Left Behind

Girl on the Hill

Girl in the Grave

The Kenzie Gilmore Series by Biba Pearce

Afterburn

Dead Heat

Heatwave

Burnout

Deep Heat

Fever Pitch

Storm Surge (Coming Soon)

Willow Grace FBI Thrillers by Anya Mora

Shadow of Grace

Condition of Grace

Hunt for Grace

Time for Grace (Coming Soon)

Gia Santella Crime Thriller Series
by Kristi Belcamino

Vendetta

Vigilante

Vengeance

Black Widow

Day of the Dead

Border Line

Night Fall

Stone Cold

Cold as Death

Cold Blooded

Dark Shadows

Dark Vengeance

Dark Justice

Deadly Justice

Deadly Lies

Vigilante Crime Series by Kristi Belcamino

Blood & Roses

Blood & Fire

Blood & Bone

Blood & Tears

Queen of Spades Thrillers by Kristi Belcamino

Queen of Spades

The One-Eyed Jack

The Suicide King

The Ace of Clubs

The Joker

The Wild Card

High Stakes

Poker Face

ABOUT THE AUTHOR

Biba Pearce is a British crime writer and author of the Kenzie Gilmore series and the DCI Rob Miller series.

Biba grew up in post-apartheid Southern Africa. As a child, she lived on the wild eastern coast and explored the sub-tropical forests and surfed in shark-infested waters.

Now a full-time writer, Biba lives in leafy Surrey and when she isn't writing, can be found walking through the countryside or kayaking on the river Thames.

Visit her at bibapearce.com and join her mailing list at https://liquidmind.media/biba-pearce-sign-up-1/ to be notified about new releases, updates and special subscriber-only deals.

Printed in Great Britain
by Amazon

29975618R10139